CONCRETE KILLA

Kingpen

**Lock Down Publications and Ca$h
Presents**

Concrete Killa

A Novel by *Kingpen*

Lock Down Publications
P.O. Box 944
Stockbridge, Ga 30281
www.lockdownpublications.com

First Edition January 2021
Printed in the United States of America

Lock Down Publications
Like our page on Facebook: Lock Down Publications @
www.facebook.com/lockdownpublications.ldp
Cover design and layout by: **Dynasty Cover Me**
Book interior design by: **Shawn Walker**
Edited by: **Nuel Uyi**

Stay Connected with Us!

Text **LOCKDOWN** to 22828 to stay up-to-date with new releases, sneak peaks, contests and more…

Thank you!

Submission Guideline.

Submit the first three chapters of your completed manuscript to ldpsubmissions@gmail.com, subject line: Your book's title. The manuscript must be in a .doc file and sent as an attachment. Document should be in Times New Roman, double spaced and in size 12 font. Also, provide your synopsis and full contact information. If sending multiple submissions, they must each be in a separate email.

Have a story but no way to send it electronically? You can still submit to LDP/Ca$h Presents. Send in the first three chapters, written or typed, of your completed manuscript to:

LDP: Submissions Dept
P.O. Box 944
Stockbridge, Ga 30281

DO NOT send original manuscript. Must be a duplicate.

Provide your synopsis and a cover letter containing your full contact information.

Thanks for considering LDP and Ca$h Presents.

Acknowledgements

First and foremost, I have to thank my Lord and Savior—Jesus Christ. I couldn't have done this without Him. Thank you for this blessing! My mother, Stacy Kirby: I love you so much. I know I haven't been the best son, but I promise I'll be that from this day forward. We never really had a close relationship, but I want you to know that you're my queen.

My grandmother, Celestine. Black don't crack! You are amazing. You took in four bad a** kids and claimed us as your own. We didn't deserve you. To this day, your voice warms my soul. I love you always.

My grandfather, aka Pawpaw. You're the one person in my life that I have never seen sweat. You showed me so much in life that I will instill into my kids. I'm proud to have your name in mines. I also want you to know that the Cowgirls suck. One love.

My Aunts—Rachel and Iesha. Y'all are like my second moms. I was bad as hell when I was growing up. Y'all came to the school atleast twice a year to put me back in school from suspension. Whenever I've needed y'all. During my incarceration, y'all showed up. I owe y'all so much, and I'm so grateful for y'all. I remember when I had failed the 8th grade, Aunt Sue snuck me into the 9th grade. Lol, look at me now!

Cordarius, my brother from another. People would always say that we were twins, yet we were actually cousins. Even though we don't have the same mother, you're always going to be my brother. I always looked up to you. I'm proud of you. One love.

Antonio, aka Tonibone. Mane, fam, people don't know the connection we share as brothers. We were both the problem children of the family. Yet we had the biggest dreams and aspirations. I want you to know as soon as I touch down, I'ma go get your kids, and pull up on you. I got them from now on. All is well.

Ca$h and LDP, I appreciate everything. I've been writing for years but never took it serious. When you told me that I had immense penmanship, I had to grab the dictionary to see what that meant. I had never seen a contract until we linked up. I appreciate everything, homie. I guarantee you that every book I put in your hands will be fire!

To my guys in the system. C Tru, Sam, C-lo, Gangsta, Rambo, Uncle Ben , Double D, Juvenile, Li'l Cali, JJ, Kenny Wayne, Uncle Marvin, Smack, Cheseray, Bigs, KudaBang, Walter, Jai, Quae, Quaky, Ivory, Big G, Chitown, Bun B, Carlos, B-Crazy, B-Gotti (West Dallas), Joshua Smart, Hustle Russle, Young Don P (Waldo), Mathmatics, Supreme, Kedric (Eastwood) Young, Christopher (Li'l Chris) Coop, Mike Prince (Mob Ties), Savage, 4Deuce, Johnny (Fattie) Fletcher, Mista, B-Hamp, Juan (JR), Bello, Deondre Torrey, Divine, Pawpaw Garcia, Swaggy Nick, Baby Boy, Money, Major (H, TX), Major (ATX).

And if I forgot about you, you're worth a mention as well because I hold you in high esteem. So sign your name here _____.

Last but not least, Asia, the woman that has held my heart since we were sixteen years old. You're my best friend and my soulmate. You have kept your promise to always be here for me. Baby, some people may think you're crazy for riding with me all of these years, but they just don't know the plan God has for us. I'm forever grateful for you.
Asia, when I'm finally able to drop down on bended knee in front of you, I don't want you to shed any tears. I only want smiles, because we have cried enough in the past. From this day forward, there's nothing but love and happiness for us, forever. I love you.

To my readers: This is my debut novel, but I'm confident you'll be impressed. I have a whole lot of heat lined up for y'all. At this moment, I hoping for a favorable parole decision. Pray for me. Until they free me, write me snail mail or email me through Jpay.
Modus:
Joshua Kirby #2003156
Beto Unit
1391 FM 3328
Tennessee Colony, TX 75880

Dedication

This book is dedicated to the love of my life, Asia, my beauty behind this madness.

Prologue

Hotboy

"God, I know I haven't called on you in a while. I know I only call on you when I fall into a pit, but I need for you to reach down and pull me out again. I promise I'll change, because you know what I'm going to do before I do it. I promise you I'll move smarter and pray more," I silently prayed as I waited on the bailiff to call me from my holding cell.

The side door opened to the courtroom as the bailiff stepped out with a pair of handcuffs and leg shackles. "You ready, youngster?" the African American asked, as he held the cuffs in his hand. I was sure he had to be the only black bailiff in the whole county.

"Yeah, let's get this over with, old timer," I said, turning my back to the door so that he could place the cuffs on me. Locking the cuffs, he secured them with a key to be sure I had no chance of escaping. Backing me out of the cell, he escorted me into the cold quiet courtroom.

As soon as I walked in, the DA smiled at me. By the smile, I was sure he thought he had this case already in the bag. I walked to the opposite table from the DA and stood behind it alone. The lawyer I had relied on to keep me out of prison ended up handling my case shoddily, and the end result was the fifteen-year sentence I was already serving. I definitely wasn't about to pay another one just to fuck me over again.

The judge's chamber opened, causing everyone in attendance to look. "All rise for Honorable Judge White," the bailiff said. The judge took her seat and the bailiff lowered his hands, indicating that we could be seated.

"What do we have today?" Judge White asked.

The bailiff handed her my case file. "The State of Texas versus inmate #2093156—name, Gianni Kingsley," he said.

Judge White looked up from the file to me. "Wow! Another inmate, where from this time?" she asked

"This one came in from George Beto, charged with one count of possession of a controlled substance in a Penal Institute, with two counts of first-degree murder," the Bailiff recited.

"And where is your lawyer?" she asked.

"Uhmm, your Honor, I chose to represent myself," I said.

She looked up from my file, shocked. "What are you? A prison lawyer?"

"No, your Honor. I'm just an innocent man that seeks his own rightfully deserved justice."

Nodding, she said, "Understandable—well, Mr. Kingsley, trial will be set for March 6th. That will give you a month to prepare your defense."

"Your Honor, if I may, I would like to request a speedy trial. The food here sucks, and I would like to get back to my assigned unit before next Tuesday. We're having pork pizza, and that's my favorite." That statement of mine drew a few laughs from the audience. The Judge didn't find it funny, as she stared at me with a blank face.

"District Attorney, how do you feel about a speedy trial?" she asked?

The DA smiled as he looked over at me. "Your Honor, if the defense wants to spend the rest of his life in prison faster, then that's fine by me."

Knowing that he already had the murder weapon, and the pound of K2 they found behind my toilet in the cell, he probably thought he already won the case. Little did he know I had a trick up my sleeve.

"In that case, a speedy trial is set for next Monday, court is dismissed," Judge White announced as she banged her gavel.

The DA looked over at me with a big smile as the bailiff came back to escort me to the cold cell. He whispered as he placed the cuffs on me, "Youngster, I want you to think about what you're doing. This isn't a game, this is your life you're playing with."

I nodded. I knew on the outside it appeared that I was giving them the rope, and standing on the chair on my own free will, just to let them kill me. "I appreciate the concern, old timer, but honestly, they ain't never met a nigga as half as smart as me," I said, as he unlocked the cell door.

"If you say so, youngster, wish you luck," he said as he unlocked the cuffs.

"Thanks for the luck, but I won't need it!" I yelled through the door, as I lay on the cold concrete slab. Placing both hands behind my head, I drifted off as I thought back to what led me here to begin with.

Newton

"Be very careful how you deal with these criminals. They are very persuasive," said the training sergeant, as he walked around eyeing us all that were training for the job. "They will try to talk about the things you like. The things that they think you like, ask about your family like they really care. Even bring up sports and politics. They will try every route to get inside your head, to get your guard down."

Some of us stared at him, and the rest looked around the spacious gym area they had for the inmates.

"These men are murderers, rapists, con artists, drug dealers, and gang members," the sergeant continued. "We are their worst enemies. We are the law. Everything that we are for, they're against. We are here to protect the children that we have at home. We are the chosen ones." As he went on and on, my mind drifted off. I couldn't believe I was training to become a correctional officer in a maximum security prison. One that was claimed to be the worst in Texas, Bloody Beto!

Grabbing his walkie-talkie off his hip, the sergeant said, "We'll line up the same way we came in. Eyes forward, and ignore the stares. Don't fall victim to them. I know some of you may be saying that you'll never, but we have a wall full of officers that said the same." He said into his walkie-talkie: "Clear the halls of all traffic. We have pre-service in the halls, pre-service in the halls."

"Girl, that was one long ass speech—his shit was longer than Martin Luther King's," Williamson said from behind me. Williamson and I became close friends while training in the academy together. She was as crazy as they came, but she was cool as can be.

"You ain't lying, I almost dozed off," I joked, as we walked down the long hallway. I tried to walk with my back straight, chest up, with my head straight ahead. The hallway was packed with a bunch of staring inmates. You could actually feel them undressing you with their eyes. I rubbed my hair to try to lay my wild hairs down. Pulling my sweat pants up, I pulled my shirt down to cover my ass; to conceal it from the lust-filled eyes as we walked to the A, B, C, D block, which accommodated the kitchen and laundry workers, along with the sex offenders who were housed on B-wing. They had their own wing because they couldn't be housed with the regular inmates.

Walking past the first block, I could see inmates from my peripheral standing on the gates—watching us. None had the nerve to say anything, seeing that the sergeant was watching over us. If they were to get caught, then they would probably get a disciplinary case.

Walking down the hallway, we made it to the E, F, G, H block. The E, F, G, H block housed the maintenance workers, and the sign shop workers. F-wing housed the offenders who were afraid to be in population. E-wing was for the religious inmates that either really wanted to change for God, or faked their intentions for whatever reason.

Just like the previous block, inmates were standing on the gates watching us as we walked by. I knew we were safe from harassment because of the training sergeant that walked alongside us. Well at least that's what I thought.

"Look out, snow bunny, you in the sweats, sexy ass!" a bold inmate yelled from H-wing's gate. Out of my peripheral I could see his face. He was black, a dark-skinned inmate who was a little taller than me. The thing that stood out to me was his boldness. He didn't care about rank right there. Who was I fooling? He really didn't care about anything, he was already in prison.

"Girl, shots fired—I know you heard that," Williamson said, as we made it to the parking lot.

"Those people really discussed me. Instead of trying to better themselves, they were staring at us like we were their next victims."

"Gabby—stop, girl, they're humans just like you and me," Williamson said, calling me by my nickname which was short for *Gabriela*.

"No, they're animals. I feel violated at how they were staring at us," I said as I unlocked my car door.

"You just mad 'cause he called you a snow bunny. All white girls get offended by that. Bitch, you better be lucky that you got a nickname. Don't let that sergeant brainwash you. This is my second unit, and to tell you the truth, it really ain't that bad."

"Yeah, that's what the rest of them females said before an inmate brainwashed them," I said, cranking my car up. "Did you see the wall of shame that they had when we walked in? They catch you messing around with an inmate, they'll dress you up in the inmate's clothes, and take a picture of you just to put it on their wall so everyone can see. I don't know about you, but I don't look good in prison white!"

"Well, today was easy, tomorrow we'll be hands on with them. Tomorrow you'll earn your stripes." She was teasing.

"Girl, you play too much—I gotta go, I have to get home to my man and kid—I'll see you bright and early tomorrow," I said, closing the door. Waving goodbye, she got inside her car. I turned my radio up as Taylor Swift played over the stereo. "*I knew you were trouble when you walked in!*" I sang as I headed home. I had a hell of a day coming up.

Hotboy

"There they go right there!" Lakewood said to me as the new class of C.O's began to walk by. Lakewood was my role dog; he was like a little brother to me. He was from Houston, the Lakewood area—that's why we called him Lakewood. You couldn't tell him shit about his hood. Even though he was only twenty-one years old, he had seen it all, and done it all, if you ask him. "Hotboy, you seen that black ho wink at me?" he said over his shoulder as I walked up behind him.

"I ain't see her, was she fine or what?" I asked, as I watched the class walk by.

"She was straight. She had a fat ass though. I could tell the bitch didn't have any panties on. Her shit was melting with every step she took." He laughed. The training sergeant walked past, causing Lakewood to back away from the gate out of fear. He always amazed me. He discharged his entire sentence in six months, with no way of anyone stopping him, yet he was the scariest nigga on the wing when it came to dealing with an officer. "You better watch out for the sergeant," he said, from behind me.

Stepping closer to the door, I said, "The sergeant better watch out for me!" The end of the new class was coming up. One of the male trainees stared at me like he wanted a problem. "The fuck you looking at, pussy!" I yelled, staring at him. That type of shit always pissed me off. They hated us without a reason, only 'cause we were locked up.

Leaning on the gate, I put my arms through the bars as I waited for the rest of the class to pass by. I noticed her before she noticed me. She had these tight, blue and grey sweats on that hugged her hips snugly. She was pretty, considering the strands of hair that stood up on her head. The glasses that she wore made her look like a college freak that was D-F-W—*down for whatever*. As she got closer to the door, I couldn't help myself. "Look out, snow bunny, you in the sweats, sexy ass!" I shouted as she passed by.

I knew she had heard me, because the chick behind her started smiling.

"Hey, get off the door!" the African C.O. working the wing yelled.

"Fuck you, nigga. Ol' girl ass punk!" I spat back at him.

"Get behind the stairs before I call rank!" he threatened.

"Spell it, pussy!" I yelled as I mean-mugged him. I walked

off, leaving him looking stupid as I ran up the back half of the stairs to get to my cell.

Making it to my cell, I placed my foot at the bottom of the door and pushed hard as I shook the door back and forth, causing it to pop open. Normally, you would need a key to open the cell doors, but this was Beto. The inmates had the keys!

"Wassup, what you about to do?" Lakewood asked as he walked up to my cell door. Lakewood was my everyday nigga. He was even my next-door neighbor. I couldn't dodge him even if I wanted to. Lakewood was about 5'8, with a chest like a ten-year-old boy's. He was sentenced to three years, which he was months away from completing. He was always in the mix, always trying to make a play. He always kept everyone laughing, especially when he got mad and started talking fast—he would end up stuttering. You wouldn't be able to calm him down, or figure out what he was saying.

"Why you always stop in front of a nigga cell?" I said as I slid the door back. "You're going to blow the spot up. You know them Africans be policing the runs and shit. Just come in." He peeped over the rail before coming in, making sure he wasn't being watched by the law man. As soon as he walked into my cell, I tossed him a Ziploc bag of tobacco. "Roll up, the papers in the bag, and don't get no ideas!" I said, as I grabbed the materials to get a light.

"My nigga, when have I ever stole anything from you? Plus you ain't really got shit to steal. When I take something, I make sure it's worth my while." He rolled up a cigarette.

I took a pencil and a razor blade, then I placed the razor into the bottom of the pencil. "I can't wait until I can use a real lighter," I said more to myself, as I placed the razor and pencil into the power socket. Using a piece of wire, I touched the tip of the wire to the tip of the pencil, causing a spark.

"Naw, nigga, I can't wait till I can smoke a real Newport—this shit here be hurting a nigga throat," Lakewood said as he twisted a piece of tissue and handed it to me. I used the tissue to catch the flame with, as I popped the socket again with the wire. I quickly lit the cigarette as I flushed the burning tissue. Taking a long drag from the square, I stared at it.

"My nigga, why do you always do that shit?" he asked, reaching for the square. I did have a habit of always looking at the cigarette as I'm smoking it. I handed the square to him.

"I hate this shit. This shit cheap as hell, and it's trash as hell, but it's the only thing that keeps a nigga sane."

"If you hate it so damn much," Lakewood said, handing it back to me, "then why you always buying it? You sho'll spend a lot of money on it."

Feeling used, I said: "Yeah, this shit crazy. I spent a hunnit just for this little ass sack. Them lame ass niggas use my money to get the shit in. So on the cool they really pimping me."

"You talking like you can do what they're doing. Like you can win a ho and make her drop out. All that pimp shit you be talking, you should've been bagged a bitch."

"It ain't hard, I had three ho's on Bradshaw," I pointed out.

He looked at me sideways. "Bradshaw, nigga, that's a transit unit. That's easy as hell. This is the big leagues. It's three thousand of different personalities, and conversations for a bitch to choose from. Bradshaw had what, almost a thousand inmates to choose from? You said you had three over there, but I can't tell. 'Cause so far, I ain't seen shit."

"Don't worry, watch, when this new class graduate, I'ma turn up!"

Gangsta

"Wassup, cuz? What you finna do today?" Li'l Tyler asked, as he sat beside me while I was seated in front of the sports TV.

I was really tired of niggas asking me the same shit every single day, like we had a lot we could do. We were in prison, there wasn't too much that we could do. There was no going to the store, or going to the club, none of the shit. To make matters worse, we were housed on medium custody, G4 status. That means that we're separated from the entire unit, and we were placed in the cell for twenty hours out of the day. We had just the privilege of walking to chow, and getting four hours of dayroom time a day.

It seemed like everyone wanted to use their dayroom time to distract me from watching TV. Without looking away from the TV, I said, "Say, cuz, don't you see me trying to watch TV, homie? We got twenty hours to talk, I'll holla at you then"

Instead of being quiet like I thought he would've, he started back talking. "So who you think going to win the NBA finals this year. The Clippers looking good already. They even beat LeBron twice this year." That was Beto for you, niggas was fucked up here. They never knew how to mind their own business, or catch a hint. I started to think that they just wanted to be around a Gangsta.

My real name is David, but I go by the name: *Gangsta*. You know, most people come to prison with a whole new persona. They come with a bunch of made-up names that they thought about in the county jail. When someone asks them their name, they just make one up right there on the spot, and everyone will start calling them that. Normally, people would come up with a super live name like *Choppa*. Or a name like *Square Business*. They never give the name that people call them in the free world. Most likely it's a bullshit name, or they got something to hide. As for me, Gangsta wasn't a name I gave myself. Gangsta was a name that was given to me.

I lived by the name, set my principles around it, and would die behind it as well. I was placed on medium custody because I beat this ese damn near to death. The crazy thing is that it was in self-defense, but no one ever believes a Gangsta!

"Li'l homie, how much time you got?" I asked.

He looked at me. "Why?"

"Coz I asked, nigga!" I yelled without looking his way. He looked back at the TV as he placed his feet on the bench that was in front of us. "I got thirty-five years," he said, sounding like he was embarrassed.

I shook my head in disbelief. "For what?"

Putting his head down, he said, "For robbing a 7-Eleven."

I shook my head again. Not because of the crime that he committed, but because he was only a kid, and was given thirty-five years for robbing a corner store. To me, that was the crime! "So what you're back here for?"

"I got jammed up with a cap of K2, and a few squares," he explained. "They didn't catch me with the two zones, and the pills I had though!" he said, feeling like he accomplished something live.

"Li'l homie, was it even your shit?"

"Well, I mean not really, but I was just about to turn up. Don-C was about to put me on!" he said excitedly.

"Don-C! Mane, that nigga can't even put himself on, he a worker too!" I yelled, getting upset. I hated when old heads preyed on the young niggas just to run game on them, only because he got a lot of time and no wisdom.

"But he—" he managed to say before I cut him off.

"But nothing! Look li'l homie, you got thirty-five years. That means you have to do seventeen-and-a-half years just to see parole. Meaning you'll be what, thirty-five—thirty-six—when you see parole?"

"Thirty-six," he answered.

"Thirty-six then. Li'l homie, it's cool to *cuz this*, *cuz that* for a moment, but how many times have a homie sent you anything back here, be it food or hygiene?"

He thought for a second. "Not once."

"I'ma show you something, homie, and always remember this. I'm a homie too, but you don't see me messing with these cats. You know why? 'Cause they lost. This place is all they know. I can't tell you how to do your time, 'cause I ain't going to do it for you, but check this. If you're going to hustle, you have to do it with a purpose. Don't do it for the fame. Whatever reason you come up with, make sure it's reason enough to sacrifice." He knew full well I was schooling him.

"I feel you, big homie. This is my first time down; I'm just trying to survive."

"Survival is in the mind, not for the fittest. So how strong is your mind?"

"It's strong," he said as if he was trying to convince himself.

"I'm not trying to tell you to hustle, li'l homie, but if you're going to get a bag, then get it by yourself. That way, you don't work for anyone, and if you have to take a loss you won't owe anyone shit." He soaked up my words of wisdom, nodding all the way.

"I appreciate ya, my nigga."

I looked back at the TV. My eyes were on the screen, but my mind was elsewhere. I was thinking about the first time I came to prison. How people tried to hustle me and crash me out. If only I knew then what I knew now, I would have beat all them bitch ass niggas up!

"Aye, Gangsta," Li'l Tyler said, catching my attention.

"Wassup?"

"How many homies sent you something back here?" he asked, looking up at me.

I laughed at his question. "None, but I got two patnas— Hotboy and Lakewood. They be looking out for me from time to time. Why you ask?"

"I was trying to see, you know they say to keep the squares out yo' circle. Maybe I need a new group of patnas like you to hang with."

"I don't know, li'l homie, I couldn't tell you about friends 'cause I don't have any. Never dealt with them squares, and I don't even have a circle. My squad so tight we like a triangle, it's only three of us with no room for anyone else to fit in. It's just me and my two bros, and in a week we'll finally be reunited!"

Chapter 1

Newton

"Hey, babe, how was your day today?" Seth asked, as I walked through the front door of our home. I gave him a quick kiss before I sat my purse down.

"It was okay. We did a few drills like we did the day before. Tomorrow though, we'll be hands-on with the inmates." Sitting beside him on the couch, I placed my feet in his lap, hoping for a foot massage.

Seth and I had been together for almost two years now. We started dating from mutual friends introducing us. One thing led to another, and we ended up falling for each other. Really, I fell in love with his six-year-old son—Jacob. He's so innocent and adorable it's hard not to love him. His mom abandoned him a few years ago, so I took up the role as his mother. My life had transformed overnight. At first I was fresh out of high school, with no kids, and a bright future. Now I'm 22 years old with a kid, and a fiancé that I'm practically taking care of.

I say *practically* because I had the only income coming in the house. The income went to the food and the bills. The correctional officer's income wasn't enough to pay the rent, but insurance was worth it.

Seth had lost his job over a month ago when his job did a random drug test, which he failed, due to him using meth occasionally. I knew that he had previously used when we first met. But he had told me he'd quit when, one time, his habit came between us. I could normally tell when he's using again, because his attitude changes. Lately he hasn't been using. He'd been in a good mood, and he kept the house clean. Plus he'd been having dinner done so that I wouldn't have to do it.

"Do you think you're ready for all of that?" he asked, concerned. That was one reason that I fell for him. He was such a caring person.

"I really don't have a choice, the bills have to get paid, and we have to eat."

Pulling me into his lap, he said, "Don't worry, babe. I know someone will call me back with a job soon."

Kissing him, I said, "Until then, I got us. But anyways, where is my little Teapot? I bought him something." I stood up to grab my purse.

"What did I tell you about calling him that? He's a boy. That name is for girls. Why do you keep buying him so many damn toys, babe? We already don't have enough money to pay the bills." Seth walked up behind me.

"He's my little teapot, don't get jealous. If I shouldn't have bought him his toy, then I should take this back then." I pulled out a cock ring that I bought from the adult store on my way home.

The look of shock registered on his face as he saw the sex toy. "I guess spending a little money wouldn't hurt," he said, hugging me from behind.

"Where's he at?" I asked.

Smiling, he said, "The little teapot is asleep."

Hotboy

"Dropping out chow, one row dropping out for chow!" the C.O. yelled over the run.

Jumping off the top bunk, I grabbed my toothbrush and Colgate. Cutting my radio on, I plugged my cardboard speaker in. "Lakewood, get up, nigga, it's chow time!" I yelled through the wall.

"Yo, I'm up!" he yelled back.

I could hear his feet hit the floor as he jumped off his bunk. "Yo' bitch ass going to cry if you fuck around and miss it. Then you going to try and blame me for it like I'm your alarm clock or something."

"Yeah, whatever, nigga. Who we got working?"

"I think it's Ms. Dean. That's who it sounded like."

"I like that old bitch for some reason," he said.

I laughed as I spit toothpaste out my mouth. "That's cause

you're fucked up, homie. That lady got you beat by at least thirty years fo'sure. She cool and down to earth, but—come on, if you were to see her in the free world, you wouldn't even look at her."

"Nigga you must don't know me well. I got a baby by my high school teacher, I like them old." He was making me laugh again.

"Two row, get on your doors; don't make me wait!" the C.O. yelled.

The doors rolled as I stepped out with my visitation clothes on, which where our best crisp whites. Considering I never went to visitation, I rocked mine everyday like I had a visit Monday through Sunday. "You ready, slow ass nigga?" I said as I stepped out the cell. Walking in front of his cell, he faced me as he was still brushing his teeth. He flipped me off as he faced the sink. Leaning my back against the rail, I let the ongoing traffic pass by. "Come on, my nigga, you know the line going to be long as hell, it's beef pizza, you know every nigga going to be in chow—even the Muslims."

Leaning over the toilet, he spat, then rinsed his mouth out. "My nigga, no matter how fast I move, we still going to be waiting. This B card, so you know Ms. Mitch going to be in front of the chow hall. You know how she is."

I nodded. He was on point. Ms. Mitch was everywhere on the unit at one time. "Fuck it, I got a square on me. Get a light and we'll smoke it while we wait." I looked around. I didn't want the C.O. walking up catching us.

"Where she at?" he asked.

Looking out, I said, "I gotcha, my nigga, she like ten cells down. Handle yo' business. I ain't going to let her walk up on you." He popped the socket and took off out the cell as I closed his door behind him. We took off down the back half of the stairs as the C.O. was trailing behind us, closing doors.

"Hotboy, wassup?" an inmate spoke as we walked by. I nodded to him and kept pushing. We walked down the stairs and waited until the C.O. walked up to three row. Walking under the stairs, we stood by the open window.

"Three row out for chow. Three row, get ready!" she yelled as she walked up the stairs. We stood under the stairs as people watched us while they walked by.

"Here, spark it up before she finishes three row," I said, handing him the square. Lakewood ducked down away from the window, so that he could light the square. When it finally caught flame, he threw the light to the floor. Taking a slow

drag, he looked around before passing it to me. Out of habit, I looked at it as I smoked. Looking around, I made sure no officer saw us smoking. It was weird because we were smoking right under a camera.

We never worried about the cameras though. The ones you had to worry about was the walking cameras. Those were the ones that could see and hear.

"What's popping? What y'all smoking?" Eastwood asked as he walked up. Eastwood was a big homie. He was real quiet. He didn't mess with too many people. He was a few years older than me, but he acted like an old school convict that had been locked up for a while. I passed him the square. Then he said, after taking a long pull on it, "I knew you two mo'fuckas was up to something, with y'all slick ass, acting like y'all was looking out the window." He passed the square to Lakewood. "Sell me one or two," Eastwood said.

I looked at him sideways. He always asked me to sell him something, knowing I didn't sell to homies, I just gave it to them. "Come on, my nigga, you know I ain't going to sell you shit. I'll shoot you some when we come back from chow. Everything put up right now."

"That's a bet," Eastwood said. "A nigga need to snatch a ho' or something. I hate Margarita got jammed up. I knew it was only a matter of time, I would 'av had that bitch dropping off like a UPS truck." Eastwood gave a short laugh.

"For real," Lakewood said in agreement, as we walked off to get in the next shot of chow.

Eastwood laughed at Lakewood. "My nigga, you don't ever talk to no ho's. All you ever do is jack off on them. I had to laugh because that was all Lakewood ever did. All jacking, no macking!

"What you laughing at, Hotboy? That shit ain't that damn funny!" Lakewood said to me, like I was the one that made the joke.

I stopped laughing to prevent myself from hurting my nigga feelings. "It's true, my nigga, that's all yo' bitch ass do."

"Naw, for real though, something gotta shake," Eastwood said, bringing us back down to earth.

"Don't worry, in due time, in due time!" I said.

Newton

"Girl, I'm so glad we ain't gotta do all that working out shit no more," Williamson said.

It was our first day in our grey uniforms with the inmates. The sergeant separated us into groups of fours. One group was in the north chow hall, and the north hallway. The other two groups were in the south chow hall, and the south hallway. Me and Williamson were a part of the group that was in the south hall, searching inmates as they passed by. "Yeah, girl, I'm glad too," I replied "I didn't know if I could take anymore of all that karate shit they were trying to teach us," I added. We were standing side by side, talking in a low tone so that no one else could hear. Actually, only my voice was low while we spoke. Even though we were close, she was still loud as hell. She couldn't whisper for shit.

"This is where it gets fun at," she said.

"How?"

She pointed to a tall dark-skinned inmate that was passing by. Curling her finger, she indicated for him to come over. He must've known the procedure, because he turned his back to her and spread his legs apart, holding his arms straight out. As she moved her hands down the front of his shirt, I noticed she put a little pressure behind it to feel his chest. She went down the length of both of his arms as well. Placing her finger in his waist band, she moved it from the front to the back. Lastly, she squatted and ran her hand down his left leg, then the right. She moved her hand up a little higher, and the inmate jumped slightly. She then stood back up and patted him on his back so that he could leave. "Girll, that nigga was packing a shank about the size of his arm. He could stab my pussy with it anytime he wants." She laughed.

I shook my head at her. "Girl, what if he go and report you? You could get into a lot of trouble!"

"Boo, he ain't going to tell nobody but his homeboys. He probably ain't had his dick touched by a woman in years."

I shook my head again. She had some nerve. She didn't even know that guy from Adam, yet she violated him. We carried on with small talk for a while to pass time. I pulled a few inmates over to search them. I was pretty careful about who I picked. I didn't want to just pick whites, blacks, or Hispanics. I picked people that I felt could be hiding something, or they at least looked nervous. I also searched them the proper way, the way we were trained to search. By the time the entire A, B, C, D block was done feeding, I was semi-tired. Plus I had searched over fifteen inmates. I could hear the Lieutenant speak into the walkie-talkie to send a shot of H-wing to chow. Thinking about the bold inmate being on that wing made my heart skip a beat. *Would he go to chow?* I wondered. *Would he even remember me? Where was all of this coming from? I mean, I did have a man at home!*

The first shot came off the wing fast. "Let's see if he remembers you," Williamson said, as if she had read my mind. Looking from face to face, I tried to make out the inmate's face. Looking at Williamson, I noticed she was doing the same thing, or maybe she was looking for her next victim to feel up. Majority of the first group looked over at us, maybe because we were new faces, but no one said a word. The other two new trainees that were alongside us called two inmates over to search, as the rest of the group went inside the chow hall.

We waited another five minutes before another group was called out. The same as before, no one uttered a word. I signaled for an inmate to come over to be searched. This time I searched him faster than I had did the rest. Then another shot came off the wing. This time a little slower, like there wasn't too many people left to come out.

"How many shots do you have left, H-wing?" the Lt. said into the walkie-talkie.

"A little under a shot," he answered back. My eyes never left the gate as I watched every inmate's face that walked off the wing. Then it happened, the C.O. closed the gate back and walked towards another wing.

"Don't worry, girl, you'll see him one day—you work here now so you really don't have a choice," Williamson said, as if she read my expression.

I played it off, well at least I tried to. "I'm not worried about that boy—I'm just ready to get this day over with," I said, denying the truth.

"Bitch, stop! You must've forgot that this ain't my first rodeo," she said. I ignored her last comment because out of my peripheral I could see the C.O. making his way back to H-wing's gate. As he opened the gate, three inmates walked out. One was a little on the heavy side. The other two were dark-skinned, although one was darker than the other one. When they turned to face the way of the chowhall, I felt my heartbeat speed up. As he walked, he looked down. I could tell that he was deep in thought. Then he looked up. He looked over at me, then he looked down again, then he looked back at me again. This time he didn't look away. He smiled a beautiful smile, sexy, yet thuggish.

I looked down because I was afraid I would smile back. When I looked back up, he was standing directly in front of me!

Hotboy

"Last call for chow!" Ms. Dean yelled, as the guard on the keys opened the door so that the remaining few could go to chow.

"Come on, my nigga, you always behind," Eastwood said to Lakewood as he ran out of the dayroom.

"I was looking at ESPN, I was trying to see about what happened with Wiseman that play with the Memphis Tigers," Lakewood explained. They went back and forth like they always did, as my mind drifted off. They always argued about sports 24/7. It killed me, because they acted like they were getting paid.

"Damn, who is that?" Eastwood said, catching my attention. I looked up quickly. I caught her dead eye. So that I wouldn't get in trouble, I checked my surroundings to see staff was working the hallway. Then I looked at her again. This time I let her see me staring. I tried to hold back the smile that was forming on my face, but I couldn't. It turned me up a notch when I saw her face get red with excitement. I guess I made her nervous. I could tell because she tilted her head down. Before she could turn back, I made my move. I was on her like a cheetah chases its prey. When she looked up I must've startled her, because she jumped back slightly.

"I didn't mean to startle you, my bad, ma—My name is Gianni, Gianni Kingsley," I said, turning my back to her so that she could search me. I spread my arms out and my legs as she went right to searching.

"I didn't call you over to get searched," she said.

"I know your mouth didn't say it, but your heart could be heard a mile away," I said as she went to my chest.

"Gianni, or whatever your name is, I didn't come here to play games. I came to do my job."

"That's good. I don't like playing games either. Never been fond of them. I wouldn't have it any other way."

She bent over to move her hand down my leg. Peeping over my shoulder, I tried to catch a glimpse of what she was working with.

"You probably tell that to every female that comes here," she said, moving to my other leg.

Telling the truth somewhat, I said, "Nah, I don't like to waste my time. You're the first I've ever invested my time in."

She stood straight up and placed her hand on the center of my back as she checked my waistband. "So what makes me so special?" she asked as she finished.

I fixed my clothes. "I don't know, I guess we're going to have to find out, huh?" I said, walking off. I gave her co-worker a friendly nod as I made my way to the chow hall, never looking back. I could guarantee she watched my every step!

Gangsta

"Ninety-seven, ninety-eight, ninety-nine, hundred," I counted, as I reached my ninth set of a hundred pushups. My body was physically exhausted, but I was mentally running a marathon. My celly sat on his bunk, pretending to read his book. "Say, my nigga, you younger than me, li'l homie, come down here and hit this floor with me and get this money," I said, trying to persuade the li'l homie.

My celly was a youngsta. I was at least ten years older than him. Being that this was his first time down, and his first time being on medium custody, I tried to help. Game him up a little bit. Plus he was a crip, so I had to look out for him.

He laid the book flat on its pages. "Nah, I'm good, Gangsta, you don't need muscles to shoot a nigga." He laughed.

I nodded in agreement. "You right, but ain't no guns in here, Quan," I said, calling him by his nickname.

"Naw, for real, I feel you," he said. Then he was, like, "Fuck it, how many more sets you got left, I'll jump in." He jumped off his rack.

"I only got one more set left of a hunnit. You can double yours up, and in between each pushup, hold for like five seconds, it'll give you a good burn."

Kneeling down in pushup position, I did my last set as the doors rolled for dayroom time. I finished my set in record timing, as I grabbed my cut-off shirt, and cup. "You coming out?" I asked Quan, as he was kneeling down doing pushups.

"I'm chilling," he said, straining. I laughed a little because he had just started and he was already hurting.

"Aye cuz, you coming out?" yelled Bingo, who was a big homie.

I stepped out the cell as I looked both ways to make sure no opp was waiting on me. I replied to Bingo. "Yeah, why? Wassup? You trying to lose in some chess or what?"

"Nigga, you know you can't fuck with me. You know what, bring a few soups and we'll gamble since you talking like you really live." He laughed.

"You got me," I said as I went back in the cell to grab a few Ramen noodles. What was crazy was that I had so many of them, but I didn't even eat them.

I used them to gamble with, and to buy cakes with. I stuck to a strict diet—mackerels and rice.

"You staying in, or are you coming out?" the C.O. asked as he walked up to my cell door.

I held my hand out to him. "Hold 'em up, bossman, I'm coming out!" I yelled, as I rushed out the cell so he wouldn't close me in. Walking down the two flights of stairs, I noticed that the dayroom was already packed. Too many niggas meant too many different personalities. I was housed on T-wing. T-wing had cameras on the run, but none in the dayroom. The dayroom was like the battlefield. Even though we only got four hours a dayroom time a day, in those four hours anything could happen.

As I walked in the dayroom, I looked around for an empty table where I could set up the chessboard. I locked C's with a few homies as we walked past each other. Majority of them walked around looking like zombies, as they were high off of K2. It amazed me that we dropped out for dayroom time at 7 a.m., and most of the dayroom was already high as hell. Majority of them only came out so that they wouldn't miss out on a free smoke.

"What's cracking, cuz?" Bingo said, as he sat across from me. Bingo was practically the only homie on medium custody that had any sense, and that didn't get high. Bingo had been gone for over twenty-seven years already. Most people that had been gone that long were penitentiary as hell, but Bingo was as free world as they came.

After locking C's, I made my first move on the chessboard. "Ain't shit, slow rolling," I said. "I finally see classification next week. It's been six long ass months. I'm hoping that they'll let me come from back here. I'm tired of this shit cuz, for real."

Bingo moved in an angle with his knight, as he tried to avoid getting it taken by my pawn. "How you think I feel, nigga?" he said. "I've been back here with these clucks for a year now, and

I've been in this penitentiary longer than most of these li'l niggas been alive, and I still got time to do." Bingo had got G4'd for using profanity towards the Warden. It hadn't been the first time he had been G4'd, and it probably wouldn't be his last time either.

Moving my bishop in front of his knight, I forced his hand so that I could gain a free piece as I studied his face. "I feel you, I would've gone crazy if they would've gave me a year back here."

"Pill lady on the wing! Pill lady on the wing! Vanilla ice cream!" the porter yelled loud enough for the wing to hear. When someone screamed *vanilla ice cream*, they were saying that a white lady was in the area. As the porter yelled it out, the entire dayroom ran over to the dayroom bars to take a look.

Medium custody wasn't allowed to have female C.O's work the wing; only the mail lady came through, and the pill lady. When they did walk through, you'd better watch out because the jackers would be ready, and they didn't give a damn who they burned up. Nobody was spared.

I shook my head as some of them walked away from the bars to finish getting high.

"Front half two row!" the porter yelled.

"Two moves checkmate," I pointed out, making Bingo look deeper at the board.

He looked up at me. "Bet double it ain't in two moves," he said, trying to roach up on an easy bet.

I acknowledged his bet. For one, I was a gambler, and two, I was a great chess player. I moved the pieces like I moved in life. I moved with patience, and perfect calculation. If I couldn't gain off the move, I didn't move it. If I was to lose a piece off a move, I made sure that I gained double from the loss. "Make your next move your best move," I teased.

As Bingo was studying his next move, a big commotion arose on the other side of the dayroom. "Bitch! Bitch! Bitch!" A voice boomed. Everyone in the dayroom stood up to watch the action. I noticed a Hispanic was bashing a black dude's head in with a fan motor that was tied tightly in a sock. All of the blacks rushed the Hispanic as a riot popped off that fast. Me and Bingo stood up and placed our backs against the wall. Bingo pulled out a shank and he tucked it at his side. I was glad that he had his because I had forgot mine when the lawman rushed me out of the cell.

When all of our homies surrounded the back wall, I knew it was the Tango Blast and the Bloods that were fighting. It was normal for an organization to find your family when shit popped off just to make sure your people were safe.

The wing boss called for backup while he watched from the run as blood splattered everywhere. As soon as he called, you could see a bunch of officers running down the hallway with riot gear on.

"Oh, shit, mask up, gas gun!" Bingo yelled as he pulled his shirt over his face. We all covered our faces as I noticed the Lt. running with the gas gun. He unlocked the latch that was attached to the dayroom window as he pulled the cover down, shooting a round into the dayroom. As soon as he shot the gun, the gas filled the dayroom instantly, and everyone started coughing and shedding tears.

Even the wing boss coughed from the strong gas. The wing boss wasn't even smart enough to cover his face as the gas burned his eyes. A few inmates ran to the toilet, fighting for water to put in their eyes to rinse the burning sensation.

As the fighting crowd dispersed, you could see the casualties. There was one black guy, and two Hispanics laid out on the floor. Half of the black guy's skull was on the floor as his dick was hanging out of his pants. The other two Hispanics were just beat up really bad. I could almost guarantee that the black guy disrespected one of the Hispanic guys by jacking off on the pill lady beside him. I shook my head at the gruesome, but normal, scene. *"Damn, this needs to fly by."*

Chapter 2

Hotboy

"Aye, Hotboy! Did you hear that?" Lakewood asked from next door.

I turned over groggily, as I looked at my clock. "What the hell you want, my nigga? It's 7:30 in the damn morning! You know I don't get up until after first drop!" I yelled out of frustration.

"I think I heard a helicopter outside. I could have sworn I heard one," he said, almost sure.

"Bruh, you bugging. It's too early to hear a helicopter, the only time they come is when a nigga gets life flighted, and I know ain't nobody then got fucked off this early in the morning."

"I know I ain't tripping," Lakewood said. "Fuck, well send me a square over here then, I can't go back to sleep now."

I looked askance at him. "You full of shit, li'l nigga. If you wanted a square, you should've just said something. Talking about you heard a helicopter—weak ass game." I reached into my shorts and pulled out a sack of tobacco. I jumped off the bunk as I handed the sack next door to him. "Damn, I hate this top bunk!" I yelled as I stubbed my toe. "Roll me one up too, bitch," I said, loud enough for him to hear. Taking my speaker from my locker, I plugged it into the radio as I turned the station to the Morning Hustle on 97.9 the beat.

I was sure that I woke up the whole wing as I turned up my radio to the max jamming *Young Dolph's* "Get Paid" song as I brushed my teeth. The aroma from the cigarette could be smelled from all the way in my cell from Lakewood's, as I saw smoke coming from his cell. "Where mines at, nigga?" He reached his hand into my cell as he handed me back the sack, along with a rolled up cigarette that was already lit. "My nigga!" I said, and sat on my celly's bunk as I inhaled the square. My celly was at school already, so I figured I'll enjoy this alone time as I listened to the wisdom that Young Dolph was spitting.

"Get paid, young nigga, get paid/ Whatever you do, just make

sure you get paid!" Dazed out from the head rush, I didn't notice the C.O standing in front of my cell until it was too late.

"Turn that shit down, and stop smoking! Stupid motherfuckas always smoke but never spray shit!" Lambo said, as he looked around the cell.

Lambo was one of the C.O's that was some-timing. He was African but wanted to be American bad as hell. He rocked Jordans, and G-shocks, hoping he'll fit in. The bad thing was that he was a straight cop. He would pretend to be cool with you when it was only you and him, but as soon as he was around another African C.O., he would change up. I tried to stay away from his bad side because he would pretend to be tough, but when shit got real, he would call for backup, or send you to lockup.

"I gotcha, Lambo," I said, hoping he'll walk off. "Where the fuck is the porter!" I yelled over the run, upset because I got caught and no one warned me.

"Fuck that! You knew better to have that shit up that damn loud anyway, especially before shift change," Lakewood said.

"Eat my dynamite pussy, and watch it blow up in yo' mouth. Yo' bitch ass was probably over there jamming my shit." I laughed.

He laughed too. "Hell yeah, that nigga Dolph be having me in the world."

I got quiet as I took a mental trip to the free world. Sometimes taking trips to the world was dangerous. It was good to be able to escape every now and then, but it was dangerous because some-times you would venture off, and it would be hard to come back.

"Don't worry, in a few more months you'll be out there, and can't nobody stop you," I reminded him.

"You right behind me. What—you got, like, ten months until you see parole?" he asked.

I smiled on the inside. It had been almost seven years since I left the free world. Time had flown by, and now time to see parole was close. "Yeah, I pray that they wake up in a good mood when I see them."

"You'll make it. You don't have a choice. You be driving them ho's crazy. They can't wait to kick you out this bitch." Lakewood laughed.

I laughed at his comment. He wasn't lying. When I first got locked up, I caused all kinds of drama. I fucked a few of their female C.O.'s, and spread a lot of dope over the unit. If only I would've been smart enough to have saved some of the money that I made, I would've had enough to get me a parole lawyer. I guarantee that the next bitch I knock, I'ma make it count.

Lambo walked back through as he counted for a second time. "Didn't you just count, my nigga?" Lakewood asked.

"Special count, fool. They had a life flight on T-wing," Lambo said, solidifying Lakewood's assumption. Shaking my head, I sent a quick prayer up. I prayed that it wasn't one of my niggas!

Newton

"Hey, chick, you ready?" Williamson asked, as we waited in line to get searched. It dawned on me that they considered all officers dirty because they searched us all as we walked into the building, like we were the ones locked up.

I answered as we moved up in line. "Yeah, I guess. One more week and we graduate,"

"Yup, but it's easier when you graduate. You'll be more re-laxed when it's just you and them."

I was next in line as I stood in front of the sergeant. "Spread out for me, sweetie," she said

Turning my back to her, I spread my legs and held my arms out just like the inmates did. Tracing her hand up and down my arms, she moved down to my legs.

"Shoes have to come off too, darling," she said.

Sitting my lunch down on the floor, I unzipped my boots and pulled them off. Handing them both to her, she looked inside of them and turned them upside down. She stuck her hand inside the shoe, hitting the bottoms together before handing them back to me. I moved to the side as I waited on Williamson to finish.

"Feels weird, don't it?" Williamson said, as she walked up beside me.

"What?" I asked, unsure of what she meant.

"You know, the whole officer shakedown shit. It's crazy because majority of the ones that be shaking us down, they be dirty too, but if they were to find something on you, they would turn you in to make it look like they aren't dirty." Her explanation made a lot of sense.

"Really, you don't think that lady is in the game, do you? I mean, look at her. She looks so sweet and innocent."

Williamson laughed at my comment. "Them the ones you have to watch, they always the main ones."

I thought about what she had just said. Looking back at the sergeant, I saw her smile at another incoming C.O. who was waiting to get searched. *Could she really be a wolf in sheep's clothing?* Pushing the thought to the side, I walked into the briefing room behind Williamson to get our assignment for the day.

"Congrats on making it out of the academy. Many people don't make it to this point," the Lt. said, as if the academy was so hard. He continued as he looked at the dry erase board, "We had a riot at seven-ish this morning. One died, and another is in critical condition. T-wing is on lockdown until the Warden says otherwise."

I shook my head. I was really starting to second guess this whole thing. *What was I doing here? Someone actually got killed, and another ended up in critical condition!"*

"Ms. Newton, are you alright?" the Lt. asked, reading my name tag. I nodded. "Yes, I'm fine," I lied with a straight face. As bad as I wanted to walk out of the room and never look back, I couldn't. I had a family to feed.

"Okay, Oakshire, you and Boadu will be paired up on the north side on T and U wing keys. Williamson and Newton, you'll be working H-wing. Very easy wing—majority of the inmates are at work already." He sounded like he did us a favor. My mind drifted off as soon as he said *H-wing*. I looked over at Williamson, and she had this cheesy grin on her face that I read straight through.

"Okay, always remember, just say no!" the Lt. said, ending his speech. Half of us headed to the south end, as the remaining half went to the north end of the unit. My nerves grew tense; I was more scared of going to H-wing than I was about the inmate that got killed.

"Girl, this is so meant to be," Williamson said, playfully bumping me as we stood in front of H-wing's gate.

"You two coming over here with me?" asked a tall Caucasian lady with short hair.

She looked to be around her fifties. Her short bob style haircut made her look younger than she was. Her wide hips and tight pants probably made the inmates go crazy as she strutted over to the gate. "I'm Ms. Dean, everyone calls me Mama Dee," she said, as she extended her hand out the gate to us. We both shook her hand,

"My name is Newton," I greeted her, as Williamson went straight hood.

"And I'm Williamson, nice to meet you, Mama Dee. Oh, and girl, I must say, you are rocking that do, it so fits you."

Williamson's compliment made Ms. Dean smile. She rubbed the back of her hair. "Thanks, sweetie, I try to stay with the style."

The turnkey boss opened the gate to let us on the wing. Looking around, I knew without a doubt I couldn't last a day in prison. Not being Williamson's first time working in a prison, the scene wasn't so bad for her.

"Come on, ladies," Mama Dee began, "let me give y'all the tour before we drop them out for dayroom time. Here, y'all can put your things in here." She unlocked a small closet. Placing our things in the closet, Mama Dee locked it back and led the way down the run.

"Prepare for dayroom time, gentleman! One row, two row, three row, get ready to drop out!" Mama Dee yelled, as inmates started to wake up. Walking close behind her, I glanced into a few cells to see how they were built.

"One row crawling, three times, soft rocks!" an inmate yelled as we passed by his cell. Walking down the long walkway, inmates placed their mirrors outside their cell to see who we were.

"Back half, two row!" another inmate yelled as we started to walk up the stairs.

"It's okay," Mama Dee said. "It used to irritate the hell out of me, but that's their way of holding down security. Sometimes it helps, sometimes it don't. I remember one time they didn't say it, and I ended up walking up on a group of guys having sex. I wish they would've said something that day, I still can't get that horrible scene outta my mind." She shook her head.

I shook my head too. That was a disturbing thought, I prayed I never walked up on anyone doing something like that.

"Ms. Dean, how you doing this morning?" a Hispanic asked.

She stopped at his cell. "I'm doing good, y'all better behave yourselves today, and don't embarrass me," she said.

Walking off, she greeted multiple inmates as we passed by their cell. Some cells had one inmate in them, and some had two. My thought was that their celly was either at school, or at work.

"Ms. Dean, I'ma be honest with you," said an inmate, "I like yo' style. You remind me of that lady—Julia Roberts."

He got a smile out of her as she walked past. I couldn't help but see who had lied to her like that. As I looked inside his cell, he looked at me like he knew me.

"Say, Hotboy, wake up, nigga, it's work call!" the inmate said out loud. Hearing his phrase, his neighbor walked up to the bars, and my heart dropped!

Hotboy

I could hear my guy shooting his shot at Ms. Dean. He did have a thing for older woman, for sure. I had just finished taking a bird bath, and covered myself with a towel as best as I could. I tried to lay my waves down as I rubbed some Blue Magic in my hair.

"Say Hotboy, wake up nigga, it's work call!" Lakewood yelled. Saying *work call* meant that there was a potential catch in the area. Walking to the bars, I took a glance to see who he was talking about.

I was sure he wasn't talking about Ms. Dean. Rubbing the grease in my scalp, I felt that I had never done it at such a special time as this. Seeing *her* face again made my heart spin. I had never felt anything so sudden for a female that I knew nothing about like I felt for her. This one *was* a prize waiting to be won. The way she looked at my body assured me she liked what she saw.

"'Damn, boy!" her co-worker said from behind her. I looked at her, and could tell she was going to be a handful. Laughing at her boldness, I sensed she wasn't new to the system.

Letting them walk by, I refused to acknowledge either of them. I knew deep down she was waiting on me to speak. I only wanted her name, and I got that once I looked at her name tag.

To seem like I wasn't thirsty for a bitch, I walked away from the cell door to finish getting dressed. I knew no man had ever turned his back on her before. I had to show her that I wasn't like any other man she ever messed with.

"Fine and cocky!" her co-worker said as they walked by. I held in a laugh until they were far away from my cell. As they made it to three row, I burst out laughing. "Lakewood, that's going to be the one watch!" I assured him with confidence.

He placed his mirror inside my cell so that he could see my face as he said, "Why you ain't say nothing? Bitch, let me find out you nutted up on me!" It was real common to use the "Bitch" word amongst friends in Texas prisons. It was wild because one word could be used for good, and bad, depending on who you were talking to, and how you said it.

"Come on, my nigga, you know the kid don't freeze up. You going hard, my nigga. See, I couldn't give her the satisfaction of being the first one to break the ice. Fair exchange ain't never been robbery. Plus, did you see that big ass ring that she had on her finger?"

"Hell yeah, that ho was big as hell. That bitch had to be fake, or her pussy gotta be the bomb."

"Check this, it's only two types of women that work in the penitentiary," I explained.

"Don't hold back, spill it," he said, looking through the mirror at me.

"Okay, so you got the ones that are married and either hate their husband, or he just ain't ever around. So they work here to have another "fake" marriage. Then you have the women that only come for the dick, and to get a little extra money in their pocket. Those are the ones that don't get fucked on a regular in the world. They get ignored by their husbands, they get tired of em."

Lakewood thought about my explanation. "You got a point, so which one do you think ole girl is?" he asked.

"She's behind door number one, just patiently waiting to be rescued. See, my guy, most people think that life is like chess—me, I think it's like poker. Chess is an even game; it's up to you to make the right moves. As for poker, see, you have no choice but to play the hand that you're dealt. You could have the best hand and not even know it. If I out bluff you, I can make you fold yo' hand. See, what you just saw was a woman playing the only hand she was dealt. She can't bluff me though, I see right through it. Right now she has a pair, but I'ma show her how to get a royal flush. Watch, when I'm done with her, she'll want to move in the cell with me!"

Lakewood smiled through the mirror. "Say bitch, you been reading the *Art of Seduction* book, huh?" he asked.

"Why would I read that? I already know everything that he's talking about. I don't need another nigga to remind me of what I already know. All I need to do is keep my own game sharp," I said, schooling him.

He laughed. "See, that's why I fuck with you. So what's the next move?"

"The next move? Shid go all in!"

Gangsta

"Johnnies, celly, you want yours?" Quan asked? I was lying in the bunk, mad as hell. Them clowns ruined our dayroom time with that weak ass riot they popped off. The Warden locked us down on a mandatory 30-day lockdown for the shit. I was glad I only had a few days until I came up before the unit classification. Especially with these weak ass johnnies they kept shooting through the bean chute.

"What's in them?" I asked, not really caring.

Quan looked inside of his brown sack. "It's beef links, peanut-butter sandwich, and some prunes."

I reached on the floor to grab my johnnie sack and I tossed it on his bunk. It was crazy how they fed us cold beef sausages that still had the condom-looking skin over it. The peanut-butter sandwiches tasted like they had mixed jelly with syrup. Then they give you prunes to help you shit it all out because they know when you eat it, it's going to leave you constipated.

I looked outside the bars with my mirror, checking for a porter. "Aye, look out, porter!" I yelled over the run.

"Who dat?" a porter yelled back.

"This 3-0-4," I said, giving him my cell number. "When you get time, pull up on me!" I yelled.

"Aye, Gangsta, you know they said that Dontae died, and that Chico got banged up real bad. They say that he might not make it either. They say that if he does make it, that his memory is going to be fucked up 'cause they stomped his skull in pretty bad." Quan was referring to the riot.

The thing about Beto—rumors started before the incident even happened. A nigga could get caught with some work, and go to lockup. If by chance the next day he gets out, he's a snitch. Or let a nigga get caught up, and the next day someone else get caught up. They'll swear the other nigga snitched to save his ass. It was one thing to put a jacket on a nigga in the penitentiary.

I always minded my business to prevent me from being in

some bullshit. If you a rat, I stay out yo' way. If you a punk, or a street nigga that mess with the boy booty, then I stay away from you. I ain't going to speak on it, or even expose you.

I was taught as a kid by my big homie that *great minds discuss ideas, average minds discuss events, and small minds discuss people.* My big homie had attributed that quote to Eleanor Roosevelt.

"How you know all this, my nigga? You weren't even in the dayroom when shit popped off. Plus I've been in the cell with you since we got racked up, so how in the hell did you find all this out?"

"I overheard the lawman telling somebody on two row about it. That shit really fucked up, bruh! Dontae was about to discharge his sentence at the end of the year, the nigga just turned 21." Quan was on the verge of crying.

"Don't spill yo' tears for that nigga! Spill 'em for his mama! He knew what could've happened when he did what he did. He disrespected another man by jacking off beside him, he fucked up."

"I feel you, bruh, that shit just made me think about my life. It ain't guaranteed to nobody."

I sat up on my bunk as I shook my head. I didn't really fuck with Dontae like that, but I damn sure didn't want him dead, but that was all a part of the game we played.

"This is the jungle, the concrete jungle. Don't ever forget it!" I schooled Quan, as I stood up to look him in the eye.

The porter walked up, cutting our conversation short.

"Wassup 3-0-4?" he said.

"Aye, I need a favor, oh shit, what's cracking, cuz? I didn't know they had you working over here," I said, happy to see a familiar face.

"Hit dat," C-lo said, holding out his "C". We locked C's and I brought it back to my heart.

"Wassup, what's the word out there? What Hotboy and Lakewood, and them niggas out there doing?"

"Them niggas good, Hotboy really been low-key. You know

he stay shooting his shot, you know how that nigga is. He ain't never going to give up until he snatch one up, or go to lockup for trying. Lakewood still on his goof ball shit, just having fun until he go home."

I smiled as I heard about my guys. I had real love for my guys. I wasn't the type to fall off, and start hating on my own team. I always wanted them to prosper. If one of us winning, then we all win. Everybody didn't see life the same way though. "Do me a favor. Tell them niggas I said, one love. Tell Hotboy I said to send me a few squares back here, if he can.

I knew I could trust C-lo with the message. He ran with us when I was on H-wing the first time. He was a real stand-up guy. "Fasho, cuz, you know I gotcha. You straight though? You need some food or something?" he asked.

"I'm straight, cuz, I got enough food to last me until I see classification next week," I assured him.

"If you need something, just let me know, I'll be back over here tomorrow. Oh, shit, I almost forgot, here—this came from Bingo—" C-lo handed me a kite. I unfolded it and read it silently: *"Shoot my money, li'l nigga, you didn't win in two moves. Better luck next time!"* I laughed at Bingo's kite. That was just like him, always trying to get over on a nigga. The only reason I dealt with him was because I knew his intentions. It's the ones you don't know their intentions that you have to worry about!

Chapter 3

Newton

"Boy, get yo' ugly ass on somewhere," Williamson said, cracking at an inmate as we closed doors.

"Two row, three row, get ready!" Ms. Dean screamed.

The inmate cracked back at Williamson. "Bitch, you ain't all that. Peanut head ass li'l girl. That's why one of yo' titties bigger than the other ones. Yoshi looking ass bitch!"

"Williamson, please don't piss them off on our first day!" I begged as we continued to close doors on one row.

"Girl, fuck them, they more scared of a piece of paper and a pen than you are of them," she said, talking about a write-up. As we walked to the front of two row, the doors rolled backwards and some inmates stepped out of their cell.

"We make them walk down the back end of the stairs to prevent a traffic jam, and to prevent anyone getting behind us," Ms. Dean says. As we continued to close their doors, I looked to where Gianni's cell is, as I noticed he hadn't come out yet. Stepping in front of his cell, he walked out looking crisp as his clothes were starched down to his shoes.

"Hey, Mama Dee, who's this you got with you?" he asked with a sexy smile. I couldn't quite put my finger on it, but there was something about him that gave me butterflies. He was so damn handsome with his starched down whites. The way his waves were spinning showed me that he took good care of his body. Even though all of the inmates wore the same clothes, his looked brand new, even his all-white Reeboks that looked like he had just bought them.

"Hey, straggler, my porter isn't coming out until later. Can you do me a favor and sweep up?" Mama Dee asked.

He smiled at her. "Anything for you, Mama Dee."

He walked down the back half of two row, as we headed to three row. I looked down to get another look at him as he walked by. To my surprise, he was looking at me too.

"See, ladies," said Mama Dee, "I'm going to put y'all in on something that they aren't going to teach you in the academy. Just because there are over three thousand men on this unit, that don't mean that you have to like one. Just because they're in cages doesn't mean that you have to treat them like animals. There will be almost two hundred and four inmates on the wing with just you working by yourself."

Mama Dee paused for a moment, then continued. "You'll be locked behind that gate with no key to get out until the keyboss lets you out. So for eight hours, you're locked up. Y'all are going to see a lot of stuff, and you're going to endure a lot of stressful days. As long as you respect them, they'll go to bat for you, trust me." Mama Dee explained, as we finished closing the doors on three row.

My mind drifted off to what she had said. *"Just because they're in cages doesn't mean you have to treat them like animals."* Walking down to the dayroom, I was finally able to get a good look at it. It was pretty small for two hundred and four inmates. It consisted of two TV's. One on the left wall, and another on the right wall. One was for whatever they wanted to watch, and the other one was for sports only. There were five small tables with four seats on each table, along with fifteen benches that faced both TV's. In the far corner was a toilet with a sink attached to it.

In the middle of the dayroom were seven blue payphones that they were able to use during the dayroom hours.

"Okay, ladies, break time for me, it's all yours. Here is the key to the dayroom, it's only good for the dayroom. Don't let anyone out unless it's an emergency, or if they have a lay in. I'm about to rest my feet, Mama Dee getting old." She handed me the keys. She went inside the small closet and she closed it behind her.

"See, girl, I told you Beto was like the club, look," Williamson said, as she directed my attention to the dayroom.

Someone was smoking; I could see scattered clouds of smoke by the movie section. "Hey, no smoking!" I yelled. Williamson stepped to the side as inmates turned to look at us. I looked over at her as she was pointing at me, letting them know she wasn't the one that yelled.

"Naw, hold up ma, don't do that!" Gianni said as he walked up. Walking to the dayroom bars, he addressed the dayroom. "Dayroom, what time do we spark up?" he asked.

"After five!" they shouted in unison.

"So if that's already overstood, then why is there smoke in the air before five? Don't be rude to the game, be true to it!" he said while looking at me.

"Thanks, I guess. You really didn't solve anything. Instead of telling them not to smoke, you only gave them a specific time to smoke."

He stared at me as if he was trying to read my mind. "You can't change the penitentiary, ma. As a man, I will never try to tell another man how to do his time, or how to live his life. I can only offer him advice on how to live his life better with fewer consequences." He held the broom in his hand.

Looking to the side of me, I noticed Williamson engaging in a deep conversation with an inmate that wore a bald fade.

"What's your name ma?" *he* asked in the sexiest tone. I raised my name tag so that he could see my name. "I can read, but I prefer us to be on a first name basis."

Putting my guard up, I said, "I'm not supposed to tell you that. You can get into a lot of trouble for asking me that."

"You're going to do a lot of things that you're not supposed to do. Get in trouble, really. Who's going to know? You ain't going to snitch, are you?"

"I'm not going to do anything that I'm not supposed to do. If you force my hand, yes, I will snitch."

He smiled as he stuck his hand into his shirt pocket, pulling out his ID card and handed it to me.

"What's this for?"

"That's for you to hold. So whenever you feel like I crossed the line, then you won't have to ask for my ID, you can just write me up."

"And what if feel you didn't cross the line?" I asked, playing along with his little game.

"Then you write my info down and take it home with you. Wait—because I'll be out soon."

I looked down at his ID as I rubbed my finger across his picture. *What in the world am I getting myself into?*

Hotboy

When she looked down a second time at my ID, I knew I had her. When she handed it back to me, she caught me by surprise. "What's up, ma? I went too far already?" I asked, wondering what went wrong. She smiled.

"No, I just remembered your info by heart. So, if you do go too far, you'll get a surprise case." She sounded more like she was joking. I placed my ID back inside my pocket as I looked over at her co-worker, who was in a deep conversation with my patna—Eastwood.

"Where you from?" I asked.

"Can't answer that, too personal," she said. She looked at me. "What are you here for, if you don't mind me asking?"

I leaned my back against the wall as I decided on if I should tell her or not. "I got fifteen years for an aggravated robbery that I did when I was a teenager. In a few months, I finally have a chance to come home."

"Did you do it?"

I looked at her and laughed. She had no idea who she was talking to. "Yeah, I did it, but I didn't deserve fifteen years for it. That was my first crime, and I was only eighteen when I did it."

"So, if I'm right, you're—what—twenty-five?" she guessed.

"Oh, snap, look at you, you can actually count," I teased.

"Boy, don't do me!" she laughed, as she playfully pushed me, catching herself off guard. "I'm—I'm sorry, I didn't—" she said, but I cut her off.

"No need, ma, you're human, I'm human. Like I told you, you're going to do a lot of shit you're not supposed to do!"

Gangsta

"Mr. Washington, you were placed on G4, medium custody, for fighting. Today marks your six-month mark," Ms. Spikes said, as she looked at the computer screen. We were sitting in a small conference room. I was finally coming up to see the unit classification as the Lt., Ms. Spikes, and Ms. Spears sat across from me. My chance of escaping the madness of medium custody was now in their hands.

"What do you have to say for yourself?" the Lt. asked

"Lieutenant, I apologize for the incident that I caused six months ago. I know now that I have to do better at controlling my temper. Seeing the things that unfold on medium custody showed me that there are two ways to do your time. You can do it easy, or you can do it hard. I can assure you, doing hard time is not for me." The Lt. nodded.

"The computer wants you to stay G4, considering your background," Ms. Spikes said, as she typed on the keyboard. I wanted to just reach across the table and slap the shit out of her. I wanted to slap her so hard that her flavorless ass gum she'd been chewing on for the past hour flew outta her mouth. She was always a hater, with her country bumpkin ass.

"I disagree with the computer," the Lt. said. "As a man," he went on, "I know that there will be conflict amongst men. As long as you'll promise me that the incident is over, then you have my vote to go back to population."

"I agree, I think everyone deserves a second chance," Ms. Spears said.

The Lt. looked over to Ms. Spikes. "Well, that's that, upgrade his custody status." Then to me, he said: "Don't make me regret it!"

I thanked him as I stood up to leave. My mind was already back at it. I was finally able to move around as I pleased. Gangsta was back!

Newton

"Girl, it's been one long ass week. I swear my feet have swelled up by all that damn walking and standing around we've been doing!" Williamson said.

We were in the south chow hall, training for our last day on OJT. I didn't think I was going to make it this past week, especially when I went to work on the north side. I have never seen so many dicks in my entire life until I went to the north side. "My feet hurts too, girl. I'm going to make Seth rub my feet as soon as I get home." It was super-hot in the chow hall. It was so packed that the line went all the way out the door like the club.

"Oh my gawd!—it's hot, I hate cake day!" she said, as she waved her hand, trying to cool off.

"It is hot. Have you seen that boy you was talking to the other day on H-wing?" I asked. She pointed to an empty table, instructing a group of inmates where to sit.

"I saw him yesterday in traffic. I couldn't talk to him though because we were in front of the sergeant, but he knew what I was thinking."

I laughed at her, she was crazy as hell. "Girl, you are something else, you know that!" I said, as I signaled for another group of inmates to get up to make room for another group. I walked around the chow hall as they all ate. When I passed by a table, they would look at my ass and whisper amongst each other.

"You're doing your job a little too hard," a familiar voice said from behind me.

I turned to the sound of his voice as he smiled at me. "Hi Kingsley, what are you doing here?" I asked as I called him by his last name.

"I mean, this is the chow hall where inmates eat," he said.

"I know, that was a dumb question. What I meant was, are you going to eat?" I said, rephrasing my question.

"I'm good, this shit nasty. What I want to eat ain't on the menu," he says as he slowly licked his lips.

His words caught me off guard, but my nipples were on point, because they instantly got hard. "Sorry, Kingsley, I'll ruin your dinner," I said, playing along.

He looked shocked by my response, but was quick with a comeback. "I'm really a dessert man—I can have my cake and eat a full meal too," he said, as he invaded my space.

I looked around to see if another C.O. could see us. The only other officer in the area was Williamson. "Well, you might have to get in line before the cake runs out," I shot back, as we almost stood face to face.

He took a step backwards as he laughed. "Oh yeah, it's like that? Don't worry, I'll get you before it's all said and done, and when I do, I'm not going to show no mercy. Have yo' fun, I'll see you when you get back."

I looked at him, confused. "Where am I going?"

"Today is your Friday, ain't it?" he asked.

He was on point as he stared at me, knowing he caught me off guard. "How'd you know today is my Friday?"

"You'll be surprised what I know, Gabriela," he said, calling me by my first name as he walked away smiling. I looked at him and wondered how he knew all of this. *Who is this man, and what is he doing to me?*

***

"Hey, love, how was your day?" Seth asked as I stepped in the kitchen.

"It was okay, I'm just glad I have three days off to spend with my two favorite men," I said before kissing him.

Hearing the sound of my voice, Jacob ran up to me with the biggest smile. "Look, mommy, look what I drew at school!" he said, showing me a crayon picture of me, him, and his father.

"That's nice, baby, is it for me?"

He handed the picture to me, as he smiled at me with his big blue eyes. "Yes, I made it for you."

I kissed his forehead. "Thank you, big man. I love it, now go and wash your hands so we can eat." He ran off to his room as I walked over to Seth. "What are we having, babe?"

He held up a pot to show me. "Leftovers with some chopped grilled potatoes."

"Really, Seth? Leftovers again! Please tell me we aren't doing this bad," I said, concerned.

Slamming the pot on the stove, he said, "It's all we have, Gabby, I mean what else do you want me to cook? He looked agitated as he stared out the kitchen window.

"What happened to the money? I mean it's only the 8th. I just got paid on the 1st."

He faced me like I said something disrespectful. "Gabby, you get paid once a month. *All* the things w*e* needed, I bought. The rent, the car note, Jacob's clothes. What do you think I did with the money?" He stormed out the kitchen.

I shook my head as I looked at the pot of stew. Even with a job, we were barely making it. I had to find another way to get some extra money.

Gangsta

"Hotboy, wake yo' bitch ass up, daddy's home!" I yelled towards his cell as I walked on H-wing. I had finally got moved to the south side. Somehow I talked the moving lady into moving me to H-wing so that I could be with my guys.

"What's good, trick? I see you survived living in the jungle. Where you going now?" Hotboy said, as he stood on his cell door.

"I'm going to 333, they gave me the bottom bunk, so I'm live. When I finish unpacking I'ma pull up on you," I said, as I carried my things up the stairs. Sliding the cell door backwards, I dragged my things into the small cell. I looked at the top bunk as my new celly was deep into a *Straight Stuntin* magazine. He finally looked up from the magazine as I tossed my mattress on the bunk.

"Wassup, my nigga? I see you made it back," he said as he jumped down to give me a hand.

"Yeah, they blessed my game and let me up. That bitch Ms. Spikes didn't even want to let me up."

"She always do that shit, that bitch is evil. She get on a nigga nerves, but I know that evil bitch got some good pussy." He laughed. I couldn't help but laugh too. I always thought the same shit about her. When I had first saw her, I wanted to fuck the shit out of her. She always wore these khaki pants, and some cowgirl boots, with her hair in a ponytail. Every time you saw her, she was chewing bubble gum. She had this walk about her that screamed "good pussy". I just figured that something was wrong with her because as fine as she was, she wasn't married.

"What the block looking like since I've been gone? Have anything live came through lately?" I asked, speaking of the new class of C.O.'s.

He sat on the toilet as he gave me a little extra room to unpack. "They got a few fuckables, a few ratchets and, like, one or two seasonals," he said.

I wasn't interested in the ratchets. The fuckables would easily fall into my lap by accident. What I wanted was the seasonals. They came to work for one reason, and one reason only—get money! "Who's the porter over here?" I asked, hoping they could be trusted. You couldn't really move without a live porter on deck.

"You know it really depends. You may have Hotboy, or Eastwood, or Time Bomb out there, it really depends on who's working the wing."

I grabbed my state shirt. "Nuff said, let me go holla at Hotboy, I'll be back later," I said as I walked out the cell. I was greeted by inmates that I hadn't seen in months. Some were on H-wing the last time I was here, and some just knew me from different places.

"Good to have you back, bitch. A nigga really needed you out here ASAP—You can't do nothing productive from back there, homie," Hotboy said as I walked up to his cell. He popped his door open to let me in. I folded his celly's mattress back so that I could sit down. I never sat on another man's mattress. You never knew how dirty a nigga was.

"I appreciate that care package you shot back there for me, the squares too."

"Stop acting brand new, my nigga—We family, that gang shit don't apply to us," he said, referring to him being a Vice Lord.

I grabbed the latest Hip-Hop magazine from off the floor. "That's love, so wassup?" I asked. "What's the play? I know you stay with some type of scheme."

Sparking up a square, he sat on the toilet and inhaled the blunt. In prison, the toilet was an all-purpose toilet. You could cook in the sink area, wash clothes in the toilet, or make your sodas cold in the toilet. The most used part had to do with sitting down either to take a crap, or sit down and chill.

"Shit slow-rolling right now," Hotboy said. "I keep buying cans from other niggas, just to stay afloat, and to have a li'l to smoke. Other than that, I'm just fishing, hoping a bitch will catch my bait."

He handed me the square. I took a pull and said, "How is that playing out for you?"

"I might got action at one. Right now she playing that stiff role. But you know that can't no white bitch get past me. I'm a white woman's dream, and a white man's worst nightmare." He laughed. I laughed too. He wasn't lying. He was a regular Hugh Hefner when it came to dealing with snow bunnies.

"Yeah, I remember how you had that white ho—Tambra—in the cell gagging." I remember how I walked up on him as she was giving him head. She was so tall that she just bent over and went that way. She had him pinned up on the wall like she was taking the dick from him.

"That white ho was *throwed* off. She wasn't cut out for the game though. All she wanted to do was fuck and suck dick. I should've pimped her. She was a straight cum freak."

"Yeah, that bitch was wild. Do you remember when you almost slapped her for fumbling the pack on A-wing?" I had to stop Hotboy that day. It was wild.

"That bitch had me hot that day. Talking about she flushed it. She knew damn well that big ass pack couldn't go down the toilet. When I came on the wing, them niggas was smoking my shit. Real shit, you saved that ho that day, because I was about to slap fire from her ass." He laughed it off.

"Whatever happened to her?" I asked as I passed the square

back to him.

"I heard from her like a few months ago. The bitch Jpayed me, talking about how she fucked up. How she missed a nigga, and how she wanted to be with me. At first, I was, like, mane—fuck that ho. Then Eastwood was, like, *mane, you better get everything you can from the bitch.* So I did, every dime, which wasn't much. The bitch was staying at a Job Corps, lame ass bitch!"

I looked up from the magazine. I laughed at him because he was really going hard. "Oh yeah, how much did you get from her?"

"I got, like, seventy-five dollars from the bitch, and a bunch of three way calls. I'm telling you she was broke as hell. Last time I heard from her, she was working at Sanderson Farms' chicken joint in Palestine, the bitch pull skin off of frozen chicken."

I knew deep down he was hurt. He would try to mask the truth, but he couldn't fool me. "My nigga, you really fucked up with the bitch, ain't you?" Hotboy was my guy, he was a fool at breaking a bitch. But he sometimes got his feelings involved. When he would get pushed to the side, or knocked for the bitch, he wouldn't show it to everyone else, but I would always know that he was fucked up by it.

"Mane, fuck that bitch," Hotboy said. We ain't finna spend our whole day talking about her sloop foot ass. Grab that red chain bag from under the bunk."

I looked under the bunk; there was a red chain bag full of bottles. "Damn, my nigga, you got enough bottles to get the whole wing drunk. Who made this shit?" I asked, pulling out a bottle from the bag.

"You know can't nobody make no drank like C-lo. That nigga shit so strong I guarantee you'll piss dirty. I had him make enough for you, me, him, Uncle Marvin, Sam, and Lakewood. You know Uncle Ben going to pull up sooner or later, so I had to have a nice batch."

I opened a bottle to smell the potent hooch. It smelled like straight orange juice. The smell would sometimes fool you, only if you didn't know who made it. Most people would think it's weak, but one bottle later, and a few squares in your system, they'll be passed out on a bench somewhere. I was happy to be away from medium custody. I had been missing out on the "good" life. I took the first bottle to the head.

Hotboy

"Who we got working?" I asked C-lo, as I walked down the stairs with the bag of hooch. Walking to the trash can, I hid the bottles under the trash bag and placed the lid over them. That way, if rank was to come, nobody would get a case for them.

"We got Ms. Bryant, that new geeky white bitch with the glasses," C-lo said, as he grabbed a bottle from out the trash can.

"She really cool, it's going to be a playa night, celebrate my nigga getting out of the jungle," I said as I looked to the main gate, making sure we didn't get snuck up on by any rank. It was like they were straight hounds when it came to hooch. It takes you, maybe, four days to make it. As soon as you get ready to drink it, here they come.

"Nephew, you back!" Uncle Marvin said as he embraced Gangsta. Gangsta tried to shake his hand after the hug. Uncle Marvin slapped his hand away. "Nephew, you ain't been gone that long. You know we don't shake hands, We been down too long, put it up there!" He held his hand up high. Gangsta laughed and did the same as Uncle Marvin slapped his hand hard.

"Damn, Unc, you ain't gotta hit my shit that damn hard," Gangsta said as he looked at his now red hand.

"Soft hand ass nigga!" Unc teased, causing us all to laugh. Uncle Marvin was one of my favorite people on the entire unit. He was always smiling, and giving people high fives. He'd been in prison for over fifteen years already. The crazy thing was that he only came to prison with a fifteen- year sentence. He ended up catching a body down here, and they slammed him with another life sentence on top of the fifteen years he already had. "I just came to holler at ya, I'ma take my leave right away coz I got some fish to fry," Uncle Marvin said.

"Peace, Uncle," Gangsta said as Uncle Marvin left, pronto. "Who is that?" Gangsta asked me. I followed his eyes to Ms. Bryant.

"That's Ms. Bryant. She new, but she ain't *new*, new. She pulled up when you got sent to medium custody."

"Is she live?" he asked.

I nodded as I took another swig from my bottle. "She'll talk, I mean I haven't seen her write a nigga up—but you know, different strokes for different folks," I said, giving him some insight.

"Fuck it, come ride with me, I need you to crank the convo up," he said, leading the way. I shook my head as I followed behind him. I was always his wingman. My job was to crank the conversation up, and when it got to going, I was to dip off.

She looked up at us as we walked up on her inside the officers' closet. "Ms. Bryant, wassup?" I asked as I felt the hooch sneak up on me.

She smiled as she walked out of the closet. "Hey, Hotboy, I see you started early today," she said, looking at the bottle in my hand. She was one of the few C.O's that called me Hotboy. Me and her had got cool one day she was doing overtime on the wing. I held jigga for her as she slept in the closet.

Even though I could tell she was a freak, I never did shoot at her. I befriended a few laws to make them, like, my play sister. That way, when I needed something, I could always go to them. Plus she wasn't my type. Ms. Bryant was super skinny. Not the average skinny, but bony skinny. She rocked a short haircut that she mostly hid under a TDCJ hat.

Her glasses only added to the geeky look she was going for. Her glasses and haircut made her look like Velma from *Scooby Doo*. The thing about prison was, as long as you had tits and a slit, you could get hit.

"Yeah, Ms. Bryant, you know I gotta celebrate my nigga coming back up the hallway," I said, throwing Gangsta into the conversation.

She eyed Gangsta as she looked him up and down. "Hey, I don't think we've met."

"We haven't, I'm Gangsta," he said.

She giggled. "I bet you are, I mean you are in prison after all, so I ain't surprised you are a *gangster*," she said.

Gangsta looked at me with a confused look as I laughed. "Naw, baby girl, my name is Gangsta, as in, G-A-N-G-S-T-A— *Gangsta*," he said, taken aback by her being so green.

"Oh, I'm sorry," she said as she laughed and then snorted like a pig.

Gangsta looked at me, and I shrugged. I had always told him to be careful what he wished for.

Chapter 4

Newton

"I hope they don't put me on the north side. I don't feel like dealing with no drama today," I said to myself as I waited for my assignment from the Lt.

"Newton, I need for you to go and relieve Ms. Bryant. She's way over her hours, please," he said.

Looking at the dry erase board, I saw that Bryant was working on H-wing, just my luck. I made my way to the wing as I held my water bottle and Ziploc bag items

"Are you my relief?" Bryant asked as I walked up to the gate. Nodding, I waited until the keyboss let me on the wing.

The light skinned C.O. smiled at me as he let me on the wing.

"Okay, so you should have an easy day today," Bryant began as she briefed me. "They partied hard last night."

"Partied?"

"Yeah, basically, they went to the club. Loud speakers, prison liquor. I even think I smelled marijuana too. But they've been asleep most of the night, so you should be good." She was in a hurry to get off the wing.

"Okay, thanks," I said as she handed me the dayroom and officer closet keys. Unlocking the closet, I placed my items inside and locked it back. Looking up to the sky, I smiled. *My first day on the wings, and you place me on H-wing, God—what are you planning?* Walking around, I began to make my rounds, making sure everyone was okay. I strolled down the run with my flashlight in hand. I woke up a few people with the bright LED light. They saw who I was, and drifted off back to sleep.

As I made it to two row, I found myself speeding up my pace to get to *14* cell. As I stood in front of *135* cell, I could see a little inside the next cell. He was lying down on the top bunk with his wave cap on. I flashed the light in his cell, causing him to stir.

I tried rushing past his cell so he wouldn't see me, but I was too slow. "Hey, come here," he requested. I closed my eyes, as I decided on what I should do. Deep down I knew that I shouldn't, but my body had a mind of its own.

"What do you want, Kingsley? Go back to sleep."

He sat up and said, "I can't when my dream is standing right in front of me."

My heart fluttered. I prayed that he couldn't see the smile he brought to my face. "Go to sleep, you still have a little over an hour until I drop out for dayroom time," I said as I tried to walk away.

"Wait!" he said, drawing me back. I turned back to his cell. "I'ma come and keep you company. Give me a minute to freshen up." he said, jumping off his bunk.

"Your door is locked, and I can't go in the picket to roll your door," I said, giving myself an easy way out.

He smiled. "Don't worry, I'll get the door open. Finish your rounds, and I'll meet you downstairs."

I walked off, laughing. He really thought he would get out his cell. I damn sure wasn't about to go all the way in the picket to let him out. As I made it to three row, I couldn't get his smile out of my head. I walked around as I continued to check on the other inmates, flashing the light in their cells, making sure they were okay.

"Oh, my God! Give me your ID! I'm writing you up, nasty fucker!" I screamed at an inmate that was lying in his bunk masturbating to me.

"Man, get your ass out front of my cell then, if you don't want to see it," he said as he kept going. "You walked up on me, anyways."

"I'm going to call for rank if you don't give me your ID!" I said, hoping to scare him into giving it to me.

"Fade that dick, bitch!" another inmate yelled over the run, causing others to laugh. I looked at the inmate as I held out my hand for his ID. He shot his sperm in the air, and it landed on his blanket. "Bye, Felicia!" he said.

I shook my head and gave up. I didn't feel like arguing with him. I was sure I wasn't going to really call rank. I didn't want them to think I couldn't handle myself on my first day. "Nasty ass!" I said out loud as I made it to the closet.

"Who?" Kingsley said from behind me, startling me.

I turned around to his sexy smile. "Kingsley, how in the hell did you get out your cell?"

He laughed like what I said was funny. "Chill, ma, if you didn't know by now, I just showed you. The inmates got the keys on Beto, fuck the Warden!"

"Well, why can't you get out of prison if you have the keys?"

He walked up closer to me. "Why leave and everything I want is right here in front of me?" He stared at me like he was chipping my walls down. I had to take a step back from him, he was making me hot.

"Kingsley, you're trouble, you know that?"

"Yeah, I know, the judge already told me. Anyway, who was you talking about? Who you calling nasty?"

"Some guy on three row was jacking off. Then he tried to pretend he didn't know I was coming. He actually kept masturbating until he came all over himself."

He laughed, but harder this time. "What's so funny? I really don't find that shit funny!" I said, letting him know I was upset.

He tried to stop laughing. "I'm sorry, it's just yo' face. You should've seen how you looked. Okay—okay, I'm through." He wiped tears away.

"Oh yeah, it's that funny? We going to see how funny it is when I put you back in yo' cell."

He stopped laughing instantly. "Chill ma, I'm done. You acting like you ain't never seen a dick before."

"I didn't come here to see no dicks," I spat.

He looked upset at how I came at him. "Well, what did you come here for then?"

"I came to make some money, 'cause I'm fucking broke."

Hotboy

Her words were like music to my ears. "So what are you going to do about it?" I asked, watching her closely.

"What do you mean? I'm going to do overtime so that when I get my check, it'll be enough to handle my bills with." he said like she had already found a solution.

"Ahhh, okay, that's it. Work twelve hours a day, just to end up broke by the end of the night. That has to be the smartest idea I've ever heard."

"At least I pay bills!" she shot back with anger. Anger—that's exactly what I wanted from her. Anger and desperation. The instant I pulled out a wad of money from my shorts, her eyes grew wide. "You see this," I said, holding it up for her to see, as I started counting bill after bill. "Just 'cause I'm in prison doesn't mean I don't pay bills. The game of life never stops and bellies never stay full." I placed the money back in my pocket.

I had caught her off guard with the money. I could tell by the look on her face. She didn't know if she wanted to snitch, or ask for some. "How did you get all that money?" she asked. "Like Yo Gotti says, *If a nigga don't hustle, then a nigga don't eat.*" Opening the closet door, she grabbed a bottle of water. I knew she was contemplating her next move.

"What kind of hustle do you have?" she asked before taking a sip from her water. I wondered if I should tell her. The last time I exposed my hand, I got turned in, and had to pay to get the case thrown out.

"I can't tell you that, ma. How do I know that I could trust you?"

Sipping her water, she raised an eyebrow. "Really, if I wanted to, I could've turned you in for what you just did."

"Fair enough. Okay then, I sell tobacco," I watched her closely. She looked at me as if I was lying.

"Tobacco, really? You made all of that, from just selling cigarettes?"

"I'm going to break it down to you. In prison, everyone has a habit. In order to feed that habit, you have to pay top dollar to get exactly what you need. See me, I don't deal drugs, it's too much of a hassle. I know for sure, that if you do any type of drug—whether it be coke, meth, weed—then you smoke cigarettes. So instead of selling drugs, I deal what I know without a doubt is going to sell. See, in here, a pack of cigarettes run you damn near one hundred dollars. In the world, you only pay ten dollars. Instead of getting a pack of Newport, I just get a can of rolling tobacco. It cost maybe thirteen dollars for an eight-ounce can. I make no less than two thousand, two hundred dollars, and that's as soon as it touches my hand."

"You're shitting me, right. You telling me you make that much money from selling cigarettes. I don't believe you." She wasn't convinced. The curiosity showed on her face as her ears got flushed red. I laughed as I watched them get red right before my eyes.

"What are you laughing at?" she asked.

I pointed. "Your ears, they red as hell, what the fuck, I ain't never seen that shit before."

She pulled on her left ear. "Oh, they always do that when I'm nervous, or excited."

"So which one are you? Are you nervous? Or are you excited?" I asked as I took a step closer. She eyed me as I invaded her space, but she held her ground.

Her words stumbled next as we stood face to face. "I-I'm nervous."

"Why are you nervous?" I said, just above a whisper.

Placing her hand on my chest, she said, as she closed her eyes, "You make me nervous."

I moved my lips to her ear. "I only want to make you feel free."

She shivered as my lips touched her ear. "Please!" she begged as my lips silenced her, as I kissed her fears away. She tried to fight the urge not to kiss me back, but the fire inside her wouldn't cease. Parting her lips, she accepted my tongue, and our tongues danced to a silent tune. Easing her backwards into the closet, she moaned as our tongues continued to make love. "Wai—Wait! Gianni, we have to stop—I mean, we can't do this, what if someone catches us?" she said as her chest heaved up and down.

I wiped her saliva away with the tip of my tongue. "When you're with me, baby, you're good. I won't put you in harm's way, I swear."

She tried hard to pull herself together. "I don't want to be one of those women on the wall of shame. I need my job! I have a family to feed." She was on the verge of panicking.

I grabbed her hand. "You don't need this job. You need the money, and if money is what you need, then I got you!"

She snatched her hand back once she realized I wasn't going to let it go. "I can't take your money; you took a chance to get it." She sounded sincere.

"Well, take a chance with me then! Help me help you. Trust me; I know what I'm doing."

She contemplated my proposal. "I can't, I just can't, I'm not that type of girl," she said as she went and sat on the ice cooler.

"That's why you're perfect. You'll be good at it as long as you follow my lead. You look like the type that'll never bring anything in. They'll never suspect you."

"I don't know, Gianni, let me at least think about it."

"I can respect that. Well, here, take this." I pulled out four crisp hundreds. "I hope it can help you in some way, that is, until you can figure out what you want to do."

"Gianni, no, I can't take that."

I put the money inside her clear bag. I wasn't taking no for an answer.

Gangsta

"I'm open, bitch!" I yelled to Hotboy as he dribbled the ball down the court. He dribbled the ball like Russell Westbrook. Recklessly, and at full speed. He bounced-passed the ball to me as I went up for a layup.

I was undercut by the opposing team player, who was supposed to be sticking me. I dodged hitting my head, but I could instantly feel the pain in my lower back from the fall. Hotboy and Lakewood were on him before I could get up. Hotboy shoved him, causing him to fall on the hot concrete. "You got a problem, bitch nigga!" Hotboy said as he stood over him.

"Mane, y'all chill, y'all know he didn't mean any harm," Savage said in his defense. Savage was a real stand up cat. He was one of those cats that ended up in the penitentiary, but could've went to the NBA.

"How the fuck he didn't mean to—he damn near killed my guy," Lakewood said, still trying to pop shit off.

Savage extended a hand to help me up, and I accepted. "I'm good, my nigga. I know li'l homie don't want no smoke." I spoke towards the nigga who'd made me fall down, as he was still on the concrete, afraid to get up.

I walked over to help him up. "You good, li'l homie?" I asked.

"Yeah, 'preciate you, Gangsta," he said.

"Let's hoop, check-up," I said as I grabbed the ball, tossing it to Savage. Hotboy and Lakewood let it go as they saw I wasn't upset about it. Moving around the court, they continued to play. I checked the ball to Savage as he passed it back. Looking around, I tried to find an open man. Lakewood ran around at full speed as I waited on an opening. Lakewood wasn't the best ball handler, but he had a good set shot.

Running past the screen that Hotboy had orchestrated, Lakewood came around the screen with his hands up as I passed him the ball. He pulled up for a jump-shot as Savage extended his hand, blocking his ball from behind him.

"Watergang fool!" Savage said, laughing.

We all fell out on the concrete, laughing at the look on Lakewood's face. "Why y'all ain't tell me that he was behind me?" he said, as he sat on the concrete beside us.

"You know that nigga long as hell! Shid, I didn't know he was behind you," Hotboy said, lying flat on his back.

"Fuck it, let's get back in rotation," Lakewood said.

"I'm done," I said, shaking my head. "I'ma walk it off, I can feel my back tightening up," I added. Lakewood helped us both up, and we walked to the grass area of the rec yard.

"So did you get any progress with Newton?" I asked Hotboy

as we took the trail.

He looked to the ground as we walked. "Can't really tell. The bitch like a rollercoaster. One minute she's up, the next she's down."

Lakewood said, on point, "Nigga, you was out there for at least two hours by yo'self. She didn't drop us out for dayroom time until about eight in the morning."

Hotboy laughed at him. "My nigga, you can't catch no fish watching my line."

"Two hours, and you didn't get nothing accomplished?" I said as we picked up our pace.

"I kissed her, but I don't think she going to drop off. She too scary. I mean, I brought it up, she just said that she would think about it."

I looked at him in disbelief. I knew my guy wasn't a liar, but kissing a new boot on the first day was abnormal. "So you kissed her, huh? My nigga, you full of shit!" I said, laughing.

"When have I ever lied? You know I'ma white woman fanatic," he said.

"Gangsta! Come here!" Bryant yelled as we almost passed her up. She was on the opposite side of the fence that blocked us from the officers.

"Skinnie Mini, what's good?" I said, calling her by the nickname I had given her.

She blushed as she stared at me. "I have something for you," she said, passing it through the gate, and I instantly tucked it. "I know that you didn't ask for anything, but I wanted to talk to you, so I got you a phone. I know that you told me you like to smoke, so I got you some weed too."

"I appreciate you for that love, for real," I said.

Smiling, Bryant said: "Uhm, I programmed my number in there. So when you get back inside and get situated, give me a call, or text."

For some reason she looked good at that moment. Maybe it was because she brought me a phone. Either way, she was beautiful for it. "Will do, and I got you for this too," I said.

She held her smile. "It's on me. What I want, you have to give it to me in private."

I gripped the package in my hand as I watched her skinny ass walk away. I was shocked because I didn't even ask her for anything, but then again I was a Gangsta, and a bitch will do anything to be in a Gangsta's presence.

Chapter 5

Newton

"Beep Beep!" The horn sounded from Williamson's car. She was blowing her horn like a mad woman scorned. I had to hitch a ride with her because Seth had used all the gas from the car, knowing I had to go to work. On top of everything else, the money Gianni had given me was missing from my purse. I walked out the front door, stressed.

I remember Mama Dee saying the job would leave us stressed out. But right now, it wasn't the job. It was my own home.

"Hey, boo!" Williamson said once I got inside the car. "You okay?" she said, reading my face.

I sighed as I looked out the window. "I hate this, ughh, I think Seth is using again," I said, feeling ashamed.

"I didn't know he messed around with drugs," she said, pulling out the driveway.

"He did at first, when I first met him. He would experiment with meth until he was granted full custody of Jacob. That was when I had told him that if he didn't quit, then I was leaving.

"Damn, so you think he's using again?" William asked.

I shook my head as I looked out the window. "I don't know, maybe it's the fact that he don't have a job, and we don't have any money. I don't really know." I was simply making up excuses.

"Everything is going to be just fine," Williamson said, changing the radio.

I looked at her and smiled. "I didn't get a chance to tell you," I said, changing the subject.

"Tell me what?" she said, sounding excited.

"Gianni kissed me," I said as I thought about how soft his lips were. She pulled the car over onto the dirt road.

"Gianni, inmate Gianni?" she asked, shocked. I nodded. "Girl, how? When? Umhuh, no you didn't keep this from me." She put the car in park. I laughed at her. She was crazy as they came.

"Girl, drive before we be late!" I said, still laughing.

She laughed as she pulled off. "Details, please."

"Okay, well I worked overtime the other day, and they placed me on H-wing. They were still racked up when I got there so I walked around doing my rounds. I woke him up by mistake with the flashlight. Somehow, he got out his cell. We ended up downstairs, and we started tasking. One thing led to another, and we started kissing." I was reminiscing about the night.

Williamson hit the steering wheel with her hand, causing me to flinch. "I knew it! I said it, you good girls are soooo slick!"

"I didn't plan for anything to happen, it just did," I said, defending myself.

"Can he kiss?" She was being nosey. I closed my eyes and leaned my head against the headrest.

"His lips felt like I'd bit into the softest peach in the world."

She looked at me out the corner of her eye. "Damn, girl, that good? Well how big is his dick?" she asked as she pulled into the prison lot.

"We didn't get that far. After the kiss, I told him that we shouldn't be doing that."

"Who are you trying to fool, Gabby? That man knows you got the hots for him. The best thing you can do at this moment is, have fun while it lasts."

"He gave me some money too, four hundred dollars. I know he had at least a few thousand on him that night."

"That's perfect for you. You already taking care of a crackhead who ain't got a job. What you can at least do is get your pussy spanked, and get a little extra money in the process." She handed her ID to the C.O. in the booth.

"He isn't on crack, it's meth." I said, defending Seth. "And I'm not having sex in a prison, that's so tacky."

"Crack, meth, cocaine—it's all the same shit. I got a cousin that sells meth, weed and pills. They don't call him the meth, weed, and pill seller. They call him a dope dealer. It's all the same, Gabby."

I laughed. She would say the damndest things sometimes. "You talking about sex in a prison," she went on. "I tell you, girl, sex in prison is better than sex on a beach. And trust, I've done both. Plus you've already kissed him, I bet you thought you'd never do that either." She parked the car. She was right. I had done something I never imagined that I'll do. And it felt damn good too.

Hotboy

"My nigga, that li'l skinny bitch is down by law. She brought a whip, and some loud, for free. I should've shot my shot at the bitch a long time ago. If I would've known she was getting down like this." I was messing with Gangsta as per my encounter with Ms. Bryant. We were in his cell, breaking down the weed as Lakewood hid behind the sheet. He was talking on the phone with his baby mama.

"Yeah, baby came through," Gangsta said as he rolled up a blunt with Bible paper. Bible paper was the best thing to smoke out of; it burned slow, like Job's rolling papers. We would always try to smoke the section without the scriptures on it, so that we wouldn't feel bad.

"Oh, that's *baby* now, huh?" I said, as I grabbed my hand mirror to check and see if anyone was coming.

Lighting up the blunt, Gangsta said, "That bitch did all this for free. Hell yeah, she baby! Wait until I put this dick in her bony ass, I bet she come through for real then."

"Hold up, nigga," I said. "Let's get rid of the whip first. We got too much going on at one time."

Gangsta looked towards the sheet with frustration. "Tell that nigga to stop cup-caking then, a nigga tryna get high."

"I'ma call you back, baby," Lakewood said, hanging up the phone. He took the sheet down and he placed the phone in his pocket.

Gangsta sparked up the blunt. "We been waiting on you, my nigga," he said. "Don't get caught up on yo' baby mama now that we gotta whip. Where was she before the whip came? She knew where you was, shid, she could've been set the blue phone up so you could've called."

I looked out the bars with the mirror again to make sure the C.O. wasn't walking around. "Security check!" I yelled over the run, asking the other inmates if they could see the C.O.

"Three row clear!" someone yelled from three row.

"Lawman at the front gate, waiting to get released!" the porter yelled from one row.

"I feel you, my nigga, but she got my kids, so I gotta keep a relationship with her," Lakewood said, taking the blunt from Gangsta as they traded spots in the vent.

Gangsta blew the smoke he had been holding in inside the vent, as he coughed uncontrollably. "Damn, that shit some gas," he said, coughing.

I looked out the bars again. Even though the porter said everything was good, I always watched out for myself. The best security *was* your own security. Handing the mirror to Gangsta, I took Lakewood's spot at the vent. Taking a slow drag, I could taste the fruity buds on the tip of my tongue.

"Check this, Lakewood—outta sight, outta mind!" said Gangsta. "So that goes for her, like it goes for every bitch. She was supposed to be down by law, that's yo' baby mama. Like Drake said, '*Lawyers and the commissary ain't gon' pay itself.*' What we about to do is, get at this money. Blow some time, and fuck some of these country ass hos, feel me?" Gangsta's words hit home, and Lakewood nodded, saying:

"I feel you, for real, you right. I tripped out." He turned on the fan, to try to blow the extra smoke out.

Pulling out a square, I lit the tip with the cherry from the blunt.

"Shift change! Chocolate ice cream!" the porter yelled. "Two row, front half, coming fast!" he said, yelling to the top of his lungs. I grabbed all the contraband that I could see, and balled it up in my hand just in case I would have to flush everything. Lakewood hid under the bunk, knowing we were three deep in a two-man cell. Gangsta grabbed the bottle of baby powder, squeezing it in the air to cover the smell. Just as he squeezed the bottle, the C.O. walked up to the door. Seeing it was her, I exhaled a sigh of relief.

"Damn, girl, don't do that shit!" I said as Lakewood slid from under the bunk.

Williamson stood there with a big smile on her face. "Where it's at? I smell it, let me inhale it!" she said.

Lakewood wiped his clothes off and sat on the toilet. "You play too much. Why you scare us like that?"

She laughed. "Let me find out y'all came all the way to prison, just to get scared," she said.

"Fuck you!" Gangsta said, laughing.

"So wassup?" I asked Williamson, hoping she'll get out front of my cell. I figured everyone on two row already had their mirrors out watching by now.

"I need to talk to you," she said, looking at me.

I caught her drift. I figured. I knew what it was about anyway. "That's a bet. Let me tighten up a little bit, and I'll be out there in a minute."

"Umhuh—and Blacky, I saw you under that bunk when I walked up here. You need a hiding spot that actually hides you." After she'd chastised Lakewood, she walked off.

Gangsta popped Lakewood in the back of the head. "Stupid ass, why you ain't let the sheet hang over the bunk so she couldn't see you? What if she was someone else?"

Lakewood rubbed the spot were Gangsta hit him. "I didn't have enough time, goofball ass nigga. That shit hurt, I'ma hit you back one day, watch! I'ma have a reflex, and slap the shit outta you." What Lakewood said sounded funny to us, and we couldn't help but laugh.

"Whatever you say, my nigga," Gangsta said to him. Gangsta looked at me. "What you think she want?"

Knowing that everything was playing right into my hands, a smile came to my face. "I think I know what she wants."

Newton

"Dayroom! Before I write y'all up!" I yelled at a group of inmates that refused to go in the dayroom. I left the dayroom door open and walked towards them. "Excuse me, do y'all not hear me saying it's dayroom time? That means, *get in the damn dayroom.*" They acted like they were deaf or something. "If you're not the porter," I added, getting agitated, "then you need to be in the dayroom like everyone else."

"We're all porters," one of the inmates said, as they all looked at me.

"Come on, y'all, it's only supposed to be two porters, and I know who they are, so just go in the dayroom."

One of the guys sucked his teeth. "A nigga don't wanna be out here with you anyway, stuck up ass bitch. I bet you stay in a trailer park." His friends laughed. That was just like any insecure man. When shit didn't go their way, they'll get in their feelings and try to clown you in front of their friends.

"Whatever, if I do live in a trailer, at least I don't stay in a li'l ass cell with another man who shits by my head. By the way, the other night I was counting, and your celly was jacking off to me by your head, so next time, sleep with an umbrella." My counterattack struck home, and the dayroom fell out laughing at him.

The inmate and his friends began to walk to the dayroom. The one with the big mouth had to get the last word in. "I don't even know why I'm entertaining you. I guarantee you won't last to next season. I bet you get walked off. You gon' be the bitch that get caught with a dick in her mouth, and a dick in yo' ass!" He sounded hurt.

As they walked in the dayroom, I slammed the door behind them. "And if I do, I bet it won't be yo' dick. Yo' shit so small it'll slip right out. Li'l dick ass li'l boy." I walked off, leaving everyone to laugh at him.

I hated the north side, but most of all I hated L-wing. The Lt. placed everyone who was ever involved in any sort of hustles or relationships with C.O.'s all on the same wing. That didn't help to stop the drug flow. It only started making the cool guys assholes. When they couldn't make money, they would act like females.

"Gabby!" A voice called me, and I peeped out of the closet to see who was calling me by my nickname. I looked to see Williamson with a big smile on her face. "Girl, don't be calling my name like that. I don't want them knowing my name like that," I said, walking to the door to see what she wanted.

She rolled her eyes. "Girl, they couldn't hear me. Don't do me, boo."

I looked down at my watch. "I'm waiting on my relief. They should be here by now."

"That's why I'm here. Can you find another ride home?" she asked.

"Find another ride home? Why?"

"Because I'ma work overtime tonight. I'm hoping they'll place me on J-wing. There is this guy who fell outta place to H-wing today, the man is fine." She looked in the direction of J-wing.

"Okay, I'll work overtime with you, I guess."

"Look at it this way. You get time and a half, and there isn't no telling where they'll place you."

"Okay, I'll meet you when the next shift is over," I said, praying that they wouldn't leave me on I-wing. I just prayed that wherever they place me, the night would go smooth!

"Shift change!" the porter yelled as I walked on H-wing. At first, I was upset about working overtime. That was until they told me that I would be working on H-wing.

As I walked on the wing, the entire dayroom looked at me. I walked to the closet, placing my things in there. I was down to one bottle of water, and some skittles. I was hungry as hell too. I practically ate everything I had while I was working on L-wing.

"Lucky me, huh?" Gianni said, walking up to the dayroom bars.

I smiled once I looked over and saw that it was him. "Why would you say that?"

"Because, my dream came true," he said with that sexy smile.

His smile kept me mesmerized as I walked up to the dayroom bars. "What dream would that be?"

"The dream of me having another chance to make you realize that I'm the best thing that could ever happen to you." He talked with such confidence. Looking at him, I realized that men were dangerous when it came to a woman's heart, but right now, I needed someone to talk to, and whatever came behind it. I placed the key in the lock to let him out the dayroom.

He looked over his shoulders and told two other inmates to come with him. As they followed close behind him, the light-skinned one went to the porter who was sitting on the trash can. The light-skinned friend said something to him that I couldn't quite make out. I could see the porter nod as he handed Gianni's friend the broom and walked towards me. "I'm going to chill and watch TV for the night," he said before walking into the dayroom.

I looked at Gianni as he nodded for me to close the dayroom door. The way his friends moved at his every command let me know that he wasn't just a nobody. My question was, who was he?

Hotboy

"So, overtime again, huh?" I asked as she walked back to the officers' closet. She was trying her best to not make eye contact.

"I really didn't have a choice this time. I rode with Williamson, and she's staying, so I had to stay too." She was still avoiding eye contact with me. I had already known the reason why. I paid Williamson $200 to work overtime, and I paid the Lt.'s porter to place her on my wing for overtime. Money well spent.

"That's good, I mean you need the money. They say too much money ain't enough money."

She ignored my statement, as she was dazed out in another world. I could tell something was really bothering her. "Gianni, why do you like me?" she asked out the blue.

I was taken aback by her sudden question. "Why not? I mean, what's not to like!" I said, still lost by her question. "You sexy as hell, ma, I can't lie. When I first saw you, when you first walked through with those sweats on, I said to myself, *I had to have her.* The way your ass switched in them pants had me. Plus the innocent look you were trying to portray interested me." After a moment's pause, I continued. "Look, ma, I've been in prison for seven years. I ain't gon' lie. I've shot at a few females here and there. But when I saw you, I saw us—outside this prison. You were the beauty behind the madness."

She couldn't help but smile. "You had me at *hello*," she said, causing me to smile too.

"I know, I have that effect on women," I said.

"Boy, shut up," she said, relaxing a little. She placed her hand on her stomach and held it there.

"What's wrong?" I asked.

She reached into her bag and pulled out a Ziploc bag full of skittles. "Nothing, I'm just hungry as hell."

"You hungry? I got some food up there if you want to eat."

She popped some skittles in her mouth and shook her head. "I'm good, I'll live."

"You should know by now that I don't take no for an answer!"

"I need for y'all to hold it down," I whispered to Gangsta and Lakewood, as she stared at me from a distance. I walked up to her and said, "You ready?"

"For?"

"Look, just come to my cell in, like, ten minutes," I said and walked off, leaving her with no room to object. I walked into my cell and placed my speaker into the radio. I scanned the stations to find the perfect song to set the mood. I landed on a country song and left it there, then I placed a red envelope over the light bulb to make the room light up red. I was sure that when she saw this, she wouldn't be able to refuse what her body desired.

Newton

I closed the closet and locked it. I looked around to make sure nobody was paying attention as I eased up the stairs. I noticed this time, no one yelled that I was walking around. A couple of people put their mirrors out their cell bars, but as soon as they saw me, they pulled them back in.

As I made it to his cell, I almost cried. The doubt that was on the inside of me was being washed away by the scene that was in front of me. The cell door was already ajar, making it easier for me to step inside. I placed my hand over my face to cover the tears that were forming. It was beautiful.

He had placed a blanket on the floor with two bowls on top of it. Inside the bowls were two deli sandwiches with chips, and a soda sat beside the bowls. In the middle of the blanket was a cup with a tissue-made rose inside. The red light that lit up the room made it special. But it didn't take away from the Chris Stapleton song that came from the radio.

Grabbing my hand, he wiped the tears away from my eyes. "Why the tears, ma?" he asked, still holding my hand.

I laughed in the midst of the tears. "It's beautiful, corny, but beautiful. I never had anyone do anything like this for me before."

He laughed. "Truth be told, I never done anything like this before either. So this is a first for the both of us. Here, sit down."

"I want to, but I can't. What if we get caught?" I said.

"Don't worry, my niggas ain't gon' let us get caught, I promise."

I sat down against my better judgment. I knew that I shouldn't have come inside his cell. I also knew that I couldn't deny the feelings I had for him. Placing my legs behind me, I smiled looking at the picnic. *"You're as smooth as Tennessee whiskey/ You're as sweet as strawberry wine/ you're as warm as a glass of brandy/ And honey I stay stoned on your love all the time—"* Chris Stapleton sang in the background.

"You want to say grace, or should I?" Gianni asked, holding his hands out to me. I was surprised. A gentleman and a thug. I placed my hands in his as he closed his eyes and tilted his head.

"Heavenly Father, thank you for this meal that we are about to receive. We thank you for this opportunity that you presented before us, to bring us closer together. I know we are doing something that we aren't supposed to do, but I ask that you protect us in the good times, and the bad times, in Jesus name."

"Amen!" I said as I let his hands go. He didn't waste any time, as he tore into his sandwich. Grabbing my soda, he popped the top before placing it back in front of me, and he did the same to his.

"Why you so quiet?" he asked.

I stared at him. "Who are you?" I asked.

He sat his sandwich down. "I'm just a man that sees what he wants, and goes after it." He placed some chips in his mouth.

"What do you really want from me, Gianni? I mean this—" I said, pointing—"It's all too much."

"I want all of you. Your problems, your smiles, your tears, your fears, your pain, and your heart. You think this is something? You ain't seen nothing yet."

The appetite that I had was now gone. The hunger that I had now was for an inmate that was clawing at my heart. "Come here!" I requested, as I curled my finger at him.

He looked up from his sandwich. "Come here!" I said, getting his full attention. He crawled over, being very careful not to knock anything over. I placed my hand on his cheek as I brought his face to mine. At that moment, I didn't care who caught us.

Hotboy

The taste of her lips was as sweet as strawberry wine. I could have sworn she said she was hungry. The way she forced me backwards on top of her food said otherwise. "Hold up, baby, let's do this right," I said, sensing were this was going. She stood up as I moved the bowls, and sodas. I opened the blanket to cover the entire floor. "Take off your boot, only one of them," I said, and she did without hesitation.

I unbuckled her pants and unzipped them as she gazed into the depths of my eyes. I began to pull them down as she held on to my shoulders. "You have to keep one pants leg on," I told her as she stepped out of her left pants leg. The sight in front of me took me to another world. Her innocence was on full display. The Victoria's Secret thong panties she wore held her vagina like a baseball mitt holds a baseball. Tracing my thumb across her slit, she jumped at the feeling of my finger against the hot cotton fabric. "I gotcha, ma," I assured her as I eased her panties down to her feet.

The smell of her scent took me over the edge. It took me to a place I hadn't visited in years. Once she stepped out of her panties with her left leg, I raised her leg, placing it high over my shoulder. She held on to me as she tried to control her balance. I squatted down and I stared into her tunnel. I looked at her in her eyes, as I kissed her sex lips softly. The wetness from her pussy coated my lips like water. I gently sucked on her clit as soft moans escaped her mouth.

She held on to the top bunk as she rolled her head back in bliss. "Shii-iit!" she moaned as I gripped her ass. Her hips found its own rhythm as she swayed with the flow of my tongue. Her juices covered my face and nose as she ground back and forth. "Right there, Gianni, right there!" She panted. Gripping her ass, I began to squeeze it. I felt her weight coming down on my face. She squeezed her titties through her shirt as she found herself on the verge of climaxing.

"Ohh, my God!—it feels sooooo good!" she said, her legs growing weak. I wiped my face with the palm of my hand and I held her up. She kissed my lips, tasting her own sweetness from my tongue. I led her to the toilet and I slid my pants down, exposing my curved hard-on. The look of shock registered all over her face. Grabbing the head, she guided her hand up and down. Her soft hand felt amazing.

Just the feel of her hand around my shaft made my dick get harder. "It curves, like a banana," she said, mesmerized. Her soft hands were driving me insane. I couldn't take it anymore, and I pulled her down on my lap. She squatted over the head as she tried to ease herself down slowly. Her walls were so tight she was barely able to get the head in. She rose up again, played with her pussy and rubbed the head back and forth against her slippery slit. Finally, she eased herself down.

"Ohh shit, baby, it's too big," she said, making it past the head. I could feel her walls stretching as she sat down more and more. She closed her eyes while I filled her up to capacity. Gripping her hips, I pumped in and out of her slowly, as soft moans escaped her lips.

"Shhh, babe," I whispered as I kissed her moans away. She rocked back and forth to match my pace. Placing her hands on my shoulders, I picked her ass up and bounced it down as skin slapped skin. "That's it, babe, right there, relax for daddy," I said as I got caught up in her tight pussy.

"Babe, ohh shit, babe, I think I'm coming—I'm coming!" She moaned as she bit her bottom lip. I could feel the nut building up as I squeezed her cheeks.

I could tell she came, as her walls squeezed the tip of my dick. That feeling alone made me shoot my load inside of her. "Ahhh fuck!" I said, a little too loud. She laid her head on my chest as she panted, looking up at me.

"Thank you, I needed that," she said.

I stood up while she was still attached to me as she eased down. "Come on, we have to clean ourselves up," I said, looking around the cell. "We went free world just then." I laughed as I looked around the cell.

Gangsta

"Damn, they been up there a minute, huh?" I said to Lakewood who was sitting on the trash can.

"Yeah, they must be running a marathon. Damn! That bitch nigga lucky. I know that white pussy good, and tight," he said, grabbing his dick.

"I bet it is, too. Skinny mini needs to work over here again—I'ma knock the bottom outta that li'l pussy, watch," I said, thinking about my li'l piece of game.

"You haven't called her yet?" Lakewood asked.

"Fasho, I call her every night. Can't leave no room for another nigga to slide in my spot. I got her head gone, I ain't got too much I gotta worry about now."

"That bitch so little though, she scare me," Lakewood said, making an ugly face.

"She scare you? What the fuck that supposed to mean?"

"Mane, that bitch too little. Little bitches like that, they make me think that they sick." A look of disgust appeared on his face there and then.

Defending Ms. Bryant, I said: "Mane, you sound stupid. That bitch is just small, that's all."

"There she goes right there!" Lakewood said, looking at Newton as she walked down the stairs. Grabbing the broom, I pretended to be sweeping. She looked over at us and blushed. I laughed on the inside, knowing my guy was the reason for her happiness.

She smoothed her hair down before walking over to us. "Hey, y'all must be really close to Gianni?" she asked.

Lakewood stood up and smiled. "That's our boy."

"Oh, that's cool," she said, smiling. "I could tell y'all are close."

I could sense the uneasiness in her body language. The feeling of knowing you did something you shouldn't have done. And to think that we knew what was going on had her nervous. "I'm Gangsta, and this is Lakewood—Me, him, and Gianni are like brothers," I said to ease her mind.

Hotboy walked up and took Lakewood's spot on the trash can. "What y'all talking about?" he said, propping his feet up on the bars.

"Shit, we just can't believe you didn't tell her about us," I said, feeling some type of way.

"Babe, this is Gangsta, and that's Lakewood," he said, pointing to us. "You can trust them with your life, because I do," he added, and she nodded.

"So, you're like our sister now," I said, making her smile. She nodded and said, "I guess so."

Chapter 6

Newton

After Williamson dropped me off at home, I tried to run to the shower to get Gianni's smell from off of me. "Gabby, is that you?" Seth asked, hearing the shower running.

I hurried out of my clothes and jumped under the water as he walked in the bathroom.

"Gabby!"

"Oh, hey baby, what are you still doing up?"

He leaned his back against the sink. "I was waiting up for you. Why are you so late getting home?"

Wiping the water from my eyes, I said, "I had to work overtime, they were short of staff."

"Why didn't you call me? I was worried sick about you." He sounded concerned. I started to feel bad about what I'd done. Here I had a man that was in love with me, and I was cheating on him with an inmate.

"I couldn't leave the building. Remember, I told you that we didn't get breaks." I tried sounding convincing.

"Oh yeah, I forgot you told me that. Well, look, Jacob's asleep. Do you have a few dollars? I need to run to the store real quick."

I noticed the redness in his eyes. I couldn't tell if it was from lack of sleep, or if he was high. "Look in my bag, I think I may have a twenty in there," I said, not really wanting to give it to him.

"Thanks, baby," he said, and he kissed me before walking out to retrieve the money.

I sighed once I heard him leave. "Damn, that was close!" I said to myself. Just the thought of what happened tonight made me feel amazing on the inside all over again. His touch, his strong hands against my ass. The feeling of him inside me. Damn, his dick felt so good. I had never been that filled up in my whole life.

I finished my shower and stepped out as I walked to my room. Jacob was lying in our bed, sound asleep. He looked so peaceful as he sucked his thumb. I loved him like he was my own son. I literally envied his real mom, Kelly. Here she had a smart, adorable son, yet she didn't even want to be around him. It pained me to see that Seth didn't want to give me a child.

Although I loved Jacob, I always wanted to have my own kid. That was the face of our arguments a lot. He stayed on me about taking birth control. He says we can't afford a baby right now. I was going to get some birth control, but now that he's sneaking around getting high again, I can't afford them!

Next Day

"I knew he had a big dick—I could tell the day we walked up to his cell and he had that towel wrapped around him." Williamson said: After telling her about our sex session, she insisted that I tell her every single detail.

"I'm still sore," I said as I handed a C.O. his vest through the small window. The Lt. had me and her working the front control booth. We were in charge of answering the unit phone, and letting people in and out the main entrance.

"I told you!" Williamson said, not caring who was listening. "Sex in prison, it makes you come so fast. The adrenaline rush and the thought of getting caught makes you so wet."

I laughed at her, she didn't give a damn. "Bitch, what are you doing over there?" Williamson asked, being nosey. I had begun to write Gianni a kite. Since our episode, I hadn't been able to get him off my mind, nor talk to him. I was locked inside this booth, so I couldn't go to him like I wanted to. So, I figured I'll write him a short letter and sneak it to him during chow.

"I'm writing Gianni a kite, if you'll just watch out for me," I said, trying to concentrate.

"Boo, you are so in love. Black dick always drive y'all white girls crazy." She was walking to the window as she spoke, to look out for me.

"No, I am not," I said, laughing like a high school girl.

"Bitch, haven't you seen? Nothing you do amazes me, I know you," she said.

I folded up the kite into a small square. "You have been on point. Now stay on point so nobody will catch me."

"Well, you better hurry up. They just called for another shot of H-wing chow!"

Hotboy

"You coming or what, nigga?" Lakewood asked as they called for a shot of chow. I was contemplating on staying in, but I figure I might as well hit the block to see if I could sneak a few words in to Gabby before she left for the night.

"Fuck it," I said as I slid my state shirt over my head. "Let's hit the A, B, C, D block first, see what's jumping down there," I added.

"What's popping?" Bigs said to me while passing. We shook up as him and Lakewood shook hands, too.

"Who working y'all wing?" I asked. Bigs was on "C" wing.

"Damn, I can't remember that nigga name. Som' white fool," he said, trying to remember.

"'Preciate it," I said as we headed in the direction of his block.

The C.O. working the keys flashed her light at me before I could make it past the crash gate. "Turn around and go back to your block before I write you an out-of-place case," Ms. Robbs said, blowing the spot up.

I hated her with a passion. She was younger than me, yet she tried to act like my mother. She was outrageously tall, and sloppy in appearance. The spandex she wore under her uniform couldn't hold all her blubber in one place. She had an awkward build. Her glasses stayed fogged up by her hot breath. She always talked with a mouth full of spit.

I was told she had Down's syndrome. She thought she was sexy because niggas would jack off on her, or they would tell her that she was sexy. Little did she know, we told every woman on the unit the same damn thang. Fat or ugly, they were all *sexy*. "You got it, I ain't going to argue with yo' cop-ass," I said before walking off.

"That bitch hates you, don't she?" Lakewood said, noticing her animosity.

"I know, I don't care. Fuck that bitch. She just mad because her husband's five feet tall, and she's seven feet tall. Instead of calling them the Robbs, we need to call them Biggie Smalls." I laughed as we walked towards the chow hall.

"Homeboy!" Lakewood said to a guy who was in the commissary line. That was one thing about prison. Being in the commissary line made everyone your homeboy, or hometown. They would call you that, hoping for a handout.

I told him, "Leave that nigga alone. You don't need shit, you got a house full of food."

"I know, I just like fucking with people. You see how he pretended not to hear me." He laughed.

"There she goes," I said, noticing Gabby in the control booth. There was a sergeant working in front of the booth controlling the chow hall traffic. "I need for you to distract the sergeant," I said to Lakewood as Gabby looked up and saw me. I raised a finger, telling her to wait a second as Lakewood walked up to the white sergeant and started talking shit. The sergeant was known for playing with the inmates a lot. He posted up with Lakewood as they started slap boxing.

I made my move, hurrying to the small window. "What's up, beautiful?" I said as she walked up to the window.

"Hey, handsome, I missed you," she said, handing me a folded piece of paper.

"I missed you more, and tell Williamson I said wassup with her nosey ass," I said, noticing she was eavesdropping.

"I gotcha, babe, be careful!" she said.

"Always," I said, before walking off, leaving Lakewood behind.

"Where's Lakewood?" Gangsta asked as I stepped on the wing.

"He should be behind me in a minute. I had to dip off, I was dirty." I explained as I sat on the trash can. I pulled out her kite and looked it over. It read: *"Baby, I enjoyed our time together, I never thought in a million years I would have done anything like that in my whole life. But I don't regret it one bit, I haven't been able to get you off my mind. I come to work now, just to see you. All I want to do is see that sexy smile, and hear your voice. I know you see parole in a few months. I want you to come home to me. If there is any way that I can help you, just let me know. Here's my number 903-555 7732, text me when I get off, yours only!"* I handed the kite to Gangsta. "Read this, G, I got her right where I want her."

Gangsta

"Damn, that bitch head sprung! Hold up, ain't she married?" I said, shaking my head. "Damn, these bitches ain't got no loyalty." I handed the kite back to him. He ripped it in half and then ripped it again before throwing it in the trash can.

"Well, Williamson told me she was engaged, she ain't married yet," Hotboy said. "She say she living with this white dude, and his son. Well, they living with her. Supposedly, he's a dopehead."

"Should've known—I figured something was wrong at home," I said, as Lakewood walked on the wing.

"Damn, bitch," Lakewood said to Hotboy, "I was looking everywhere for yo' ass. I stood up on the chow hall table screaming yo' name and everything."

"My bad, bitch, I had to burn off. Job well done, though."

"So what she talking about?" Lakewood asked him.

"We in business, that's all you need to know," Hotboy said, walking off.

Lakewood walked behind him. "Good, 'cause we haven't had a square in days, I'm feining hard."

"Where the fuck y'all think y'all going?" I asked as they tried to walk away. They turned around.

"What?" Hotboy asked.

"Grab the broom, I need to take care of some business," I said, looking towards Bryant. They understood without me having to say another word.

"Overstood, where yo' celly at?" Hotboy asked. I looked around the dayroom for my celly. He was sitting at the poker table, losing all his money to Kuda, *2-3*, and Memphis.

"I'm good," I said. "He in the dayroom. If somebody comes, scream loud, you know my cell all the way in the back." I walked off afterwards.

"Aye, bitch, hold up!" Hotboy said, stopping me in my tracks. "What do I need to tell Ms. Bryant?" he asked. "Or do she already know the play?"

I laughed. "Yeah, fool, she knows. You know I dot my i's and cross my t's. Y'all just hold it down, I got this."

***

"Damn, you a fool," I said, as I fucked Bryant's mouth. Her head game was superb. She looked like a slutty school girl, with her glasses on, as her head bobbed up and down.

"Ahh!" she gasped as she came up for air. She wiped the spit from her mouth, and spat on my dick as she jacked me off. She traced her tongue down my shaft as she found her way to my balls.

"Freaky ass bitch, suck this dick and stop playing," I demanded. She was good at following orders. She slapped her tongue with the head of my dick before sticking it back inside her mouth. I fucked her mouth like a tight pussy, making her gag as tears fell from her eyes. "Nasty bitch! Stand up, have you ever been fucked by a Gangsta?" I asked, feeling myself.

She shook her head as she stood up. She unbuckled her pants; they freely fell to the ground. I turned her, making her bend over the toilet, then I raised the bottom of her shirt above her ass. Smacking her on her pink ass, I knew for a fact my neighbors heard it. She reached behind her to guide my dick inside her hole. Grabbing her arms, I held them up as I rammed my dick inside her. I moved in and out with determination. I had been waiting for this for over two weeks. Every night we had phone sex, and now I was finally digging in the real deal. I arched her back and slid my hand up her shirt.

Her backbone poked out of her back like a dinosaur's. That shit had me grossed out, so I slid her shirt back down. I can't lie, her pussy was so good I could get out of it.

"Gangsta, hurt this pussy." She moaned as she held on to the sink. As ugly as she was, she was turning me on. I went into my second wind, as I pulled out and turned her facing me. I picked her up, and she wrapped her legs around my waist. My dick snuggled right back into her warm cave.

"Fuck me, fuck mee-e-e-e," she said as she bounced up and down. She was so light it felt like I was throwing her. "Don't come inside me," she said, catching me at my peak. I lowered her down and she slid to her knees. She opened her mouth wide like I was her dentist. Bouncing my dick head on the tip of her tongue, I shot my load all over her face and glasses.

"Ahhh, fuck!" I groaned. It felt so good that I could barely move. Walking to the toilet with my pants still down, I took a piss while she put her pants back on. I grabbed a clean towel and wiped my dick off before handing it to her, so that she could wipe her glasses off.

She kissed my neck as I pulled my pants back up. "You're mine, for life!" she said, hugging me from the back.

Newton

"Mommy, where's daddy?" Jacob asked as we sat on the couch, watching TV.

I rubbed his head. "He went to the store. He'll be back before you go to sleep. I promise." I was now 100% positive that Seth was using again. I found residue inside my car.

"Mommy, can we watch The Lion King again?" Jacob asked, looking up at me.

I smiled. He really loved that movie. "Sure, baby." I turned on Netflix. Leaning his head against me, Jacob waited on the movie to start.

My phone rang just as the movie was about to start. "Jacob baby, can you hand mommy her phone? That might be daddy." I pointed to the phone on the table. He jumped up to retrieve my phone, and handed it to me. "Hello," I answered.

"Hey, you busy?" Gianni said, just above a whisper. I jumped up from the couch, accidently pushing Jacob over as I walked into my bedroom.

"Hey, boo! I was hoping you'll call. You didn't call last night like I asked you to,"

"I know, we didn't have a good third shift last night, so I couldn't. Seeing that you're free to talk now says you're man isn't home."

"Yes, he's out, again!" I said, defeated.

"Why you say it like that?"

"I don't know, he's just changed since I started working at the prison. He's back getting high again." There was a brief pause in our conversation until Gianni said:

"I can't actually say I'm sorry to hear that. I mean, he's my competition, and the worse he's doing, the better we'll be."

"I really hate it here now," I said. "It's like our relationship went downhill, fast. I really don't know what the problem is."

"You know exactly what it is. He ain't me. After being around me and going home to another nigga, it'll drive you insane. That's like having your favorite ice cream, and someone comes and trade it out for your least favorite. It just ain't the same, even if it is ice cream."

I laughed. "Shut up, that is not it!" I said, killing his pride.

"Then what is it?"

"I don't think I'm in love with him anymore," I said, shocked that those words actually came from my mouth.

"How you figure?" he asked.

I laid back on the bed and said, "Because I'm in love with you."

"Prove it then."

"I thought I *did*," I said, thinking about what we had done in his cell.

"Naw, ma, sex ain't love. Rats have sex, dogs have sex. Actions show love."

"So what do you want me to do?" I asked, ready to take on the world for him.

"Leave him!" he said, catching me off guard. I didn't expect for him to say that.

"How, Gianni? I live with him. The house is in both our names. Plus, I'm like the mother to his son, I can't leave Jacob."

"Then you don't love me. Love will sacrifice. Can't you see— I'm sitting in this cell on a cellphone. If they catch me, I could get some more time. So I'm sacrificing my life, just to talk to you. That's love!"

I felt bad by those words of his. "I understand, baby." I sighed. "Calm down, I mean it's not that easy. Where am I supposed to stay? I'm broke, I don't have any money."

"Give me a month then," he said, like he had a plan. "We hustle for a month; you'll have enough money to buy your own house, and a car."

"One month?" I said, thinking about it. "You promise?"

"My word."

Three Weeks Later

Hotboy

"You really think she's going to come through? She's been saying she was going to bring you something for the past three weeks," Lakewood said as we waited in the commissary line for shift change.

Watching the officers' faces as they came through the front door, I answered. "Ain't no doubt in my mind. The only thing is, will she make it through with it?"

"If she do make it through, bitch, we on!" he said.

"Shut up, nigga, damn!" I said, getting frustrated. I was trying to concentrate, and he wouldn't stop talking. He kept right on talking like I hadn't said a word.

"Yeah, she needs to come through fast, 'cause you need a square, bad."

Laughing at him, I said, "Alright, my nigga, keep on." I saw Williamson as she walked through the door. I figured Gabby couldn't be too far behind. "There she go, damn, she made it," I said, excited as she walked in.

"Damn, that bitch is built Ford-tough," Lakewood said.

I said, as she headed in our direction, "She just well-trained. Took me three weeks to get her comfortable with doing it. All we had to do now was watch and see what wing she would work on."

"I know she ain't about to hand it to us right in the open," he said, making me nervous. The way she was looking made me think the same thing, Until she walked past us walking to the E, F, G, H picket.

"Damn, she scared me," I said, relaxing.

"Look, she the picket boss. That mean we ain't gotta fall outta place to get it. All you have to do is go up to three row, and have her hand it to you."

I nodded in agreement. "Bitch, you ain't so stupid after all huh," I teased as Lakewood and I walked to the wing.

"Fuck you, fool, I happened to be the smartest nigga you know. I just play dumb." He laughed.

Officer Wade opened the gate to let us in as I saluted Officer Little, who was working the wing. He was cool, so I didn't have to worry about a bullshit C.O. all in my business. Running up the stairs, I rushed to three row to get Gabby's attention. "Look out, picket boss!" I yelled, hoping she heard me. "Picket!" I said as she stepped in front of me smiling.

"Bae, I did it!" she said, excited.

"Were you nervous?" I asked.

"At first I was, but the spandex kept it from falling. I practiced at home, like you told me to do so I could get comfortable walking around with it. Once I got searched, and she let me pass, I saw how easy it really is."

"I'm proud of you. Where's it at?"

She smiled. I still have it down there." She pointed to her private area. "I didn't want to go directly to the restroom, just in case someone was watching me."

I was really proud of her. What she did wasn't an easy task. What I'd taught her, she took it and ran with it. "We should be good now. Go ahead to the restroom, and get it ready. Come back here, and give it to me. When I get everything put up, I'ma come back and holla at you."

"Okay, bae, can I have a kiss?" she asked, smiling. I looked back to make sure no one was watching as I put my face to the bars to sneak a kiss. "I love you!" she said.

"I know. You just showed me!"

"Damn, that's a lot—I thought you told her to only bring eight ounces?" Lakewood asked as he broke the pack down into a bowl. Grabbing a brand new razor, he split the pack down the middle, cutting through the thick black tape.

"I told her to bring half. She had said something about buying some vacuum seal bags so that she can put more in them. I didn't think she would bring the whole sixteen." I was amazed.

"Wonder Woman," Lakewood said, making me laugh. I had to admit, she was bad.

"Naw, for real, huh." I agreed.

"So how much you going to send her for all this?" he asked.

"This is two cans. Right now, considering how the game is, with it being a drought on tobacco, I can really tax niggas. I can do two for fifty dollars. That's an easy four thousand dollars."

"Yeah, but you know you smoke. Shid, we smoke. So you can't say four thousand dollars." Lakewood was making a point.

"You right, matter of fact, get that empty Ziploc bag over there so we can go ahead and put a smoke sack up."

He grabbed the bag and walked to the bars to make sure no one was coming.

As he came back over to the desk, I said, "I told her to come through at least three days a week. That way, we can keep a steady flow of blend. We gon' have this bitch flooded, watch."

"That's smart though. You gotta get it while the getting's good."

I looked up at Lakewood. "Where's Gangsta?" I asked, noticing I hadn't seen him out and about all day.

"He's in his cell. He talking about he thinks he got some type of virus or something."

"That nigga just getting old," I said as I taped up the remaining of the pack. "Here—" I handed it to him. "Give this to the hold man. Tell him I'm gon' bless his game next shift." I popped out the cell. I had to go check on my guy. It wasn't like him to not holla at me all day.

Gangsta

"You ain't coming in? Why not?" I asked Bryant as I whispered into the phone.

"I have shit to do," Bryant said like she had an attitude.

"Damn, I wanted to see you, but it's cool."

"I'll be back in a couple of days, I promise," she said, as though that was supposed to make me feel better. I ought to be getting another drop from her when she came back. The bitch kept calling in, saying she had to go check on her mom in Dallas. Like I gave a fuck about her mama.

I was tired, sick, and I wasn't trying to hear any more excuses. "Whatever, I'ma holla at you," I said, hanging up before she could utter another word. I put the phone up and grabbed my book that I was trying to finish reading.

"What's good, nigga? You straight in there? Hotboy asked as he stood in front of my cell.

"Yeah, I'm straight. Trying to get this virus up off of me."

"Wassup, did she come through?" I asked.

"Yeah, she did. I got everything put up right now. I'ma send you a smoke sack by the porter. Get some rest, nigga, you look sick as hell, I'ma come back and check on you later."

"I'm good, my nigga. It ain't that serious. I was just about to chill and read this book." I held the book up so that Hotboy could see it.

"Which one is that?" he asked, trying to read the cover.

"*Trust No Bitch 3*, by Cash and Nene Capri."

"Oh yeah, I haven't read part three yet. Part one and two went hard though. Who got next in line for that one?"

"'This my celly's, but you can read it, he ain't gon' trip," I said, feeling a sharp pain in my stomach.

" Take heed to the title," Hotboy said, laughing.

I nodded. "For real. Trust no bitch. Them hos will get you killed."

"Or kill you," Hotboy added.

"Straight up!"

"I gotta go though, I told baby I would come back and holla at her while she was still in the picket. I'ma send you something to smoke in a second."

"Tell sis I said wassup," I shouted after him.

I shook my head at him. He was deep in love. He always said that he wouldn't fall in love with a bitch that worked in the penitentiary, but he couldn't fool me. I knew that look from anywhere; that was pure love.

Picking the book back up, I jumped back into it like it was a movie. This junt was so live it was hard to put it down. I had the perfect thing to cap it off with. A cup of coffee, and some cappuccino. Jumping off the bunk, I felt another sharp pain that ran from my stomach to my heart. This time the pain took me down to my knees.

Clutching my chest, I hunched over in severe pain. I looked up to see the porter standing at my cell door. "Aye, Gangsta, you alright? Cuz, Gangsta! You straight?" he kept asking. I couldn't gather enough strength to answer him as I held on to the bottom bunk. "Man down! Man down!" was the last thing I could remember.

"Mr. Washington, can you hear me?" the nurse asked, as she shone a light in my face.

I looked around the room as another nurse wrote something down on a clipboard. I nodded to answer her question, but I was too parched to speak.

"Mr. Washington, you've been out for a whole three days. We

couldn't figure out what the problem was, so we ran some blood tests."

I looked around the room for a clock. I was sure she mistook the word *days* for *hours*. Handing me a cup of water, she said, "I looked at your file, and it says that you were clean when you first entered TDCJ's system. Now I'm going to ask you some very important questions. I want you to be truthful with me, and with yourself." I downed the water like I was dying of thirst. "Mr. Washington, have you had any fights recently?" she asked.

I shook my head. "No, uhh—" I said, straining to talk. "It's been over six months since my last fight," I answered.

"What about tattoos?" she asked.

I shook my head, now worried.

"Have you ever participated in any homosexual activities?" she asked as she drained the blood from my face with her questions.

"Hell naw!" I shouted, feeling dizzy.

"Mr. Washington, your blood work came back, I'm sorry to tell you, but you've contracted the AIDS virus," she said with pity.

I looked at her like she was crazy. She must've mistaken me with someone else. Then I saw my legs were cuffed to the bedrails. This was serious. I couldn't have AIDS. I didn't have a fight. I didn't fuck around with the fuck around. I hated needles. So how? I thought back to the last time I had sex. That skinny bitch!

Chapter 7

Newton

"Fuck! I can't be!" I yelled at Williamson as we sat in her bathroom. I had just taken two different pregnancy tests, and they all came back positive. "Pass me the other one," I said, ready to try again.

"Gabby, stop! The first two ain't lying. You're pregnant!" I didn't want to believe. I covered my face as the tears fell freely.

She placed her hands on my shoulder to console me. "It's going to be okay. This is exactly what you wanted, a baby," she said, trying to make me feel better.

I sighed. "This is what I wanted, but how am I supposed to tell Seth that I'm pregnant, and by another man? An inmate at that. What if Gianni don't want a baby. I completely destroyed my life."

"Come on, boo, don't say that. Seth hasn't been home in almost two weeks. Your mom has been taking care of Jacob while you've been at work. That man is down bad, and you know it. Gianni loves you! I don't think that he's the type to abandon his child."

Wiping my face, I looked at the smiley face on the pregnancy test. "I'm pregnant!" I laughed, with tears falling.

She laughed with me as she gave me a hug. "Yes, bitch, you're pregnant!"

"I wonder what he's going to say," I said through sniffles.

"There's only one way to find out. You have to tell him."

"Yeah, you're right. I'll tell him tomorrow at work, face to face. I don't know how I'm going to break the news to Seth. And Jacob, oh my God, Jacob. I don't wanna hurt him. He's innocent in all of this."

"Well, first Seth has to come home," Williamson said, helping me off the bathroom floor. I looked down at the test again. I couldn't help but wonder. *Where was he?*

Next Day

"Gianni, I'm pregnant. Gianni, babe, you're going to be a dad. Gianni, I'm sorry, but I'm pregnant. I'm sorry, ughh—just calm down, Gabby!" I told myself as I stood in the chow hall, rehearsing the best way to tell him we were having a baby.

An inmate walked with his tray in his hand. "Hey sexy," he began, "I've been trying to get at you for a while. I can't seem to get you to work G-wing to save my life." He eyed me like I was a piece of meat.

"Would you sit down? If I had to work G-wing to save your life, you would be a dead motherfucker," I said, annoyed. He sat his tray down on the table in front of me.

"It's like that, bitch?"

"I got your bitch, bitch!" I spat.

"Sexy and feisty. Is that pussy as angry as your attitude?"

"Fuck you, punk loving ass faggot. I heard you got caught the other day in that punk cell eating *his* ass. They should've ran yo' gay as off the unit." I yelled as people watched.

He walked up as he grilled me. "You don't know what the hell you're talking about, bitch! You trying to put a jacket on me. I should smack yo' trash ass." He stepped closer to me.

"Aye, homie, this yo' tray?" Gianni asked from behind him.

The disturbing inmate turned around and saw who it was, and took a step back. "What's popping, Hotboy?" he said, sounding friendly.

"Yo' skull if you don't get you some business!" Gianni said, mean-mugging him.

The inmate held his hands up and stepped back. "Didn't know that was you, homie—My bad!" he said as he grabbed his tray and walked off.

I relaxed a little as Gianni stepped closer to me. "You alright, ma? What are you doing getting into it with that nigga? Can't you see ain't no cameras in here? Some of these niggas got a lot of time. They don't give a damn about you."

"I know. I'm sorry. I just didn't feel like being bothered. And he kept messing with me."

100

"What's wrong?"

It was now, or never. "I'm pregnant!"

Hotboy

"Say what?" I said, hoping I heard wrong.

She put her head down. "You heard me, Gianni, I'm fucking pregnant!" she said, on the verge of tears. As bad as I wanted to console her, I couldn't. She was still a C.O., and I was still an inmate.

"Maybe I should never have told you about it at all," she said, feeling bad.

"I didn't mean it like that. I was just saying you caught me by surprise. I mean we only had sex, like, once."

She looked at me like she wanted to slap the spit outta my mouth. "So what are you saying? I'm not a ho, Gianni, and I haven't slept with Seth in almost two months."

"I thought you were on birth control?"

She grilled me. "You know what, fuck you!" she yelled as she turned her back to me.

I grabbed her arm, making her face me. I didn't care who saw. I didn't want to hurt her. "I'm sorry, this is all just so sudden, that's all. I do want kids; I just didn't expect the baby to be a penitentiary baby."

She tilted her head towards the floor. "What! You think this is how I wanted it to happen? I didn't plan any of this, but what's done is done, Gianni. I'm telling you now, I'm having my baby!"

I sat on the top of the table and rubbed my head. "I'm not the type of nigga to let you do it alone. I'm going to be there for my kid. It's just that we just started stacking up for a house. Now we have to put up for a baby too." I hoped she got the hint.

"I can keep doing what we've been doing—until I start to show," she said.

"Naw, we have to change it up," I said, thinking about the next play.

She looked up at me. "What do you mean?" she asked.

"The tobacco is good money, but it's slow money. We need some fast money. The only way to do that is to fuck with some K2."

She shook her head. "No, baby, I told you I didn't want to bring any drugs, especially that K2 stuff. Do you see what it's doing to people?"

"Do you know how much money we can make? We can make anywhere from fifteen to twenty grand, easy. It's the same amount as if you're bringing the tobacco. If we don't do it, somebody else will. So it wouldn't matter. We might as well get this money one way or another—that shit still going to hit the unit."

"What if I get caught? That's a felony!" She looked scared.

"Regardless—tobacco or K2—if you get caught, you're only going to get fired. Look, we not even going to talk like that. Do you trust me?" She nodded, looking at the ground. "Look at me, Gabby." She looked up, afraid. "I love you!" I said for the very first time.

She smiled as though she'd been waiting for that her whole life. "I love you too!"

Three Weeks Later

Gangsta

"Don't! Don't you dare, bitch! I told you that I didn't want any medicine!" I yelled at the nurse as she tried to inject some medicine into my IV bag. I had been moved to a cell in the back of the infirmary. I knew my guys have been worried about me. I sent a kite to them a week ago, telling them I was okay, and that I had a stomach virus. I lied and told them that they were holding me in detox until the virus passed over me.

I felt bad lying to my guys, but I was too ashamed to tell them that I had contracted the AIDS virus from that dirty ass bitch. I should have taken heed from Lakewood when he had said she looked sick. I was so caught up in getting some pussy, I didn't pay attention.

The nurses did their best. The prison didn't fund enough money to provide good medicine. The medicine that they provided only made you feel worse than better. Lately, I haven't been able to stomach any food; it's been almost a week and a half since I actually ate anything. I know I've lost over 30lbs in the past week.

"Washington, you have to let me give you this medicine, honey. If you don't, the virus will eat you up from the inside."

I cried for the first time in over twenty years. "Bitch, look at me! It's already eating me up. I'm already dead! I can't go home like this, they'll swear I slept with a punk." I cried.

She must've felt my pain. Grabbing a cold towel, she dabbed my forehead to cool me down. "Everything is going to be okay, I promise!"

***

"Trash, you got any trash in here, homie?" the porter asked as he peeped inside my room. Walking inside, he grabbed the trash can and emptied it as he looked over at me. "Gangsta! Is that you?" Kuda asked. Kuda was a Puerto Rican who was from Fort Worth. He was housed on H-wing when I was over there.

I was pissed. I told the nurses not to let anyone in my room for anything. I was afraid someone would see me and tell everyone what I looked like. Now look what happened.

"Damn, Gangsta, what happened? You look bad, homie," Kuda said.

I pulled the blanket over my chest to hide the bones that showed. "I'm good, I just got the stomach virus."

He looked at me with disgust. "That's a bad stomach virus. The worse I've seen. What the doctor say?"

"He say I'll be good in a week or two." I went from being a Gangsta to a liar.

That's wassup then. I'll tell Hotboy that I saw you. They been asking about you every day. I didn't know which room you was in at first, but I'll tell them I saw you." He grabbed the trash can.

"Tell them I'm good, and I'll see them soon." Deep down, I

knew I wasn't willing to see my homies at all. What hurt more was the fact that I was lying. The thought of that caused a tear to roll down my cheek.

"No doubt, big bro. Feel better!" Kuda said as he closed the door behind him. As soon as I heard the door click, tears poured down like a waterfall. *"Look at you now, Gangsta, you're a shadow of your former self!"*

Newton

"Thank you, mama, I really appreciate you for keeping an eye on him while I'm at work," I said as I handed my mother $200 for keeping Jacob for the week.

She accepted it and stuck it inside her bra. "It's no problem, sweetie. He's so quiet half the time, I don't even know he's here. By the way, have you heard anything on Seth yet?"

"Your luck is as good as mine. He's had the car for over a month now. I can't report it stolen because it's in his name."

She gave me a much needed hug. "Don't worry, baby, he'll come around when he's ready. Men just seem to have prideful issues sometimes. Your daddy was like that too sometimes."

"Mommy," Jacob said, looking up at me.

"Yes, sweetie."

"I miss daddy," he said as we walked to the car.

I placed him in his car seat and sighed. "I know, baby, I know."

***

"Okay, sweetie, go get your things ready for bed while I prepare your bath water," I said to Jacob as I placed the keys on the stand—keys to the car Gianni bought me. I walked in the living room and sat my purse on the couch.

"Gabby," Seth said, scaring me.

I turned to the sight of him sitting in the dark on the love seat. His clothes looked like he had been lying in the mud. His face looked like he hadn't shaved in weeks. "Seth, what the hell! Where have you been?"

Jacob ran in the room as he heard his father's voice. "Daddy, you're home!"

"Yes, daddy's home, now go get ready for bed like mommy asked you to," he said, nonchalant.

I waited until Jacob was out of sight before tearing into Seth's ass. "So, you're not going to answer my fucking question. And where is our car? I didn't see it in the driveway?"

"I've been busy," was all he said.

"Busy! Really, Seth, busy! Fucking busy! That's all you have to say after being away for almost two damn months." I yelled.

"Look, not now," he said, standing up. "I didn't come home for this shit." He grabbed my purse.

I walked up to him. "What the hell are you looking for in my purse?" I asked, reaching for it.

"I need some money, Gabby," he said, pulling out my wallet. I snatched it from him and yelled. "No, the hell you don't! Is that why you came home? For money? So what, so you can run back out, and get high again?" Jacob stood at the doorway, watching in horror. He had never seen either of us act like this. "Seth, where is our car?" I asked again.

He sat on the couch and put his hands on his head. "I sold it."

I looked at him with so much hatred. "You sold our car? Are you out of your fucking mind, Seth! I'm here, every day, with your son, *your son*! Every night, making sure he goes to school. Making sure he's well taken care of, while I still go to work. Here you are getting high. You're no better than his mother!" I spat.

"I'm sorry, Gabby," he said, sobbing as he looked over at Jacob.

I walked away from him and led Jacob to his bath. "No, you're *not* sorry, but you will be!"

Hotboy

"I bet we beat them hos, what you wanna bet?" I yelled at JJ as we sat in front of the sports TV, watching the Grizzles play the Mavericks.

JJ replied immediately. "Come on, my nigga, them hos trash. All y'all got is Ja Morant. Other than that, y'all ain't got shit. He can't beat us by himself."

"Well—bet, bitch! That's my squad, fuck that gay pony shit you be cheering for. Luka trying to be like Curry and shit, shooting the ball from half court. Let him try that shit tonight, I bet y'all lose."

"Man, sit yo' ass down before you owe me your whole life," JJ said. "I know we going to win," he added.

"Well, this should be easy money for you then," I said, longing for a bet.

"You know what, since you talking so damn much, what you wanna bet?" he asked.

"Make it light on yo'self," I said.

"Bet a dollar," he said, codedly referring to $100.

"I want my money too, bitch. I know how you are. You'll drag a nigga forever." I laughed as the game tipped off. I don't know why I even bet the fool. If he was cool with you, he would take forever to pay you. They even came up with a phrase for paying a nigga late. They called it, *the JJ drag game.*

"We up by ten now, y'all dead," I yelled as JJ walked away from the TV. "Second half, Ja gon' come out and dunk on Luka pale skin ass, watch. Make a poster outta that clown." I was teasing. I couldn't really watch a game without talking shit. It was no fun to watch the game and be quiet. To me, if you wanted to watch sports quietly, you should've just watched a movie.

I stood up and walked to the window beside Lakewood, to hit the square he was smoking. "Let me tap that," I said as I kneeled down beside him.

Kuda walked up and tossed a kite by my foot. "That's from Gangsta," he said.

"Word, how my nigga doing?" I asked, picking up the kite.

It had been over three months since I last saw my nigga. He even stopped replying to my kites. I tried numerous times to get back there to see him. It seemed like every time I got a chance, it was a bullshit law working back there. Kuda shook his head and said, "The nigga looking worse and worse every day I see him. To me, it looks like he's dying."

"Dying? The nigga got a stomach virus. How serious can that be?" I asked.

"I think it's more than that," Kuda said as he walked off.

I sat on the table and unfolded the kite. It read:

"What's good, homie? I hope you charge it to my head, and not my heart for not writing y'all back. I ain't been in the right mindset to really respond. As I'm sitting here putting all this together, I had to shed a few tears. I've been thinking about all the good times me, you, Lakewood, and them shared together. All the plans we had lined up for when we touch down. It's heartbreaking that I won't be able to see y'all in the free world. It was crazy how that day you told me to trust no bitch.

We sit in this bitch, and plot. We plot on how we're going to break a ho, and all along they be plotting the same damn thang. I know you're wondering what the fuck I'm talking about. I was given the AIDS virus through that skinny bitch Bryant. They say that everything that glitters ain't gold. I was thinking that I was the man for getting some pussy in the penitentiary. Really I was in last place. I was better off staying on medium custody!

This virus is killing me slowly, homie. It hurts me knowing that I let a bitch take a Gangsta down. Laying in this hospital bed, day in and day out, it hurts. This shit ain't me, homie! I'ma Gangsta! Gangstas don't lay down until they're tired. I have to say that I'm tired, homie. My body is tired, my mind is tired. Tell Lakewood I said to take care of them kids when he goes home. Tell C-1o and Eastwood I said one love.

Tell Uncle Marvin I said to stay up, we've been down too long. And for you homie, I'ma watch over you every day. All I ask is that you don't let that skinny bitch get away with what she did to me. I love y'all, Gangsta!"

Tears started to fall onto the kite as I let the cigarette drop to the floor.

Chapter 8

Gangsta

"Hey, Mr. Washington, how are you feeling?" Nurse Davis asked. Nurse Davis was a cool white chick who had been working on the unit for a while. Everyone wanted to fuck her because she was so laid back. Even though she was white, she considered herself a redbone. She had some hips, but no ass. I could tell she was a straight freak. Even while I was laid out with full-blown AIDS, she was still dick-watching.

If she didn't know any better, I probably could've bent her over this bed and fucked the shit outta her. I know she liked that rough shit; she looked like a straight nympho. I raised up on my elbows and said, "I'm doing a li'l better," even though I was lying through my teeth.

She took my vital signs and jotted something down on her clipboard. "Vital signs seem to be looking good. Did you eat anything today?" she asked as she pushed the machine to the corner.

"Every drop," I said.

"Good for you. You getting better depends on you. Before I go, do you need anything?"

"I could use another sheet, it's getting cold in here," I said.

"Sure honey, I'll be right back," she said, closing the door behind her. She had to go upstairs to get the blanket, so I only had a li'l time. I jumped out the bed on weak legs as soon as she left. Grabbing the sheet that I had got from another porter earlier, I walked over to grab the chair from the corner. I locked the wheels on it so that it wouldn't move. Stepping on the chair, I tied the sheets together, then tied them to the pole hanging from the ceiling.

Once I made a tight loop, I placed it over my head to my neck. Contemplating not to go through with it, I hesitated. I looked at myself through the reflection in the mirror. I wasn't close to who I used to be. I wasn't Gangsta anymore. I looked around to the machines that they had me hooked up to. I thought of the constant drinking of that nasty ass nutrition shake.

The Gangsta that had once terrorized the streets was now a pile of bones. "Look at yo'self, look at you now, Gangsta!" I said to myself as the tears started falling. "At least go out like a Gangsta! Finish what you started!" My conscience spoke to me. *"You can do it! You're a Gangsta!"* Closing my eyes, I rocked the chair from side to side until I couldn't feel it under me anymore. It felt like I had jumped off the Empire State Building. My body fought a good fight, but my mind had gave up a long time ago. Gangstas don't die, we multiply!

Newton

"Gabby, are you alright?" Seth asked as I read a text from Williamson that said Gangsta had hung himself. Once Seth found out that I was pregnant, from me constantly throwing up, he didn't quit doing meth, but he did come home every night. I never gained the courage to tell him that the baby wasn't his.

Wiping the tears away, I said, "Yes, I'm fine, umm, I just got a text from Williamson saying someone we knew killed himself."

"Damn, that's sad. Was it a C.O.?" he asked.

"Yes."

"Damn, that sucks, I'm here for you if you need me," he said, patting my leg.

"Thanks," I said, really wanting to be there for Gianni.

"Baby, I know that this isn't the right time to tell you this, but I want to let you know that I'm so grateful that you didn't give up on me. I want to let you know I'm trying to get myself cleaned up, for good this time. For you, for Jacob, and for our unborn." Seth's words fell on deaf ears. The only thing that I could think about at the moment was Gianni.

Hotboy

"He good now, he in a better place," Lakewood said as he

wiped his tears away. "I know he's in a Gangsta's paradise."

I took a sip from the bottle of hooch as I let the effects take the pain away. "Damn, my nigga tripped out. He could've went home and went to the best doctors in the city. They could've helped him." I hit the bottle again. I usually didn't drink to get drunk, but today I was already on my fifth bottle.

"Come on, my nigga," said Uncle Marvin. "You know Gangsta. He wasn't going to go home and go to no damn doctors asking for their help."

"Unc, you remember that time Gangsta and B-hamp was slap boxing in the dayroom after we all had got drunk," Lakewood said, bringing up old times.

I spit the hooch out as I laughed, thinking back to that day.

Unc said, laughing, "I remember that he had got out there with B-hamp. Then afterwards when Six-Five started laughing, he called him out. He hurt Six-Five so bad, he had his lips swollen as a mo' fucka."

"Oh, you remember when he beat that *ese* up on A-wing?" Lakewood asked.

"Yeah, he hurt that *ese*. He had that nigga looking like the pumpkin head." I laughed as we reminisced about our friend.

"'Damn the penitentiary! It always takes out the good ones," Unc said before walking away. He never liked people to see him in his feelings. I could see that Gangsta's death hit everyone really hard, especially me.

I hadn't stopped drinking yet. I had to celebrate for my nigga. He was always the life of the party. "Damn, I miss my nigga!" I said out loud.

"We have to get that bitch for what she did to my nigga," Lakewood said, upset. "She knew her shit was sour," he added

I twisted my face as the hooch made my stomach churn. I said to him, "You ain't gon' do shit but take yo' ass home to yo' kids. You got two weeks until you discharge, go home!"

"That was my nigga too!" he said, obviously upset.

"Lakewood, I can't lose y'all both to the system, homie. We need you in the free world. Your daughters need you too. Do that for Gangsta, go home, and take care of your business like he asked."

He took his bottle to the head and said, "Don't let that bitch get away with that shit, Hotboy, or I'll never forgive you."

I took the rest of my bottle to the head. "Over my dead body!"

Newton

"Hey, have you seen him?" I asked Williamson.

"Naw, they had me in front of the infirmary earlier today. Aren't you doing moves? Why haven't you went to see him yet?" she asked.

"I've been moving a lot of G4's. I haven't had the chance to go down there yet. I actually have to move someone to his wing now. So I'm headed there now."

"Tell him I said I'm sorry for his loss, and when I get the chance, I'll pull up over there."

"I'll tell him. I know he's hurting. I just hope he don't take it too hard." I walked down the hall in a hurry. "H-wing in!" I yelled at the African keyboss. I swear, they got on my last nerve. They were always gossiping. I was trying to check on my babe, and this nappy-headed ass bitch was taking all day to open the gate. She looked over at me as she took her time walking over to the gate. I swear if I wasn't pregnant I would've told her something. I rolled my eyes as I walked past her, she was beneath me.

"229 bottom, you're moving to 214 bottom," I said, noticing Gianni's celly was moving. "You're going to 229 bottom," I said to the inmate that I brought from G4. I walked to Gianni as he sat on the trash can. "Hey, you okay?" I asked.

He looked at me with anger in his eyes. "Do I look okay?" he answered, smelling like a liquor store. "Ain't this your day off, what are you doing here?" he asked.

"I came to do overtime. I wanted to make sure you were okay. Williamson texted me, telling me what happened. You know, with Gangsta."

He grilled me like I had done something wrong. "That was

two days ago. You just now seeing if I was okay. Get the fuck outta my face!" He spat on the ground in front of me.

"Gianni, don't act like that with me right now, don't shut me out," I pleaded.

"Did you know that bitch Bryant had AIDS?" he asked.

"No!" I said, shaking my head. "I swear I didn't know. I didn't even know who she was until all of this happened."

He looked me up and down. "Do I need to get checked?" he asked. I felt so low. I wanted to slap him so bad.

"Really, Gianni, you're really going to ask me that!"

"I'm just saying, you're the one sleeping with a dopehead. I bet you still haven't told him who the daddy is, have you?"

Shaking my head I said. "It's not that easy."

He stood up, mean-mugging me. "Well, let me make it easy for you. Don't fuck with me until you leave him. Fuck you, and fuck that baby, it probably ain't mines anyway."

The Next Day

"You think he meant it? Or was it the hooch talking?" Williamson asked as we waited in the doctor's office lobby.

"I really don't know. Maybe that's just how he grieves," I said, trying to soften the pain.

"You know, they say a drunk mind speaks sober thoughts," she added, not helping matters at all.

"I don't know. Him and Gangsta were like brothers. Then Lakewood caught chain to go home last night. So now, he's all alone." I was thinking deeply about Gianni.

Sipping her coffee, Williamson said, "Damn, that man's luck is bad. I'm glad you got him and not me."

I shook my head as I tried to ignore her. She didn't have no idea what a filter was. "What am I going to do?" I asked, rubbing my stomach.

"You have an easy choice to make. You're just making it hard. Someone will get hurt in the end. You just have to make sure that someone isn't you."

"Ms. Newton," a nurse said as she emerged from the back room. I raised my hand. "You can come with me," she said, and I stood up. Williamson grabbed my purse and followed me into the back room. The nurse said to me, before closing the door behind her, "You can sit on top of the table. The doctor will be right in to see you."

"So what do you want? Boy or girl?" Williamson asked.

Rubbing my belly, I said, "I don't really care. I just want a healthy baby. But—a mini-me would be nice." I smiled.

"Girl, if you have a daughter, I'm going to spoil her rotten. I'm going to be the best God-mama in the world."

"God-mama? Who named you the God-mama?" I joked.

"Bitch, don't play with me, you know I'm the God-mama." She laughed.

"I'm just playing girl, you know I love you." We laughed together.

The doctor walked in. "Okay, I'm sorry to keep you waiting so long," he said, shaking my hand, then Williamson's.

"It's okay, Doc," I said.

"Okay, let's get started. Can you lay back for me and raise your shirt above your stomach," he instructed, and he rubbed a cold gel over my belly. "Are you excited to know the gender?" he asked.

"I am," Williamson said before I could answer.

"Yes, Doctor, I am," I said, laughing at Williamson.

"Well, let's find out then, shall we?" he said, turning the monitor on. Looking at the screen, I tried to make out what it was, but I couldn't tell. "He's shy," the doctor said.

"He?" I said, smiling.

"Yes, and he's very shy. Let me move to the other side so that you can see him clearer." He moved the tube over my belly. "There he is," the doctor said, and a smile crept on my face.

I could see *his* face clear as day on the screen. "Oh my God, look at him," I said, as Williamson held my hand.

"He's going to be a big boy," the doctor said as he captured the baby, smiling. He handed me a paper towel, and I cleaned the goo off of my belly. "I'll get you a few copies of the sonogram to take with you. Make sure you keep taking your vitamins, and eat healthy. Remember, your baby's health depends on your health."

I smiled. "I will, Doc, and thank you," I said, shaking his hand before he left out the room.

"So, are you going to tell him?" Williamson asked as soon as the doctor left.

"I think I'm just going to send him a picture of the sonogram and let him decide."

"He'll be there for y'all. His first kid, and it's a boy. I know men; they'll kill to have a son."

"I sure hope so!" I said.

Hotboy

"Come on, nephew," Uncle Marvin said, "you gotta get outta this bunk. You ain't been out the cell since Lakewood went home." Uncle Marvin got moved into my cell the other day. He tried hard to bring me outta my funk. After Lakewood went home, I kinda lost myself. First, Gangsta; then Lakewood.

As best as Unc tried, I just couldn't shake back. "Nephew, get out that bunk. You about to go home in a few months. You can't enjoy life like this. Got the cell smelling like ass and feet." He threw a dirty sock at me.

I laughed at him 'cause I could smell myself. "My bad, Unc, I'm tripping," I admitted as I jumped off the bunk.

"You got niggas looking for you trying to get some work, and you locked up here in the cell. Gangsta gone, homie, you gotta live yo' life. Plus, you got that li'l girl pregnant. You got a whole family to take care of now, nephew. Get yo' shit together."

Sitting on the stool, I thought about what he said. The last time I had talked to Gabby, I went hard on her. I was so upset with the death of Gangsta that I used her as a punching bag. "You right, Unc. See, that's why I love you, fam," I said, trying to give him a hug.

He backed away. "I'm old school penitentiary, we don't hug.

We give high fives. Put it up there, we've been down too long!"

Later that night, I sat on the trash can, hoping babe would work on my wing so that we could talk. She walked by the wing door and looked in my direction as I began to walk towards the gate. "Are you working over here?" I asked.

I noticed her baby bump had started to show. "No, I'm working on G-wing," she said.

"Cool, I'll come over there. I need to talk to you about something."

She nodded before walking on G-wing. I had butterflies fighting inside my stomach as I wondered how this was going to play out. I just hoped she could forgive me.

Newton

I was glad to be working on G-wing, so that Gianni could come over, knowing that they didn't have any cameras.

"Hey, Newton," the porter said as I walked on the wing.

"Hey, Jackson," I greeted back.

"I see you finally showing," he said, making me rub my belly. That had become a force of habit.

"He's been so much trouble. All he wants to do is eat." I smiled.

"Oh, word—it's a boy. That's live." He was happy for me.

"Hey, Jackson, I need a big favor, if you don't mind," I said.

"Anything, you name it, I gotcha."

"Could I use your cell? Gianni's coming over so we can talk. I don't want the dayroom in my business."

"Come on, you know Hotboy family. Go ahead, the door already open. I ain't got a celly, so y'all good."

"Okay, thanks. Where's your cell at?"

"327."

I slid the door open, and I pretended to be doing a cell search as I waited on Gianni. I really hoped he had finally come to his senses, because I really missed him.

"You waiting on me?" he asked from behind me. I smiled,

knowing the voice belonged to a man that my heart desired. I turned to face him as he stepped inside the cell.

"I'm so—" I said, but he kissed my words away.

"I was stupid for how I treated you." Looking down at my stomach, he placed his hand on my belly. "I'll never leave y'all again," he said

"I think he'll be glad to hear that." I smiled.

He looked up at me and smiled. "He! You're kidding! It's a boy? How you know?" he asked, excited.

"Shhh, babe!" I hushed him as I laughed. "Me and Williamson went to the doctor the other day. I texted you a picture of the sonogram, you didn't get it?" I asked as he hugged me.

"Damn, I didn't even check the damn phone. I haven't been myself lately, but I'm back now. And I'm not going anywhere." He kissed me.

"I missed you," I said as I kissed him from his lips to his neck.

"I missed you too." He pulled me in tighter.

"Can I have *some*?" I asked as I licked his lips.

"Oh, you did miss *me*, huh?" He laughed.

Reaching down, I grabbed his dick through his pants. "I've been feining since our first time," I said, feeling hot as I gripped his dick that was growing in my hand. We kissed a slow passionate kiss, as I moved my hand up and down his length. His hands found my pants, and he unbuttoned them. Walking backwards, he led the way while my hand never left his dick as he sat on the toilet.

"Turn around," he demanded. I did as I was told, and I faced the bars. I turned back to look at him. "Strip for daddy," he said, turning me on.

I bit my lip as I slowly pulled my pants down. I brought them back up, just under my ass cheeks, and he slapped my ass. That shit made my pussy so hot. Letting my pants fall, I eased on his lap as I ground on his dick. He placed his hands between my legs as he found my center. Moving my panties to the side, he fingered my swollen clit while I ground on his lap.

"I missed your touch, babe." I moaned as he stuck a finger

inside. "Please put it in before we run out of time—I need to feel you," I begged as his finger did wonders. Lifting me up, he pulled my panties down, and I found the perfect seat on his lap. "Ommm, babe, you fill me up," I moaned, playing with my clit as he fucked me slowly.

He leaned me forward and had a full view of his dick pumping in and out of my wet box. "Damn, you got the best pussy I've ever had," he said, as he spread my ass cheeks, sliding his thumb to the center of my back door. I had never experienced anal before, but with him I didn't care what he did.

As I felt his thumb break the crease of my ass hole, I went into another dimension. "Daddy, oohh shit, what are you doing to me? Shiit, that feels so good." I moaned as I bounced up and down on his dick. He gripped my ass as we tried to match each other's motions. "I love you babe, shit I love you," I moaned as he hit my spot. I could feel his dick growing inside me.

"Work that pussy, babe—work it for daddy—yeah, right there," he said as he pumped faster.

Leaning my head forward, my ass spread wider, and he slapped it, making me come instantly. "Shit, babe, I'm coming!" I moaned.

"Let it out, babe, I'm there too," he said as he came inside me. His dick jumped as his seed shot inside me. I could feel the cum sliding down my leg as he held on to me. Kissing my back, he said, "I love you too!"

I smiled as I panted. "I know!"

After he left to go back to his wing, I went to the restroom to clean myself up. I couldn't get the big ass smile off my face as everyone kept wondering why I was so happy. Only me and Jackson knew the inside joke. As soon as he saw me smiling, he said, "Dick will drive a bitch crazy!"

I laughed. "I don't know what you talking about," I said, grabbing the mail from the closet to pass out. "I'll be back if someone comes looking for me," I said, walking up the stairs.

"Mail call three row!" Jackson screamed as I walked up the stairs.

"305, you got mail," I said, passing an inmate his mail. "310, you have mail," I said, walking up to another cell.

"Do I have mail?" another inmate asked as I was walking by his cell.

I double checked to make sure I didn't look over it. "Not today, sorry," I said. I walked to 3-26 as I noticed the back light was out. I couldn't remember if the light was out when I came to three row earlier or not. "Damn, I didn't bring my flashlight." I said to myself. "Umm, 3-28, you have mail," I said, trying to read the name on the envelope. It was so dark that I could barely make out the name. When I faced the cell I thought I had seen a ghost.

The inmate said, smiling, "So we meet again. Finally got yo' fine ass on my wing, huh?"

I noticed that his door was wide open and his celly wasn't in there with him. "What is your door doing open? You know that's a major case, attempt to escape." I said, trying to mask my fear of him.

"Says the bitch that was just fucking in the next cell," he said, grinning.

"I don't know what you're talking about."

"I ain't gon' say nothing. I just want my turn." He grabbed my arm.

Slapping his hand away, I dropped the rest of the mail. "Don't you fucking touch me!" I said as I tried to get away.

He grabbed me harder, forcing me closer to him. "What, you think that nigga better than me or som'? What, cause he got more money than me or something!"

My heart raced. I was beyond scared now. "Please, let me go!" I begged.

"Naw, don't beg now," he said, pulling me into his cell.

I tried snatching away from him, but he was too strong. "Let go of me!" I yelled. No one could hear me because someone had their speaker up so loud.

Kissing me on the neck, he went for my pants. "I don't like sloppy seconds, but today it'll do," he said, snatching the button off.

"Please don't!" I begged. He ignored me as he pulled his pants down. I shoved him hard as I tried to run. He ran after me, snatching me by the arm. "No, stop!" I yelled, hoping someone could hear me.

"If I can't have you, then he can't either!" he said as he pushed me over the rail. All I could think about was my baby. *Lord, take me, just save my baby!*

Chapter 9

Hotboy

"Hotboy! They just ran over to G-wing with medical, and all the rank," Unc said, standing in front of our cell. I was just looking at the sonogram picture that Gabby sent me.

"Here, hold this down for me," I said, handing him the cell phone. I popped out the cell and headed down the stairs.

I could see a crowd of inmates in the dayroom looking out the window towards G-wing. "What they saying happened?" I asked the C.O. who was working the wing.

"I'm not sure, they said someone fell from three row," he said. His words stung, and I prayed that it wasn't Gabby. Hugging the main door, I waited to see who would come out on the gurney. The rank filed out first to clear the hallway. You could hear the helicopter landing outside.

"Clear the halls, we have an officer down!" the captain yelled into his walkie-talkie. My legs gave out as I heard what he said. As they wheeled the gurney off the wing, I could see her face. She wore a neck brace around her neck. They had her tied down to the gurney as they pumped her with an oxygen bag.

Uncle Marvin pulled me away from the gate as the tears fell down my face. "Come on, nephew. You can't let them see you crying like this. They'll put two and two together like that."

I looked at her face as they rushed her past the wing. I couldn't really see if she was breathing or not. He face was covered with blood. "I just—I just left from her, Unc. What happened?" I questioned as I cried on his shoulder. I'on know, nephew, but we'll find out. Just calm down, and pray!"

One Month Later

"Have you heard anything new on how she's doing?" Uncle Marvin asked.

I had been texting her phone every day, hoping she'll text me back, but she never did. "Naw, I haven't, Unc. Williamson says she is gon' pull up on her at the hospital today. So I'm hoping she'll bring back some good news." I lay in my bunk.

"Just keep yo' faith, nephew. Sometimes, that's all you need."

Newton

"You have a visitor, sweetie," the nurse said, letting Williamson in. She walked in with a huge teddy bear and some balloons.

"Hey, boo, how are you feeling?" she asked.

"I'm doing a little better. Still can't feel my legs. And my neck is still sore as hell."

She looked over at Seth who was sitting at my bedside. Since the incident, he's been by my side every day. He even stopped using drugs again. "I'll leave you two ladies to your privacy," he said, excusing himself.

"Gianni has been worried sick about you. Why haven't you answered any of his calls, or replied to any of his texts?" Williamson asked.

"I can't. For one, I don't have my phone. I don't know where it is. What am I supposed to tell him? That I'm not pregnant anymore?"

"You have to tell him something. The man is going crazy thinking about you."

I laid my head back on the pillow. "Don't you think this is all a sign? I mean, it's like everything I wanted, I got. Then, it was all gone before I could even enjoy it. It was like God was showing me that I was making a big mistake."

"Girl, what are you talking about?"

I sighed. "I didn't fall over the rail, Jasmine," I said, calling her by her first name. "I was pushed," I added.

She looked at me, confused. "By who?" His name was Jamie Dougwell. I still remembered his name from his mail.

"Some guy named Jamie, Jamie Dougwell," I said.

"Wait a minute, you saying he pushed you, and you didn't say anything!" she said, upset.

"I couldn't say anything. Me and Gianni had just finished having sex in the cell next door from the guy. He threatened to tell on us. He tried to force me in his cell to have sex with him, but I fought him off. He said that if he couldn't have me, then Gianni couldn't either." Tears began to fall from my eyes.

"This is some Lifetime Movie Network shit here. You have to tell Gianni."

"I can't, it's no use, I'll never see him again," I said, hating myself.

"Why not?"

"I'm not going back to work ever again. I shouldn't have been working there in the first place."

She looked down at her phone. "Well, somebody has to tell him something. Because he's calling right now."

Hotboy

"What she say, nephew?" Unc asked as he put the mirror down.

"She says she's still asleep. She said she talked to her when she first got there, but they came in and gave her some pain medicine that knocked her out."

"What she say about the baby?" Uncle asked.

"Nothing, she said she would talk to me when she comes to work." I sighed.

"Think positive, nephew. You'll be okay. Well, until then, you need to take care of yo' business. You still got that pound of K2 under the damn toilet. You need to get off that shit, instead of leaving it down there."

"I'll take care of it later. I ain't really in the mood to be doing no hustling." I felt depressed.

"Overstood, what you need to do is chill until Williamson gets here. I'll call you when she lands." He patted my mattress.

I grabbed the phone and scrolled to the pictures. I silently prayed for my son. "God, have mercy on me," I said silently.

The Next Night

Me and Unc stood at the gate as Williamson recited every-thing that her and Gabby talked about. "She said she's going to stay with her fiancé and move away when she gets well."

Dropping my head, I couldn't believe what I was hearing. "Dirty bitch!" I spat.

"Don't say that, Gianni, you know deep down that girl loves you, and I know you love her too," Williamson said, upsetting me even more.

"Love don't love nobody! To hell with her!" Deep down I was hurt. I couldn't believe she abandoned me like she did. "I gotta get the nigga back for what he did. Not for her, but for my li'l nigga. Do you know who's working G-wing right now?" I asked her.

She looked at me. "Bryant!"

Creeping up the stairs, I made sure no one was awake to see me. My mind was already made up. Somebody was going to die tonight. Careful not to wake anyone up, I crept along the wall with the darkness. Making my way to the back half of three row, I could hear faint moans. Walking in front of my destination, I looked to see the door wide open. Both of my targets were in the same cell. They were in their own fantasy world.

Stepping into the cell, I was careful not to alarm them. Bryant was bent over the toilet as she was getting fucked from the back. "That's my spot, baby, my asshole, ohh shit, fuck my asshole, daddy," she moaned. We always said he was a booty bandit. He fucked her ass like he was taking it from her.

I wasn't a cock blocker, but I had to break their li'l party up. Punching him in the back of his head, he fell on top of her.

"The hell man!" he said, confused as he rubbed his head. As I stepped into the dim light, he saw my face. "Ohh, shit man! I'm sorry, I didn't mean—" he said, but I stuck a shank under his chin. Pulling it out, I rammed it in his throat over and over as he choked on his own blood. Bryant screamed as she felt his warm blood splatter all over her face. As his body fell, I snatched her up by her shirt, and stuck the shank in her stomach several times, looking

124

her in her eyes.

She had taken one of my best friends away from me, and I came to avenge his death. She grabbed at her stomach as I plunged the shank in her over and over until I lost count. The smell of shit lingered in the air as her body collapsed on top of her secret lover.

I eased off the wing unnoticed. The only one that saw me was the keyboss, and Williamson was a gangsta!

One Week Later

"Hey! Get up, and get out of them right now!" McFee yelled as he stood in front of my cell. McFee was the unit Lieutenant. He was also a pain in the ass. Uncle Marvin shot up outta his bunk as he looked towards the toilet. I shook my head as I thought about what was under there. I never got the chance to get the K2, plus I had stashed the shank that I killed Bryant and her man with.

Unc must've read my mind, and he suddenly grabbed his baby oil from the night stand. He started squeezing it all over the floor by the door.

"What the hell do you think you're doing? Get your hands behind your back and face the toilet!" McFee screamed. He stood at the door along with five more officers. They looked like they came to handle business. They thrive for moments like this. Running in a nigga cell to bend us up and possibly break a nigga arm or some shit.

"Nephew, whatever happens, don't get off yo' bunk," Uncle Marvin said, stripping down to his boxers. Once he did, he grabbed his New Balances and put them on. I knew he was preparing for war too.

"What the fuck you mean? I'm riding. This our cell, fuck them hos!" I spat, getting off the top bunk. I had to be very careful not to slip as I got down.

"My last warning, get to the back of your cells, and face the damn toilet!" the Lt. screamed as he placed the master key inside our cell door. I wanted to grab the drugs and the shank from under the toilet, but either way, they would still charge me for it. All they had to do was see it, they didn't need physical evidence to charge me.

"Fuck it!" I said as I bent down to grab the shank. I could take a possession charge, but two counts of murder in the penitentiary—That was an expiration date. I would never see the light of day again.

"He's flushing something!" a C.O. said from behind the Lt.

You could hear the loud click as the Lt. opened the cell door. They tried to rush in to stop me, but instantly started sliding from the baby oil. As soon as the Lt. slid in Uncle Marvin's direction, Unc caught his ass with a bad ass right hand, sending him sliding backwards.

Another C.O. rushed in behind the Lt., trying to be a captain, but Unc landed him a punch that sent him reeling. By then, I already flushed the shank. I just had to find a way to get the dope down the toilet. It was wrapped so tight with the black tape I would have to fight with it just to get it opened. My dumb ass double wrapped it, which made it harder to open.

As soon as I reached down to grab the dope, all the officers took a chance as they bombarded the cell, not caring if they fell or not.

"Get the fuck off me!" Unc screamed as they jumped him. My hand was moving back and forth as I tried to feel for the pack. "Ahhhh, bitch!" Unc screamed again. I knew he was in pain as they beat him up. I jumped up and tip toed over to help him. The cell was only big enough for four of us, so I had to give Unc a fair chance. I reared back as far as my arm would let me, and came back with full force. I knocked the C.O. out on impact. His body fell on top of Uncle Marvin's. I posted up, waiting for the next C.O. If I was going down, I would go down with a bang!

Two Days Later

"Hey, wake up, chow time!" the African C.O. yelled, banging

on the cell bars.

I looked around the cell and wondered how I got in here. I had to be on X-wing because it was only one bunk in here with me. My mouth was dry like I hadn't had any water in days. Sitting up in the bunk, I reached over to the bean slot to grab my food. "How long have I been back here?" I asked the C.O.

"Today makes two days. When you finish eating, get ready. The OIG wants to see you."

I bit into the hard biscuit as I looked up at him. The OIG was the unit free world officers. You only went to them if you were about to get a free world charge. So I'm assuming they must've found the dope. Looking down at my clothes, I had dried up blood all over me. "Whose blood is this?" I asked the C.O.

He laughed. "It's yours, you don't remember? The back of your head was like a fountain. It was blood everywhere. You lucky, you could've got brain damage."

I felt the back of my head and found a knot. I could feel the scalp peeling where the blood had dried up. I still can't remember how it happened. All I could remember was fighting with the laws until McFee stormed in with the baton in his hand. Somehow, he got behind me and started choking me with it until I passed out. They must've jumped on me while I was passed out. They had to.

I finished up the breakfast and went to wash my face. I didn't have any of my property, so I couldn't even brush my teeth. They were probably going through all my shit.

"Nephew!" I could hear the sound of Uncle Marvin's voice through the vent.

I stood on the toilet to get closer to the vent. It was pitch-black once you looked inside it, but you could hear people talking on the other side. "Yooo!" I yelled back to Unc.

"Can you hear me!" he yelled back.

"Yeah, I hear you!" I screamed back.

"The OIG called me down to his office. Looking for some answers, huh! I hit him with that espanol—*Me no speak English.*" He laughed.

I joined in with a laugh too. I knew Unc was a gangsta, he

wouldn't rat on me. "What else they say?" I asked.

"They found the dope. He said he's going to charge us both with it unless one of us come forward to claim it. I told him he can eat my dick. I ain't never going home after all."

I shook my head. I didn't want Unc to have to go through this shit, behind my mistakes. I didn't want to fuck up my parole, but the way it was looking, I could kiss parole goodbye.

I couldn't let Unc go down for what I did. "Don't worry, Unc, I'll take care of it!" I yelled loud enough for him to hear.

The C.O. walked up to my cell with a pair of cuffs. "Kingsley, the OIG is ready to see you," he said.

I nodded before turning back to the vent. "I gotta go, Unc, they calling for me now!" I yelled before stepping off the toilet. I backed into the door and held my arms behind me to get cuffed. After the C.O. placed the cuffs on me, the door opened and I stepped out. I was greeted by Lt. McFee.

He had a bandage on his right cheek, and a black eye on the left side. He still wore a grin on his face through all the pain. "How's your head feeling?" he asked with a light snicker. I knew it; they did me dirty once I passed out. Filthy pigs, they wasn't man enough to get a one-on-one.

"Oh yeah, that was you, huh? I'll get the last laugh, watch!" I said as he escorted me to the school house, where the OIG's office was.

"I'm going to get you for what you did to my officer," he said as we made it inside the school.

"How's his jaw doing?" I teased.

"Oh, I'm talking about Bryant. Ohhh, you didn't know! We found your little shank in the pipe chase. Even still had traces of blood on it." He knocked on the OIG's door before we walked in.

The OIG was a middle-aged black man. He stood behind his computer as he gestured for me to sit down. The Lt. kept the cuffs on me as I took a seat.

"How are you doing, Mr. Kingsley?" the OIG asked.

"Besides the pain in my head from your officers beating me half to death, I'm good," I said, looking towards the Lt.

"Do you know why you're here?" the OIG asked.

I shook my head.

"Well, you were staying on H-wing, in cell 2-14. My officers found a pound of synthetic marijuana, known as K2. It was wrapped up in black tape, found under your cell toilet." He showed me pictures of the pack. "Also, my officers claimed that they saw you flush something down the toilet. After doing a thorough search, they found this behind your wall, in the pipe chase." He pulled out the shank that was inside an evidence bag.

My eyes grew double its size once I saw the shank. The dope was the least of my worries. That was petty time considered to what the shank could do to me. "Whose is that supposed to be?" I asked, playing dumb.

"That's what I'm trying to figure out. See, it didn't make it all the way through the pipe; it actually got caught up between your cell, and your neighbor's cell. I still have to send it in for prints. I just figured that if you had something to tell me, you could save me a lot of time, and work." He tutted, then continued:

"Look, brother, I hate to see my black brothers go down this road. You're young. You have a lot of time to get your life together. You can't do it from this penitentiary." He was throwing the black card at me.

"*I ain't your brother, your mama ain't had me, pussy-ass nigga, I don't know your pappy,*" I said, reciting Money Bagg Yo's song.

The OIG's face was twisted. He couldn't believe I'd disrespected him like that, in front of his fellow officers. "Do yo' fucking job, I ain't getting paid for this shit. I ain't got nothing to say, now can I go back to my cell?"

He mean-mugged me as he nodded to the Lt.

"Come on, get up!" McFee said, snatching me by the cuffs.

"Mr. Kingsley, when the judge bangs the gavel, there is no more room for dealing—so think about it, and let me know," the OIG said. I looked at him and grilled him. He was an Uncle Tom. Shooting that brother-brother shit my way, and had the nerve to have me want to snitch. Who was I going to snitch on? Myself?

"Fuck you, the judge, yo' C.O.'s, and the bitch that birthed yo' Uncle Ruckus ass." I spat as the Lt shoved me out the door. I knew I was dead when it came to the shit they found. My prints were all over everything. Fuck it. I guess now all I needed to do was, get comfortable. I was never going home again.

Chapter 10

One Month Later

I was sitting in the courtroom, looking like a bum. The county that I was held in gave me a shirt that was too big. Along with some pants that were too tight. I looked like I got my clothes from the Goodwill. My lawyer was, more or less, non-existent, so I had to stand up and present my defense, looking like a complete idiot. I didn't care though. I had something for them.

"Mr. Kingsley, are you ready for your witness?" the judge asked.

I stood up, fixing my clothes. "Yes, your Honor, I would like to call a Mr. Marvin Dallas to the stand," I said, looking at the DA. Uncle Marvin walked out the side door with his crisp whites on. He nodded to me before taking the stand.

The bailiff walked over with a black Bible in his hand, and Uncle Marvin placed his right hand on the Bible to swear in.

"Mr. Dallas, do you swear to tell the truth, the whole truth, and nothing but the truth, so help you God?" the bailiff recited.

Uncle Marvin nodded, "I do."

The bailiff looked over to me. "He's all yours."

I stepped closer to the witness stand. "Mr. Dallas, how long have you known me?" I asked.

"For almost three years now," he answered.

"And during those three years, could you say that I was a violent man? A man capable of killing someone?" I asked.

The DA stood up. "I object! Your Honor, he's leading the witness!"

"Sustained! Mr. Kingsley, be more specific with your questions, please," the judge said.

"Yes, your Honor. Well, Mr. Dallas, you were my cellmate, right? Have you ever saw me do anything harmful to anyone?" I asked.

"Objection! Your Honor, he's doing it again," the DA yelled.

"Overruled, carry on, I want to see were this is headed," the judge said.

"Thank you, your Honor. Mr. Dallas, on the day that they found the weapon, known as a shank, could you say that it was mine?" Uncle Marvin shook his head. "And why would you say no?" I asked.

"Because it was mine," he said, causing the crowd to gasp.

"So, if I'm understanding you right, you're saying that the murder weapon that the DA has—belongs to you?"

He nodded and said, "Yeah, and they got my dope too."

He caused a few laughs from the jury booth. The judge banged her gavel. "Order! Order in the court!"

The DA was hysterical as he stood up in a rage. "Your Honor, this is all rehearsed. That was his cellmate, they made all this stuff up!"

"Overruled! Mr. Donaldson, if you have another outburst like that again in my courtroom, you will be asked to leave, and your assistant will be asked to conclude the case," the judge said. The DA sat down in defeat. "Mr. Dallas," the judge said, addressing Uncle Marvin, "you do know that you are under oath. If you are caught lying under oath, you could be given some more time added to your sentence."

"I know, judge," Uncle Marvin said, looking up at her. The judge nodded at me to continue, until Uncle Marvin spoke up. "The man that y'all came to try today is innocent. I haven't been able to sleep since the incident happened. The DA wants to say that I'm making all this up. I literally stabbed the man in his throat several times. Afterwards, I shoved it under his chin and I watched him choke on his own blood."

The judge banged her gavel. "That's enough, Mr. Dallas," she said, but he kept going.

"I stabbed the C.O. in her stomach over ten times as she stared at me in my eyes just before I shoved the shank in her throat. Is there anything else that y'all want to know?"

I laughed on the inside. Unc could've won an Oscar for his performance. "No further questions, your Honor, I rest my case," I said and walked back to my seat. Looking over at the DA, I was sure he would lose his job.

Uncle Marvin winked at me before he was escorted back to the holding cell. In the beginning, I was prepared to take my own bid. Then Unc told me that he would rather take it for me, so that I could go home. He already had a life sentence without a chance of parole. I looked behind me to see the OIG and McFee sitting in the crowd. They both grilled me. I knew I had just made another two enemies. I didn't care. I was sure I was going home when parole presented itself.

The OIG and Lt. McFee walked up behind me as the bailiff was placing me back in the handcuffs. "We'll see you back on Beto soon. We have some unfinished business to take care of!" McFee said, as I was escorted out.

Seth

"Hey, I'm Jake. Is this your first unit?" he asked, holding his hand out.

I shook his hand. "Yeah, never really been into this kind of work, I'm Seth."

"This is supposed to be the worst unit in Texas," Jake said.

"So I've heard," I said as we got in line to hear the sergeant's speech.

"Welcome to Beto," the sergeant began. "Be very careful how you deal with these criminals. They are very persuasive. They will try to talk to you about the things you like, the things they think you like, they'll ask about your family, they will practically try every route to get inside your head. These men are murderers, rapists, con artists, drug dealers, and gang members. We are their worst enemies. We are the law. Everything we do, they are against it. We are here to protect the children we have at home. We are the chosen ones."

The sergeant's speech ended there and then. The voice I heard next was Jake's.

"Seth, you coming?" Jake asked, snapping me out of my trance. I looked at the sonogram on the screen. "Gianni Jr.," I said to myself as I read the screen on Gabby's phone before placing it back in my pocket. *Gianni, I'm coming for you!*

One Month Later

Hotboy

"When we reach the back door, I want everyone to remain seated until I tell y'all to get up," a C.O. said as we pulled up to the George Beto unit. I was actually happy to see Beto again. More so glad that I beat the murder case and possession case that they had me dead to the wrong on.

Thankfully, Uncle Marvin took the rap for me. I'll always be in debt to him for it too. Even though he knew it would've gotten him in a worse state than he was already in, he still took the rap for me. He didn't care; he had already had a life sentence without parole. All they did was add two more life sentences stacked with his other one.

I guess the judge thought he would never die. Unc wasn't bothered though. He had already spent most of his life in the system. The penitentiary had grown to be all he knew. Sad to say, he was content with it. As the bus pulled up to the back door of the infirmary, I silently prayed to God that this would be my final time pulling up to this place. The next time I leave, I was never coming back.

"Who's that?" my riding buddy asked. We were handcuffed together, his right arm to my left arm.

Looking past him outside the window, I saw a group of inmates walking back to the main building. "That's the sign shop workers, they probably just now getting off work," I said as the engine to the bus cut off. The officer who was sitting in the back of the bus hopped out as he walked to the infirmary's back door. He knocked for at least five minutes before someone answered.

"Is this your first time?" my riding buddy asked.

Shaking my head, I said, "Naw, I just left this unit a month or so ago. I had to clear up some legal issues. My riding buddy

134

looked to be at least eighteen, or nineteen years old. Sitting down, he was neck in neck with me in height. He could've fooled you into thinking that he was Hispanic by his skin complexion. I knew like every other nigga in the penitentiary knew. It was something about them white boys. No matter what they did, they couldn't hide that red neck.

"Was it live here?" he asked. "I mean to be prison," he added.

"Yeah, when I left, this bitch was turnt up. I did hear that they had got a new Warden since I've been gone, so we'll see."

The bus driver stood up to address us. "Cut the damn talking out and listen up. When I call your name, I want you to line up at the back door down there." He pointed in the direction of the door.

I cut my eyes at the bus driver. He talked like he was really about that life. Deep down, he was as soft as they came. He knew mostly all of the inmates on the bus were either new to the system altogether, or just new to Beto. So he tried to make himself look stiff to intimidate them. He wasn't fooling me though.

"Marillo, Sanchez," he said, calling the first two names. "Smith—and White, follow behind them." As an inmate dragged his chain bag down the steps, the driver yelled, "Y'all need to move a little faster, I'm not trying to be messing with y'all all damn day." After a moment's pause, while staring at me like he knew me, he said, "Goff, Kingsley, y'all are next."

I picked up my bag with ease, unlike my riding buddy whose bag was full to the top with commissary and paperwork. He tried carrying the bag, but us being cuffed together made it impossible. As we finally made it down the stairs, the sun punched me right in the face. It was something about East Texas weather. When it was hot outside, it was like the sun was getting a tan. When it rained, it was like a tsunami.

"Aye, Hotboy, I see you made it back, bitch!" JJ yelled as he walked by with the sign shop workers.

I remembered once I saw his face that he never paid me my $100. "Yeah, I'm tryna get back on H-wing with y'all if I can!" I yelled as I lined up behind the other inmates.

Sergeant Tatum walked out of the infirmary back door with a

handful of files. "Hey! Quiet in my line," he said, walking up to me. I grilled him as he looked me up and down. I had to shake my head at him. The man still had the same pair of wrangler jeans on that he wore the day I first got on the unit years ago. He practically wore the same pair of pants every single day.

Looking over me, he said, "You've had enough time to talk during your bus ride. It's my time now, and you are to listen, you hear!" He stood at a measly 6'10 that no one feared. He wasn't muscularly built. He was just tall and lanky.

I knew without a doubt I could knock him out with one punch, but this was his world, I was just passing through. "You got it, *bossman*," I said.

Once the last pair of inmates made it off the bus, the sergeant walked to the front of the group. "Inmates, offenders, convicts, whichever you prefer to be called, welcome to the George Beto unit. I'm Sergeant Tatum, and until you take parole, or discharge, this will be your new home!"

Newton

"Hey, Ms. Newton, how are you feeling?" the nurse asked as she walked into the room. It had been over three months since I was pushed over three row. I was finally moved from ICU to a regular room. Over time, I started to get feeling back in my right leg while my left leg took its time.

"I'm fine, Ms. Debra, still no feeling in my left leg though. I was able to do some leg exercises with the doctor's help earlier."

She smiled. "That's good, honey. You have to keep it up. Just keep your faith, and everything will work out for the greater good. If you believe you can be healed, then it shall be." She walked up to my bedside, looked to the monitors, and jotted something down on her notepad. "Where's Seth? I haven't seen him at all today," she said.

I smiled at the sound of his name. Seth had stepped up in ways that I never would've imagined. He took care of home, me, and Jacob. "He's at work. He should be up here later."

"Where does he work, if you don't mind me asking?"

"Oh no, I don't mind," I said. I was actually happy that he had a job. "He works at Sanderson Farms, the one in Palestine," I said, recalling what he had told me.

"That's good for him. He's a good man, you better hold on to him."

"Trust me," I said, "I'm going to keep him for life. You have no idea what we've been through. Yet he's still here, thank God!"

"Relationships aren't meaningful without a test or two. That's why you have to get past this together. This is where love counts." Her words made me think. "Well, okay sweetie, it's about time I clocked out. Do you need anything else before I go?"

I shook my head. "No, ma'am, I'm fine." As she kissed me on the cheek, I added, "You just make sure you get home safe, and I'll see you bright and early tomorrow."

"Tell Seth and Jacob I said hello. If you need anything, just be sure to buzz the front desk."

"Will do," I said as she closed the door. Reaching under the pillow, I pulled out my motivation—the one thing that gave me that extra drive. It was my poison that reminded me of the man that deep down really had my heart. It was the one thing that kept us bonded together forever. Our son's sonogram!

Hotboy

"Damn, I hate the feeling of handcuffs," my riding buddy said as Sergeant Tatum removed the cuffs. When he removed mine, I rubbed my wrist as I looked around for a familiar face. "Damn, who is that?" my riding buddy pointed to a nurse passing by. I was so focused on finding someone else that I completely ignored his question. "Oh, I see, you trying to keep all the hos to yo'self, huh?" he said.

I faced him. "Word of advice, homie. Before you get to where you're going, learn to talk less, and mind your own fucking business."

He looked at me like he wanted to test me, but changed his mind. "My bad, bro. I'm just nervous, that's all. I didn't mean any disrespect. I'm Archie, by the way." He held out his fist.

"Hotboy," I said as I dap'd him up.

"So where do you think they'll house me?" he asked.

"Depends."

"On what?"

"Depends on if you're gang-affiliated, and if you're willing to work."

"I don't bang!" he said, as I looked him over.

"What does those five point stars mean that you got tat'd on you?" I asked.

He looked at the stars that were tat'd on his arm. "They're just stars," he said as he looked at me with a concerned look.

"The Blast are going to want to look at you for them stars for sure. So prepare yourself." I looked at the tats.

"Wait, the Blast?" he said, staring at me.

"Yeah, Tango Blast. They own almost every Hispanic in Texas prisons. They carry the five point star, so unless you wanna blast, you better cover it up."

"So, what if I wanna be a solo?" he asked.

I laughed at his inexperience. "Just 'cause you're a solo don't mean shit. Technically, there ain't a such thing as a solo in the penitentiary. You gon' get a solo check as soon as you come through the door. The solo's gon' beat yo' ass. Then the Blast gon' beat yo' ass. The Mexicles get their shot at you too. So, look at it this way, the solos get it worse."

"So, basically you're saying, I might as well get down with someone. The way you're explaining it, I really don't have a choice."

I managed to laugh. "What I'm saying is, regardless, today you're going to get yo' ass beat." I looked around at all the other inmates that caught the chain with us. Majority of them heard me talking to Archie, and they wondered what the outcome would be for them when they finally got to their wings.

"So what about the whites? Do we get the same treatment?" a young Caucasian asked.

"Nah, whites are different," I answered. You can either join the woods, or join a family."

"What do you mean, *woods*? *Family*? Dude, I'm eighteen, I don't know anything about nothing." He looked scared. I felt for youngsters like him. They came straight from the county with no clue as to what was ahead of them. A bunch of cats in the county jail telling them fake war stories about prison, gassing their heads up. They get more time in the county than their actual age all because their lawyer convinced them it was the best deal he could get.

They probably thought they'd sign for their time, and make parole from a transit unit, never actually going to the "big house". The chances of someone making parole in Texas were slim to none. Texas prisons made so much money from free labor that they never wanted to release anyone. Behind the free labor was a bullshit job certification that only said we went to work because we didn't want to end up on the bad side of the unit.

Here you have an eighteen-year-old who was told by a court-appointed lawyer that he had no other choice but to go to prison, so that he could get his $500 check and be on his merry. Having being the youngsta's first offence, he probably thought he would make his first parole, so he went ahead and signed. Now he's sitting in one of the worst prisons in Texas, about to get punched on for being white. The system was broken, and no one actually cared.

I explained, "A wood is a white person who went against the grain, saying that they didn't want to be a part of the families. So they stood up against the families banging the color of their skin as their own gang. They're like the white version of the Tango Blast. In yo' case though, youngsta, you can either join the woods or one of the families, or get ready for the three F's."

"Three F's?" The white youngster was confused.

"Fight, fuck, or bust a fifty," I recited. A few inmates started laughing. A young black kid that was sitting beside Archie looked over at me like he wanted to ask what would happen to him, but he was too afraid to find out.

"Don't worry, my nigga," I said, trying to allay his fear. "All the blacks get a pass on Beto. We don't believe in doing heart checks on our own people. So consider yo'self lucky." He relaxed a little. He looked like the world had been lifted off of his shoulders.

"Hotboy, bitch, leave them young niggas alone, scaring them and shit," Kuda said, walking up behind me.

I stood up to embrace him. "Bitch, you know I was just making fun. It's good to see you again. Yo' fat ass lost some weight. I see you still working in this dirty ass infirmary." I smiled

"As much time as I got, I gotta stay busy. Plus ain't nothing like being around some hos all day every day. You couldn't beat that with Mayweather's hands." He laughed. It was only three months ago that I was feeling the pain he was feeling. The pain of knowing I would have to wake up in the penitentiary for the next ten or so years. That was beyond cruel and unusual pain. If it wasn't for Uncle Marvin taking the rap, I wouldn't know where I would've been mentally.

"I was just looking for you, my nigga," I said, stepping out of ears reach.

"What's up?" Kuda asked.

"I'm trying to get back on my feet. You know the li'l bitch I was fucking with before I left. She took off with all my bread. I'm due to see parole real soon, I ain't tryna go home broke. You know this ain't me." I looked down at my dirty clothes.

"Shit's different now, fam. The game then changed since you been gone. We got this new warden, he's a straight Klux. He even gave McFee the keys to the unit to do whatever he wants. McFee got this bitch dry, all the hos scared to fuck around."

I already knew who McFee was. He was a straight cop, top flight. Word around the unit was that his old lady got caught fucking an inmate back in the day. Ever since that shit happened, McFee's been after every inmate that had a name that was doing anything that wasn't in the TDCJ handbook. He was already on my hit list for that shit he said in the courtroom.

"So you saying ain't nothing going on? You gots to be kidding me!" I said.

"You got a few niggas that be jugging with the visitation blast, but you know how that shit goes. You may hit, you may miss. Bruh, I'm telling you, this new warden ain't no joke."

By virtue of Kuda's explanation, I was starting to get upset. Damn, why'd they send me back to this shithole.

"Mane, fuck the warden!" Kuda said, noticing my uneasiness. "If the last warden couldn't change Beto, what makes this nigga think he can? Until they start giving these hos raises, then we always got a chance. These hos broke as hell, taxes only come around like Christmas. After that, they gon' be looking for some help."

I looked at him and said, "It's still bitches working on the unit ain't it?"

He looked at me sideways. "What kind of question is that? Well, yea!"

"If it's still bitches working on the unit, then there is still a chance. All we have to do is knock the right bitch."

"Bitch, you know I'm with you. You have to see how the unit is now. Niggas be telling, writing 1-60's and shit. You don't even know who the real enemy is because they be hiding and telling."

"Niggas been snitching, that ain't gon' ever stop," I said. "They wait until they come to the penitentiary to start snitching. If they would've done it in the world, they wouldn't be here."

"Yeah, you're right. So what, how are we gon' play it?" Kuda asked.

"Let me see how shit is moving around the unit first. I'ma see where they house me at, and I'll let you know the next play."

We embraced again. What was understood didn't have to be explained. Kuda had always had my back, even down to the darkest moments.

Chapter 11

Seth

"Hey, beautiful," I said as I walked into the room. Gabby fumbled with her pillow as she turned and smiled at me.

"Hey, baby, I didn't think you were going to come. It's so late I thought you were going to wait until tomorrow." She noticed I was alone. "Where's Jacob?"

"He's with your mom. I wanted to come by myself this time. I'll bring him tomorrow."

"Daddy wants me all to himself, huh?"

She knew how to get me every single time. I smiled as I walked to her bed. "I guess you can say that. I do miss you."

"Oh, really, do you miss me, or do you miss this?" she said, pulling her blanket back, revealing her bald pussy.

My face turned red as I admired her boldness. "Chill out, baby, before you start something in here."

She frowned. "Baby I'm horny, I'm hurting, but I ain't dying. My vagina still works, you know." She laughed. The sight did intrigue me. I was tempted as hell. It had been a long time since we had been intimate. I looked at her lying in the hospital bed. I had failed her as her man. I even failed at being the only man she desired.

Leaning forward, we kissed passionately as my fingers grazed her folds. Her body arched at the feeling of my fingers slipping into her center. "Baby, ahhhh! I told you she still works," she said as my fingers came out coated in her juices.

The bulge in my pants rose as my dick strained against my zipper. Her hands roamed to my pants, and she squeezed my dick through the thick fabric. "Baby, chill, what if the nurse comes, in?" I said as she gripped my hard-on.

"All you have to do is, lock the door, come on, please," she begged. She may have lost her ability to walk, but she didn't lose her spunk. I walked to the door and peeped outside to see if anyone was coming, before locking it shut. Turning around to face her, I remembered why I fell in love with her in the first place. She was beautiful, flaws and all.

As I walked to the bed, she scooted over to make room for me. "Don't take it easy on me. Don't treat me like a cripple. Make me feel my legs again, hurt me." Her voice sounded seductive. I pulled my shirt over my head and climbed on top of her, placing her legs between mine. Her gown eased off, exposing all of her glory with a purpose. She tugged at her pretty nipples as I tried to unzip my zipper. The sight of her playing with her nipples was so distracting that I couldn't get the zipper down.

"Let me help," she said, and she took control, moving my hand to the side. I had to stand up to let her do it, but as I came down to her level, our lips stuck together like magnets. "Baby, hold on," she said, grabbing the remote for her bed. With a grin, she pressed a button on the remote, bringing the bed in just a little at the bottom area. I couldn't help but smile. Baby was a straight freak.

Pulling her body to the curved section of the bed, she gritted her teeth in pain. "Are you okay?" I asked.

She smiled. "Never better, now give me some of that dick."

I laughed as my thumb connected with her pearl. It was poking out like a ground hog on ground hogs day. Her back arched as my thumb brought her to a quick climax.

"Right there, baby," she moaned as she closed her eyes. I stopped just as she bit her bottom lip. "What the hell Seth! I was there, you better—"

I didn't let her finish what she was gonna say, for I shoved my dick to the bottom of her pussy in one thrust. Her mouth was shaped like an "o" as her pussy clamped around my dick. "Is this what you wanted, huh, pain?" I said as the bed began to shake. She could only nod as I raised her right leg above my shoulder.

"Fuck, it feels good, baby," she said as I gripped her titties. The position I had her in gave me action to dig deeper than I ever had before as I worked up a sweat. With her leg placed on my shoulder I leaned forward as we kissed again.

"Seth, ahhhh—shhiiitt, baby! I missed you so much, shit baby!" Her moans sent me into overdrive as I raised her left leg, placing it over my other shoulder. She winced in pain, but I ignored her cries, giving her exactly what she asked for, pain. I kneeled in her pussy like I was saying my prayers. The only difference was, she was the one speaking in tongues.

I must've made a mistake and hit a button on the remote, 'cause her bed laid down flat. I was so determined to get my nut that was building that I didn't miss a beat. Gripping her ass, I pulled her in closer as we tongue-kissed.

"Ohh, baby, I feel it—I'm coming," she said as her right leg twitched. My hand slid under her pillow as I felt myself on the edge.

My fingers touched something as I was sliding my hand from under her pillow. I couldn't help my curiosity as I stuck my hand back under her pillow to find out what I had touched. As I pulled my hand out, my eyes went from pure passion, to pure regret. Without even trying, I climaxed inside of her, then as my dick went limp instantly. I was sure she had already come as she pulled me to her and our lips met again. As we kissed, I eased my hand back under her pillow, returning what I had just seen.

"Baby, that was amazing," she said as we ended our kiss.

I slid off the bed and rushed to put my clothes back on. "Yeah, it was, huh!"

"You okay?" she asked as she noticed me rushing.

Trying to mask my new emotions, I replied, "Yes, baby, I'm good. I needed that. You just don't know how that motivated me."

She smiled as she covered herself with her gown. "I'm glad that I could help," she said.

I smiled as we kissed. "You have no idea!"

Hotboy

"So what they say?" I asked Archie as he walked out of the GI's office. He leaned against the wall and said, "They think I'm a part of the Tango Blast. I told them that I wasn't, but they wasn't trying to hear shit I was saying. They said that if I wasn't already a part of the blast, then I would be by the end of the night."

A lady who was a part of the committee walked out of the room. "Kingsley," she said, reading my name from her file. I walked slowly as I placed my hands behind my back. I already knew the procedure. Look innocent, until proven guilty. As I walked in, I noticed a few familiar faces amongst the committee team. The head GI, Sergeant John. His assistant—Ms. Raylette. Then there was Ms. Spikes, who worked in classification. The second warden in charge was also there.

All eyes were on me as I stood in front of them. I noticed the uneasiness that the warden plastered on his face as he noticed me.

"Mr. Kingsley, welcome back," the warden said. "Rumor has it that you came away innocent," he said, like he was shocked with the results. I ignored his statement. For some reason, I never respected him. He never rubbed me the wrong way personally, but he also never did anything for the inmates. He never spoke up for us in any way when the officers fucked us over; he just let them do it. So, to me, he was like every other warden in Texas. Overpaid and worthless.

I guess the GI noticed that I wasn't about to respond to the warden, so he decided to play the black card on me.

"Wassup, King," the GI began, "I don't want no shit from you this time. Your file says you are due to see parole in a few months. If you plan on going home, you better stay out the way."

The C.O.'s knew that speaking about an inmate's parole was like talking about a kid's mama. It was a really touchy subject. I tried to hold back a laugh at him.

Sergeant John wasn't stocky, nor was he fat. He had a slight stoop in his back that made it look funny when he walked. When he talked he sounded like Mike Tyson. The only reason we never clowned him was because he didn't really cause any ruckus on the unit. The only time he ran down on someone was if you were making too much noise without trying to hide it.

Personally, the only reason I respected him was because he had bagged a bad young bitch. I had to admit, for an old nigga he had a nice wife that flaunted it every day at work.

"I'm good, Sarge, just trying to get this day out the way so I can knock another one out and go home," I said, making him smile. He liked to think that he had clout with the black inmates. Really, he didn't have shit but a badge.

"Any new tattoos?" Ms. Raylette asked. It was the GI's job to keep documentation on everyone who was on gang file. They also kept documentation on our tattoos as well. I had over a hundred tats, and counting. When I had caught chain to get the case behind me, I ended up getting two new tats. Under my left eye I got two teardrops. One for Gangsta, and the other one for my Jr. I was so black though, I was sure they couldn't see them.

"Naw, no new tats, I decided to finally call it quits, for now," I said as Ms. Raylette stared at me. I favored Ms. Raylette for some odd reason. She really wasn't my type, but I just knew she was a down-to-earth freak. She wore a tongue ring to work every day, knowing what we considered the true definition for it. She even had one that glowed up in the dark. She was the first bitch I'd ever seen with one. I wanted to blow the power out just to make her put that bitch to work.

She was a tall Caucasian lady, thick for her height though. She always wore a long body shield that covered her body. You could look at her legs and see that she was fine. The thing that threw me off was her double chin. I knew, when she gave a nigga head, he would be in severe pain.

"Has Sarge been treating you right?" I asked her, just to make Ms. Spikes feel left out.

Raylette smiled and said, "You don't have to worry about him treating me right, you have to worry about me treating him right."

I could see Ms. Spikes getting irritated as she tap'd her pen on the table. "Okay, now that the reunion is over, can we please get this over with? We still have a bunch of other inmates to interview, and I have better things that I could be doing."

"Okay, well, as of now Mr. Kingsley," said the warden, "you'll be staying on L-wing until further notice, per McFee's request."

"Wait, L-wing? I didn't do shit. I just got back, ain't that the trouble wing?" I asked.

He nodded and said, "So to say. It's only temporary. That's until McFee can assure that you aren't up to your old tricks."

"That's some bullshit!" I spat.

The whole room looked at me like I was crazy. "You can either go to L-wing, or X-wing, your choice," Sergeant John said.

I had too much to do to go to X-wing. X-wing was segregation. "L-wing it is!" I said.

"As soon as you're cleared," Ms. Spikes said, grinning, "you can get a job and move back to the south side. So the best thing to do is to stay out of the way. Seeing that it's you, that'll be hard to do."

I ignored her slick comment. Deep down she was just a nigga lover in denial. I nodded as I walked out of the room. I damn sure didn't want to go to L-wing. There was too many chiefs, and not enough Indians.

"What did they say?" Archie asked once I walked out the room.

"Basically, they said I'm a menace to society!"

Seth

"Incoming, Mr. Kiles," the keyboss said as she let a new inmate on the wing. Peeping around the closet, I was able to see who was coming in. A young kid—who I couldn't tell was either white, or Hispanic—stood by the door as he clutched his mattress over his shoulder.

Closing the closet, I said, "Where are you going?"

"I'm going to 1-27," he said, looking around the dayroom. I could tell that this was his first rodeo by how nervous he was. He looked out of place. A few inmates walked up to the dayroom bars as they grilled him.

"Where you from, homie?" an inmate asked the lad.

"I'm from Houston."

"Put your things up and come holla at me. I'll be over there." He pointed to a section with a group of Hispanics. He nodded as

148

he looked at me. I didn't care what went on. I had one agenda, finding Gianni!

"I'll get your cell open, just go stand by the door," I said. The lad walked down the run as the porter gave him a hand with his mattress.

"Look out, Deon, you got a new celly," the porter yelled before getting to his cell. I shook my head at their penitentiary ways. This place was really a world of its own.

"Picketboss, can you open up one, twenty-seven?" I asked. The African C.O. looked at me like I had asked him to loan me $500. "Excuse me, sir. I need one, twenty-seven opened!"

He looked from me to his newspaper, then back to me. He huffed, then stood up. I couldn't stand laziness, and it seemed like almost every African that worked on the unit was lazy as hell. I walked away as I'd seen him open the inmate's door.

The new inmate walked in the cell and came out as fast as he went in. He walked up to me and just looked at me.

"What?" I asked, wondering why he was looking at me.

"I'm trying to get in the dayroom," he said nervously.

"Why didn't you just say that then?" I said as I unlocked the dayroom door to let him in. As he walked in, I locked the door behind him and placed my foot on the bars. I watched him walk up to the group of Hispanics. I took favor in watching the inmates discipline their own. Especially the Hispanics, they didn't show mercy.

They conversed back and forth as the new guy kept shaking his head. I noticed that majority of the inmates were looking in their direction, waiting to see what would happen.

"Looking in the dayroom!" an inmate yelled as he noticed me watching. Everyone looked at me.

I couldn't help but speak coldly there and then. "Let me make myself perfectly clear. I don't care what the fuck y'all do. Smoke, drink, even kill each other for all I care. I just ask that y'all do it in your cells, or in the dayroom. Don't bring that shit to my run."

A few inmates nodded in respect. I could hear scattered conversations about how I was a law, and how they didn't trust me. I really didn't care what they thought. In the end, I was the one who could give them a pass, or take them down.

The Hispanics broke up their li'l meeting, maybe until I left for the night. I watched as the new inmate walked up to the domino table. "Can I get next?" he asked. The loser got up, and the new inmate sat down to play.

"What do you play? Man's hand, or graveyard?" he asked as he shook the dominos.

"Big six calls it," his opponent said.

"What they call you?" the new inmate asked.

"Li'l Nine," his opponent said as he placed big six down.

"Pull or no pull?" he asked Nine.

"Man's hand," Li'l Nine said.

Playing a domino, the new inmate said, "I'm Archie."

Nine slammed a domino down so hard that the entire dayroom looked back in their direction. "Ella, Bella, and Stella! Bitches do whatever I tell 'em!" he yelled, laughing.

Archie laughed too, hearing the phrase for the first time. "Where you from?" Archie asked.

"I'm from Dallas. Where you just coming from?" Nine asked.

"Bradshaw transit unit. I was just on Gurney though, then I went to Byrd, then here."

"Long ride, huh?"

"Hell yeah, that bitch took forever. I had a cool riding buddy though, so time went by fast."

"Yeah, what's his name?" Nine asked.

"They call him Hotboy. He says he used to be over here a few months ago."

Nine looked at him, surprised. "Hotboy, you talking about *Hotboy*, Hotboy? He short, with wavy hair? Black as hell, got a lot of tat's?" Nine questioned.

"Yeah, I think that's him. If I'm not mistaken, his last name is King som',"

Archie caught my full attention at the mention of that name. "Did you just say King?" I asked.

Archie looked at Nine, wondering if he should answer me. I

noticed Nine kicking him under the table, telling him not to answer, but Archie didn't know that the kick was intentional

"Did you mean Kingsley?" I asked.

He nodded and smiled. "Yeah, that's his name, he was cool as hell." Archie said, looking at Nine. Li'l Nine shook his head and laid it on the table. One thing you never did was give an inmate's name away to a C.O., especially an inmate like Kingsley.

Walking away from the stairs, I planned my next move. I had been searching for an inmate that wasn't even on the unit. Now all I had to do was find out what wing he was staying on, and make his life a living hell. Tupac was right, revenge was like the sweetest thing next to getting pussy!

Hotboy

"Aye, my nigga! Wasssuupp, biiitchhh!" Major yelled as I walked on L-wing. As bad as I wanted to be on H-wing, I still had some live niggas I could fuck with until I got my name cleared. Like Major—he was one of the homies. Not like a regular homie because he was part of the pyramid.

Major was like family, with me being a Vice Lord. The only thing—Major was throwed off. He was the type of cat that banged the five with his last breath. If he wasn't screaming about some gang shit, or smashing some ops, he was reppin' the southwest. Major stood at an even 6 feet. He was on the heavy side, but he disguised it with heavy clothes. His bald head added to his already menacing vibe. His tattooed face only made him look just like his reputation, tough.

He always kept people laughing, especially when he saw you for the first time for the day. He had a special way at greeting people. He never changed up, unless you tried to play him for stupid. I sat my mattress down and walked up to the bars to shake up with him.

"Bitch, I heard you got away like OJ Simpson," Major said, making me laugh.

"Som' like that, how'd you hear?"

"Come on, bitch, you know I keep tabs on the fam. You my baby, I found out the same day you got shipped."

"Shit was fucked up for me at first, but you know I had to weave that bullshit with my Mayweather defense."

Major pretended to be weaving punches as he moved his head from side to side. "Bitch, I already know how that shit goes. Where they put you at?" he asked.

"They put me in two-eighteen. Who's my celly?" I asked, hoping I didn't have a dope fiend, or a crash dummy for a celly.

"Bitch, you live, you and Li'l Cali cellys," he said

I had to remember who Cali was. There were so many Calis on the unit. I just hoped he was talking about my day one Cali. "Which Cali are you talking about?"

"Crip Cali, light-skinned, mixed breed Cali," Major said.

"Oh, shit," I said. "I gotta go holla at my guy. Let me put my shit up, I'll be back to fuck witcha." Me and Major locked up again, then I grabbed my mattress and tossed it over my shoulder. I noticed the porter coming my way, but I couldn't make out his face.

As I took the front half of the stairs, I heard my name being called by a familiar voice, "Hotboy, ahh, my nigga, bitch, you back," Four Deuce said as he walked up behind me.

I dropped my mattress and we embraced. I had known him since I first pulled up on the unit. He was just like me, wild and outspoken, when it came to getting money; nothing could get in his way. When it came to knocking a nigga out, he did it with ease. "You looking like you ain't missed a meal," he said as I rubbed my belly.

"A nigga books stay full," I said, "so I'ma stay full. On the up and up, I'm tryna get some issue."

He helped me with my mattress. "So what you saying, my G?" he asked.

"What I'm saying is, we need to take this bitch back over. We convicts, we ain't no saints. Just 'cause the unit change, that don't mean we change. A nigga got mouths to feed, especially you." He nodded as we stepped in front of the cell. Cali was behind the sheet, and he peeped over the curtain.

"Say it ain't so! Bitch, you coming in here?" Cali said, as he snatched the sheet down. He had water all over the floor, so I could tell he had just finished taking a bird bath. I slid the cell door back as I laid the mattress on the top bunk.

Trying not to step in the water, I maneuvered to the back of the cell to embrace my day one. "Good to see you, bitch," Cali said. "That shit was crazy, all the rumors that went around the unit about you, I knew my nigga would be back in the flesh with the full scoop," he added.

I tossed my chain bag on the top bunk alongside my mattress as I sat on Cali's bunk. Four Deuce posted up on the door as they both stared at me, hoping I'll give them some insight. I was true to the game, and a believer of the code. I was taking my demons to the grave. "It ain't shit to tell. As you can see, I'm free, well free from that bullshit. I didn't have anything to do with those bodies."

Four Deuce smirked. "Bitch, kill that noise. You ain't gots to tell us the truth, but you ain't gotta lie to me either, 'cause surely, I know the truth."

I laughed. "If you don't want me to lie to you, then don't ask," I said. Cali cleaned the water off the floor with a towel, and squeezed the water in the toilet.

"So what's the plan?" Cali asked. I shook my head. I didn't even have to tell him what I was on. He was my guy, he knew me. I had known Cali since the free world. We had bumped into each other in Dallas a few times.

Back then, he would carry a pistol that was bigger than him. He was only 5'5. He was built like a middle schooler. He was mixed with black and Asian traits, so he had a light skin complexion. You couldn't tell him he wasn't Magic Don Juan. He swore he could bag any bitch that stood in front of him.

The thing I liked most about him—he had heart. As small as he was, he would fight a giant. He knew he didn't have shit from the shoulders, but when it came to defending his name, he was a champ.

"The plan is to flood this bitch from end to end, and everything a nigga want, we'll have," I said, hoping they were with me.

"My nigga," Cali said, "do you know this is McFee's wing? Ain't shit coming, or going, through this bitch without him knowing and catching it. He got like three snitches on this wing alone."

I replied promptly. "It's snitches everywhere, that's a part of the game. The thing is to feed the snitches so that they won't snitch on you. They got habits too. I just want to get the ball and pass it to y'all, I'ma team player."

Four Deuce agreed. "It can be done," he said. "All we have to do is get in position. You know I can make this bitch shake."

I thought about how I was going to get on my feet without any money. I was hurting financially since I had sent all my money to Gabby. After she left, she never sent it back. That was my mistake, playas fuck up. Now I had to start from the bottom. "Y'all just stay ready, 'cause I'm about to flood this bitch!"

Seth

"Lieutenant, do you mind if I use your log in? I have an inmate that I need to write up that refused to give me his housing," I said as I walked into the Lieutenant's office

He eased from behind his desk. "Perfect timing, I needed a smoke break. If they ask where I'm, tell them I went to the restroom." He walked out the room. I sat in his chair and rolled myself behind his desk. He left his password in the system, so that I could go straight to the database and get exactly what I needed. I typed in *Kingsley*, and two inmates' names popped up on the screen. Seeing the initial "G" in front of one of the names, my blood boiled.

I clicked on the name as his file popped up. Using the Lieutenant's database, I was able to see all of his prior cases. I had to shake my head as I strolled down his file. I couldn't believe Gabby would cheat on me with a criminal like him. To think of her sleeping with him, even almost having his kid, just made me want to kill her too.

He was in prison for committing an aggravated robbery when he was a teenager. The aggravated robbery was the only case that he had under his name. The list of disciplinary cases that he had was longer than a kid's Christmas list. He went from a fight case to an attempt-to-riot case, then to an actual riot case. He even had a possession of contraband, which was for a hundred dollar bill.

What hurt was to see that he had a previous established relationship case with a female officer in the year 2017. That meant Gabby wasn't his first, probably wasn't his second either. Scrolling to the top of the screen, I looked at his picture again. His mugshot made him look harmless, even with the face tattoos. I knew he wasn't harmless. He had broken up my family. He had caused two happy people to lose trust. What he did was, create enmity.

I looked under his mugshot as it showed his housing. L-wing—two-eighteen top. I printed off his mugshot and closed out the screen.

"Mr. Kiles, what are you doing?" Lieutenant Tru asked. Lt. Tru was a short bulldyke who every inmate liked because she was hip to their schemes and tricks. She always took her anger out on the C.O.'s, especially the female C.O.'s that didn't want to sleep with her.

I tried to conceal the mugshot as I placed it behind my back. "Oh, um, I had to get an inmate's housing. I tried to write him up earlier, but he wouldn't give me his cell number, so I asked the other Lt. if I could I get it from the computer."

She walked behind me to the computer and she sat in the chair. She clicked the screen, trying to be nosey. Thank goodness, I had already closed out of the screen. She looked up from the screen with a suspicious look. Before she could interrogate me any further, I was gone.

As I walked out the office, I peeped over my shoulder to see the Lieutenant watching me walk away. I was sometimes confused. Who were the real criminals? Headed in the direction of L-wing, I tried to form a plan. I knew I just couldn't walk up to him and kill him. I couldn't walk up to him and expose my hand. I had to do it right. I could've easily said that I saw him with a phone, just to get him locked up. That wouldn't soothe my soul. I wanted him to suffer, and suffer in a way he could never be healed.

While I walked down the hallway, two sergeants were escorting a shirtless inmate to X-wing. As they waited to get on the wing, I did my best to be nosey.

"What you got, sarge?" I asked. The inmate looked at me as he shook his head. Whatever he had done, he wasn't proud of it.

"Caught this little fucker with a chip bag full of K2. He even had the audacity to fight me for it. Hit me with a pretty good left too. If only he would've followed up with the right, I would've been down for the count, and he would've got away. That damn K2 shit then fried their brains. One of my officers, your fellow co-worker, had to bring it in. This is too much for visitation."

The sarge finished his explanation. Another officer stood behind them with a camcorder as she recorded them walking on the wing. I saw the chip bag full of K2 that the sarge possessed. My plan fell into place like a Tetris game. All I had to do was supply someone with product, in exchange for them getting Kingsley out the way. Two heads were always better than one.

Chapter 12

Hotboy

"Aye, bitch, you staying in or what? They about to drop out for dayroom time," Cali said, hitting the bunk.

I yawned as I uncovered my head with the blanket. For my first night back on the unit, I slept pretty good. When you're money-motivated, it's always easy to sleep. "Who working?" I asked as I stretched out on the bunk.

"Ms. Gall, the Mexican chick. You remember her, don't you?"

I recalled. "You talking 'bout crazy lady. How could I forget! We bumped heads one time so bad that I almost slapped the shit outta her. The bitch tried to slap me 'cause I asked to go to church."

"She working with a new boot. They just walked by not too long ago."

"Who she training, a hard head, or a female?" I asked.

"Som' li'l chick. Li'l bitch look alright though. But training with Gall, she ain't gon' be good."

Jumping of my bunk, I said, "The bitch already got her mind made up about what she gon' do. All she waiting for is a boss nigga to tell her that it's the right decision." I rubbed the bottom of my socks before stepping into my shower shoes. Grabbing my toothbrush and Colgate, I pressed the water button until it got stuck.

Cali sat on his bunk, giving me room to get ready. The cell was so small; it was hard for two people to move around at one time. "So what?" Cali said. "You about to try yo' luck with Gall working? You's a fool, you know she don't play that shit."

I rinsed my mouth out before spitting into the toilet, and replied. "She just gon' have to go with the flow today. It's make or break season. She can either get on the ship, or get left behind."

The doors rolled just as I finished wiping my face. I hung my towel up on the clothes line and slid my feet into my new low-top

Reeboks. Cali stepped out the cell first, and he looked both ways before taking the back half of the stairs. I followed behind him and I closed the cell door.

"Hotboy, bitch, when you move over here?" T-man asked as we walked down the stairs. I shook up with him as we walked to the dayroom door,

"I got here yesterday. After I got done unpacking, I was too tired to come back to the dayroom, so I stayed in and went to sleep. I can't believe you still on this lame ass wing, you ain't tried to move around yet?"

"I was gon' move, but shid, I then got used to being over here. It really ain't that bad though. McFee tried to put all the hustlers on the same wing to hurt us, really he ended up making this ho live. The only thing is the hos, they be scared to fuck with us, seeing that we're under the radar."

As I watched the new boot walk down the stairs, I told T-man: "They ain't scared. This wing just like any other wing. Look, all you have to do is find me some cash, I'll show you how to shake the spot."

"Some cash, my nigga?" T-man said, looking askance at me. "What you tryna do? You just got back, bitch, don't do nothing stupid."

"I'm trying to win, now what you tryna do?" I asked.

He looked at me before shaking his head. "Bitch, don't get us killed," he said.

"I don't get people killed, I do the killing," I said as he walked off to retrieve some cash.

"Dayroom, bitches!" Ms. Gall yelled. She was one of the few laws that loved to call inmates *bitches*. Call her one back, and see if she likes it. She would curse the blacks. Spit on the Mexicans, and smile at the whites. The bitch had all her morals fucked up. I couldn't blame her; well, not today, only because I needed her. I needed her to let me stay on the run so that I could shoot my shot at the new boot. "That means you too, Kingsley! You're not exempt," Ms. Gall said. I mean-mugged her as I walked up to her.

"I didn't come because I ain't no bitch. You know me and you don't get down like that. I ain't the rest of these niggas."

She placed her hand on her hip. "I didn't call you a bitch, I called *them* bitches, now get yo' ass in the dayroom like I said."

T-man ran up behind me as we walked into the dayroom. "Did you get it?" I asked. He pulled out a hundred dollar bill wrapped in Saran Wrap. I eyed the new boot down before walking away from the bars. She looked at me before putting her head down. I knew without a doubt she couldn't stand under this thunder for five minutes. "Aye, look out, Bama, I need a favor," I said to Bama as I walked up to the wood section. Bama was a tall white guy who worked out every day all day. He was originally from Alabama, but ended up in prison with an interstate compact, He was tat'd up with a full beard, just Ms. Gall's type.

"What's up, Hotboy?" he asked as he shook my hand.

I was one of the few guys on the unit that did business with every race. I mainly did business with every race but blacks. Doing business with whites and Hispanics gave me a little insurance. They mostly always came through on time just to avoid a racial riot.

Doing business with your own kind could be like tossing a coin in the air, hoping it lands on heads. It was fifty-fifty.

"I need for you to take off your shirt, and work out," I said, drawing a confused look from Bama. He laughed.

"What?"

I explained: "I know it sounds weird, but you know like I know, Ms. Gall likes you. Right now, I need that bitch out of my way. You're the only one that can get her off guard."

He laughed again. He knew like we all knew she was into him. "Man, that bitch is crazy, bro. I know she cuts for me, but still, she's bipolar, out-of-this-world bipolar. That's a lot of work."

"Look, when have I ever asked you to do something for free? I got you—you know if I win, we all win."

He contemplated it for a second. "Okay, but don't forget me when the pack flies. All I want is some Hydroxycut." He walked towards the back. I shook my head. All he wanted was some weight loss material. Nigga didn't even want to make any money.

Bama popped his top to reveal a wife beater and a bunch of tat's. He kneeled down and started doing pushups. I lost count at eighty as he continued to go. I watched Gall as she watched him. Normally, she would tell people to stop working out.

Seeing that it was him, she enjoyed the show. She couldn't take it any longer as her legs crossed each other. I knew her watching him made her pussy wet. "Bama, come here!" she said, and he stood up from doing, God knows, how many pushups!

He walked over, his body glistening with sweat. "What's up?" he asked as he made his pecks jump. Her smile couldn't be hidden as she showed all thirty-two.

"What did I tell y'all about working out in my dayroom?"

Bama looked down at her as his body towered hers. "You didn't tell me anything. You know if you would've, I would've stopped."

"You heard me tell them to stop earlier," Ms. Gall said, trying to play hard.

"I'm not them, but I gotcha, I'm done. So is that all you wanted?" he asked as he made his pecks jump again.

She eyed his chest, and looked back at the new boot she was training. "No, I actually could use a little company. My trainee is boring."

Bama looked back at me, but I pretended not to be looking "You the one with the keys," Bama said to her. "You know I can't talk to you all day from here. Let me come out and play porter."

"Okay, but when it gets close to shift change, you have to go back in the dayroom," she said.

"That's cool, but let my homeboy come out with me so he can watch my back."

"Who you talking about?" she asked, looking around the dayroom.

He looked over at me. "Hotboy."

"Oh, hell naw. That boy is not coming out here to get me put on the hot list." She said that loud enough for the whole dayroom to hear.

"Shhh, damn, why you gotta be so damn loud? He ain't hot,

shid the whole wing hot, we all under investigation. Look, the only way I'm coming out is if he can come too."

She looked over at me, weighing her options. She had been after Bama for a while now. He stayed far away from her because he wasn't into loud and crazy bitches. Now that he was giving her conversation, she couldn't pass up the opportunity.

"Look, he better stay off of two and three row. And stay off the main door too. I swear to God, if y'all get me in trouble—"

"I got you," he said, waving me over.

I walked over like I didn't know what was going on. "What's up?" I said.

"Come out with me, watch my back," Bama said, playing along.

She shook her head like she didn't really want to let me out. Unlocking the dayroom door, she let us out. I instantly eyed the new boot as she leaned against the wall.

"Figures," I said. Bama and Gall moved their conversation by the closet; that was just what I needed.

"Figures what?" the new boot said.

"I just figured you was scared, that's all." I said.

"Scared? Boy, please! Of what? You, y'all, stop it." She rolled her neck.

"I just figured you were scared of an opportunity," I said, throwing the bait. I walked up closer to see if she would stop me. I didn't get too close to scare her, but I got close enough to smell her perfume. She eyed me, but didn't budge. I was told I was sometimes too bold. I took chances; that's why I was always winning.

"An opportunity like what? 'Cause this place is only a stepping stone." She crossed her arms.

"The opportunities to have everything you've ever dreamed of," I countered.

She hunched over, laughing at me like I said something funny. "Boy, you crazy! Good try, but I'm not the one. Try another bitch."

That was the reason why I didn't fuck with black hos. Either they've been played by a nigga like me, or they had brothers like me that's game-tight just like me.

"What are you talking about?" I said, playing dumb.

"That li'l line you just used on me. Don't let it happen again."

"No need, I never use the same line twice," I said.

"Boy, what do you want?" she said, like I was irritating her.

"Your name."

She had no choice but to tell me her name, seeing that she didn't have on her nametag. "Sanderfield," she said.

"I'm Kingsley."

"And I'm not interested," she said, killing my vibe. I was two seconds from telling her that she wasn't even my type. I didn't do it because I didn't want to mess anything up, just in case she was playing hard to get. She wasn't ugly, but then again she wasn't up to par with my standards. She was a yellow-bone with long curly hair that was hers. She also had nice hips, but with a white girl ass. She had a huge ass clown nose that looked like it came off with her glasses.

"Sanderfield, are you ready?" said a new boot who I had never seen before. When I saw her, I just knew she would be the one. She must've felt it too because she couldn't keep her eyes off of me. She was my type. Long-haired, short with just enough hips and ass.

My favorite thing was, she wasn't black. Which meant she didn't have a brother like me. She had a beautiful smile and a gullible personality. Sanderfield walked to the door, and they started conversing back and forth.

The whole time they were talking, she kept looking over Sanderfield's shoulder, smiling at me. I didn't want to seem thirsty, so I walked away to let them talk about whatever they were talking about. When I looked back in their direction, she was still staring at me. I knew I had her. I didn't win the barbeque sauce, but I did win the ranch dressing.

Newton

162

"Okay, Newton, you have to try harder, doll, come on, try to take a step," the doctor instructed. My forehead was covered with sweat as I stood on my right leg. My right leg moved with a little stiffness. My left leg seemed to be stuck on stupid because it wouldn't do anything my mind told it to do.

"I'm trying, doctor!" I screamed in frustration. I strained hard as I held myself up with the help of the side rails. My left leg started moving, barely. It took everything in me to make that happen. The doctor must've noticed the slight movement as he tried to give me some encouragement.

"There you go, Newton, you can do it, one more time!" he screamed, sounding more like a football coach than a doctor. My left leg dangled as I squeezed my eyes shut, hoping it would give me some sort of superhuman strength. At the moment I damn sure needed it.

With everything I had in me I moved my right leg as my left leg got some act right, and followed behind the right leg. I was able to take two steps before crashing to the floor.

The doctor rushed to my rescue. "It's okay, sweetie. You're okay, you did really good." He helped me off the floor onto a wheel chair.

"Good job, Gabby, I knew you could do it," Ms. Debra said, wiping sweat from my forehead.

Looking down at my legs, I tried to catch my breath. My heart raced like I had just ran a marathon. "I did good, doctor?"

"Sure, you did. You did awesome, darling, Look at it this way—it's only been three months, look how far you've come. I'll give you another month. With your dedication, and willpower, you'll be walking like normal."

"You mean that?" I smiled.

"Sure, your recovery depends on you, and how hard you work. Our staff will be here around the clock to help you recover."

I nodded as I thought about me being able to walk again. I could finally be myself again.

"We will need your fiancé to sign a few papers to ensure that his insurance will cover the cost of your therapeutic treatments. When he signs off, we can get you started as soon as you're ready."

"Okay, doctor," I said, nodding as I tried to remember what kind of insurance Seth said he had. I had tried to call him earlier, but he didn't answer. Lately he's been working overtime almost every day. I figured he was working double shifts to be able to cover the cost of my medical bills. "I'll have him down here first thing in the morning. I can't wait to get my life back to normal." I smiled

"Good," the doctor said, returning the smile. "Until then, just rest up. You did good today."

Ms. Debra unlocked the wheels on the wheelchair. "Look at you," she said as she began to wheel me back to my room. "Come next month, you and Seth will be walking down the street with Jacob running behind y'all. You never know, y'all could finally walk down the aisle."

I smiled at the thought of us finally getting married. After all we've been through, we deserved a happy ending. I would have to talk to him about it. That was if he brought his ass up here.

Seth

I smiled as the Lieutenant read the rosters. I was finally going to be working on L-wing. I couldn't hide my excitement. I had worked overtime every day, hoping they'll place me on L-wing. Considering we could only work twelve hours straight, I was only left with four hours to get my mission accomplished.

As I walked on the wing, I got a quick briefing before sending the C.O. on her way. I placed my things in the closet, and grabbed a bed book roster to see if he was still housed on the wing. Scrolling down the list, I found his name as it showed his job, age, height, weight, and custody status. Placing the roster back in the closet, I locked the door as I looked around the dayroom for my victim.

"Shift change, hard head!" an inmate yelled while pushing the broom in my direction. "One row crawling!" he shouted as I began to walk his way. As I got closer to him, I wished that this job required us to carry a gun.

Seeing his face for the first time in person made me want to kill him right then and there. As we stood a short distance from each other I was actually at loss for words. Everything that I had planned to say went out the window.

"You working over here?" he asked. I just stared at him. He was close to my height, maybe a little shorter. He was dark-skinned with wavy hair. He was clad in a wife beater, which I suspected was contraband. His tattoos covered almost his entire body. He was well-built for his height. You could look at him and tell that he worked out a lot.

His shoulders were squared perfectly with his chest. I tried to imagine what made Gabby want to cheat on me with him. I wasn't physically fit like he was. I really had nothing that I could see physically in comparison. I guess the only thing that we had in common was our preference in women.

"Just for four hours, I'm doing overtime," I managed to say.

"You new here?" he asked.

I laughed in his face by mistake. Here was the convict that ruined my life, and he didn't even know it. "Yeah, well, not really. I've been here for maybe two months or so. Actually, this is my first time working this wing."

"How you like the unit so far?" he asked.

"I've had good days and bad days. I hate working medium custody though."

He laughed. "I bet you do, them niggas be tripping."

We stood by the stairs talking like we were old friends. "I haven't seen you on the unit before. Are you new here?" I asked him.

"Not really, I used to be over here. I went on chain to take care of some issues."

"Like what?" I asked.

He hesitated before he answered. "I was falsely accused of two murders. I'm not sure if you heard about it. Some months ago, two people were stabbed to death on G-wing. An officer, and an inmate, they tried saying I was the one who did it."

"I think I heard something about that. Was that around the same time that female C.O. was shoved over the rail on three row?"

"Yeah, that was around the same time," he said, his mind drifting off. I had no idea he was accused of killing two people, one being the guy who shoved Gabby over the rail. He had to really care for her to be willing to spend the rest of his life in prison. Then again, her fall had killed their love child.

"So what happened with the case?" I asked, being nosey.

He leaned against the stair rail. "The guy who actually did it came forward and cleared my name."

I knew he was full of shit. He was good at hiding it too. That's probably how he got Gabby to cheat with him. "Glad you didn't go down for it then. It would've sucked to go down for something that you didn't do."

He sighed like he was thinking about the guy who took the rap for him. "Yeah, that would've sucked. God's plan though—I guess he had something else in store for me."

"Like what?" I asked.

"I don't know, I'm about to see parole in, like, two months. So the plan is to just stay out the way until it's time to go home. I'm preparing myself for the free world, so I'm chilling."

"So what are you going to do for money? You can't survive in the world without cash. It's hard to survive out there right now. Especially when you're coming home on your dick." Undoubtedly, I caught him off guard.

He looked at me, stunned that those words actually came from my mouth. I had a plan. And even though I wanted to kill him, I couldn't do it without him. My plan was simple; give him enough rope to hang himself!

Hotboy

I looked at him, stunned. I had to be misreading the entire

conversation. Normally, the inmate would be the one to initiate the topic about making money. Yet, this new boot, so to say, was shooting at me. He didn't come straight out and say let's make some money, but basically in prison terms he said, let's make some money.

Just to make sure I wasn't tripping, I sidestepped his comment, and waited on him to counter. "Yeah, you right, a nigga can't go home broke. They used to have ways for inmates to make money legally until they shut the craft shop down." He smirked like he knew something about me that he wasn't saying.

"Come on, bro," he said, "I'm white, not green. Everyone knows who you are, that's all they talk about. It is only one reason everyone knows your name. You got the juice! Let's just say that I got a family to feed, and this job don't cover my family, and tricking expenses, if you know what I mean." He winked at me.

"Fam! Don't ever, ever, ever, *ever*, wink at me again. I feel what you're saying, but you're starting to scare me," I said, taking a step back from him.

"Come on, bro, I'm not that type of guy. I don't want to do business with just anyone. I wanted to make sure that when I did get at some money, that I did business with the right person. He had to be stiff."

I nodded in agreement. He was right; you couldn't get money with just anyone. Niggas would scream that they were money getters, but the truth of the matter was, they ended up bringing unwanted heat.

"So let's just cut the bullshit then. What are you insinuating?" I said. I was tired of the run around he was doing. If he was talking business, I was all ears.

He placed both of his hands in his pocket and faced the day-room. "I'm trying to hustle, but I don't know what I'm doing."

I laughed on the inside. I had never hustled with a male C.O. before. In all of my years hustling in prison, it was only with females. Not that I had a rule against hustling with a male C.O. It was just I normally finessed a bitch, fuck her, then get her to drop; all in that order. Now, this falls into my lap.

"So let me get this straight," I said, still trying to avoid incriminating myself. "You trying to help me, help you?"

"In so many words, yes," he said.

Hoping he was in sync with it, I told him, "Look my nigga, this shit ain't no game. Either you're going to come with it, or stop bumping about it. I usually pay for the first drop, but seeing that I don't know you, we gon' do shit different. Bring me the first drop outta yo' pocket, and I'll sell it, and send you your half. How the game is right now, we'll make a lot of money. It's all up to you."

"So what, how would I do it?" he asked.

"My nigga, you got a dick, don't you! It ain't like you a female, it should be easier for you. All you have to do is wrap it up good, and pretend that it's yo' dick."

"I got that part, but you not telling me what you want me to bring," he pointed out.

He was right, I was slacking. I wasn't used to everything moving so fast. I was used to play-by-play action. "Can you handle tobacco? Like a can at a time?"

"I should be able to," he said. "Not sure what a can is, but I'll find out." Never having a male C.O. took away from some of the game's advantages. Most females wouldn't bring certain shit. I always wanted to break a law that wasn't scared to deal with hard drugs. I could finally be able to jump a point.

"Are you scared to bring hard drugs, like Ecstasy and meth?" When I said *meth*, his eyes lit up like he had some buried skeletons in his closet.

"I can do it. It's all the same to me."

"What about phones? We can break the bank with them!" I said.

"I don't know about phones, you know they got metal detectors up front where we come in at."

I already knew they had metal detectors. I just wanted to see were the line would be drawn.

"Don't worry about that. What we need is some grade *A* ice. Some shit that will make a mo'fucka stay up for weeks at a time, I want niggas to be grinding their teeth when we finish with them."

He smiled like he knew what I was talking about. I knew he did, I could see the sweat forming on his forehead as I talked about it. Once an ice-head, always an ice-head. I had to be careful with this one.

"So when do you want to start?" I asked.

"I'm off tomorrow. I can pick up the ice and the tobacco tomorrow, and come in and do overtime the day after to bring it."

I liked the way the white boy moved. He was persistent, and money-motivated. "That's a bet. That gives me enough time to get everything set up. Until then, make a cash app. When you wrap the pack up, make sure you put your cash app information in there with it, so I can shoot you yo' half of the bread."

He nodded in understanding. "Overstood, and make sure you be careful," he said.

"Don't worry about me, you just be careful walking through that door with that shit on you. Keep yo' mouth closed. Your business is *your* business, not the unit's business."

"Aye, Kingsley, I appreciate you, man. You have no idea."

"Naw, I appreciate you, homie," I said as he walked off to do his rounds. As he hit the steps, I realized that he called me by my last name. I couldn't recall me telling it to him. Then again, he said my name was ringing all over the unit. I wonder who put him on me. Shrugging, I brushed the thought off. I didn't care who did it, I appreciate whoever did it. I was back like I never left!

Chapter 13

Seth

"Daddy, where are we going? Can we stop and get McDonald's?" Jacob asked as we parked the car.

I texted my old supplier, letting him know I was outside. I had no other choice but to bring Jacob. I was going to leave him over at Gabby's mom's house, but Gabby insisted that I bring him to see her first thing in the morning. "We'll get some as soon as we leave," I said.

"Who lives here?" Jacob asked.

"Just an old friend of daddy's. We'll be out before you know it."

"Isn't that our car," he said, pointing to Gabby's old car that I sold for some dope.

I felt lower than low. I had traded happiness for a temporary high. "Looks like it, but it's not. We traded ours for this one." My supplier hit me back, saying I was good to come in. "Okay, listen, Jacob, when we get inside, I want you to stay behind me, and don't ask any questions. As soon as we leave, I'll buy you a happy meal."

He smiled and said, "Can I get a large drink this time?"

"Whatever you want."

"How about an apple pie?" he said, trying his luck.

"Sure, anything else?"

He thought for a second. "No, that will be it!" He was too smart for his own good. I locked the car doors as we got out. We wasn't in the hood, but there was ice heads everywhere, looking for a come-up. Knocking on the door, I could hear the deadbolt unlock.

"Straydog, been a minute, what brings you back?" my supplier said as he let us in. *Straydog* was the nickname they used to call me when I was doing meth. I would always end up on some dopeboy's doorstep, so they gave me the nickname Straydog.

"You know I don't go by that anymore," I said as I stepped

inside with Jacob close behind.

"Who is this you got with you?" he asked, finally seeing Jacob. Jacob tucked his head behind my legs. He always pretended to be shy when he met someone for the first time.

"He's not even here. I just want to get down to business, so that I can go," I said as we walked to the bar.

"So what are you trying to get?" he asked.

"I need a quarter of your best shit. I got five hundred dollars on me right now. I'll have the rest by the end of the week."

He eyed me as he sat on his barstool. "Stray, I thought that you were done fucking around. I know you said it once, maybe twice, shid, maybe even three times. I figured with your ole' lady being all broken up and shit that you would be done for good. I guess I do have that ultimate temptation. I should start calling that shit *sin* instead of *ice*."

"Cut the bullshit, Dub, I'm clean now. I got this side hustle with this new job, so I'm in need of some product."

He raised his eyebrows curiously. "New job, huh? Put me in with the details."

"I work at a prison, so I'ma going to drop off a little extra work on the side to make a little money," I said.

He smiled mischievously. "I like what I'm hearing. So Stray-dog is trying to step up and be a top-dog, hmm!" Walking to his light stash, Dub said, "I tell you what—I'll do this for you, but you have to do something for me too."

"What is it?"

"I have a cousin that's locked up on the unit that you work on. I need for you to take him this." He pulled out a sack of fluffy buds.

"I didn't even tell you what unit I worked on. Your cousin could be anywhere in the system."

"You didn't have to tell me. You must have forgot, I keep tabs on my best custos. You work on Beto, that's where my cousin is at. His name is Carlos, he goes by Los. You may or may not know him. It'll be hard to miss him. He's probably the only one on the unit with ten thousand dollars' worth of diamonds in his mouth."

I looked over at Jacob as he started to play with a 6 foot bong. "Jacob, stop!" I yelled as I tried to think things through.

"You do this for me, and I'll give you a deal on the ice. We'll get money together. Who knows, you might make enough money to be able to buy your car back." He laughed.

I weighed my options. I was already going to be dropping off for Gianni, but only for a purpose. Now I was stuck between getting my revenge, and getting some money.

"I'll do it. But not for long, so don't make it a habit."

He smiled as he tossed me the weed and another package that looked like crystals. I eyed the dope as I twisted it in my hands. The last time I had this much dope at one time, I had sold our car, and abandoned my family. This time I was determined to double what I'd lost. I wasn't going back to what I used to be.

I pulled out the $500 that I promised him, and tossed it to him. "I'll call you in a couple of days," I said.

Tucking the dope in my pockets, I patted Jacob on the head so we could go.

"Before you go, Stray, I must say I'm glad I ran into you again. Guess who stopped by the other day."

Curiosity forced me to turn around.

"Who?" I asked.

"Your baby mama. Can't lie, she was looking good too."

"Come on, Jacob, let's go," I said as we walked out the door. I hadn't seen Kelly in over two years. She had abandoned me and Jacob all for the sake of a high. I had always wondered where she was. I would think about what I would say to her if ever given the chance. It didn't matter, I had too much on my mind to add her to the list.

"Daddy, what's a baby mama?"

Newton

"Mommy!" Jacob said as he ran and jumped on the hospital bed.

I hugged him tight like I hadn't seen him in years. "Hey my

little teapot, did you miss me that much?" I said as I looked up at Seth. He hated for me to call him a teapot. Seth stared at me from a distance. "No kiss?" I asked him.

Jacob kissed my cheek as he smiled in my face, "Not you, silly, I know you love me." I looked at Seth. He walked over to me and leaned down to kiss me. As we kissed, I closed my eyes. Once I opened them, he was looking at me. "Are you okay?" I asked him.

He walked over to the recliner and sat in it, "Why would you ask?" I shrugged. "Just making sure. So, Jacob, baby, have you been good with daddy since I've been gone?"

Jacob smiled as he looked around the hospital room. "I'm always good, mommy," he said. I laughed at his innocent face. In just a few months he had grown so much. I felt like I was missing the most important days of his life.

Seth leaned his head back as he stared at the ceiling. "Have you been getting any sleep?" I asked Seth. He sighed like I was irritating him.

"I really haven't slept lately. I've been working overtime every day. I have to make sure Jacob is up and ready for school every morning. Plus, I have to pick him up from your mom's every day. So yeah, I'm tired, Gabby." Jacob looked up at me, waiting on my response. He could always tell when we were about to argue.

"I used to do all that too, Seth. I know how you're feeling, that's why I asked." Jacob grabbed the remote that was attached to the bed, and started pressing buttons. "Stop, Jacob!" I yelled out of frustration.

Seth sat up in the chair. "What's that supposed to mean, Gabby, huh?"

"Nothing, Seth, look, I don't want to argue, I really don't. Can we have a good day? I really had some good news to share with y'all."

The nurse walked in before I could continue. "Ms. Newton, did you call?" Ms. Debra asked. She smiled as she noticed Jacob sitting on the bed with me. "Hey, Jacob baby, I didn't even see you come in. Look at you, you're getting so big." Her compliment made Jacob blush.

I smiled at how Jacob pretended to be so innocent in front of her. He stepped over me as he climbed down to give her a hug. "Hey, Ms. Debra," he said, hugging her thick legs.

She hugged him back as she leaned over. "Come to see mommy? Did she tell you how good she's been doing?"

"I didn't get a chance to tell them yet," I said.

"Well, I'm just in time then," she said, smiling.

"Baby, I took a step the other day, with the help of the doctors, and Ms. Debra. After we finished, the doctor told me that I could be walking normal in a few months, if I put in the necessary work to get healthy. He said that I could start this treatment program that they have. Some kind of therapeutic treatment that teaches your bones how to move properly again."

Seth looked around like he didn't even care. "That's good, baby, so when do you start?" he asked. I knew he was just saying that because Ms. Debra was in the room. I knew Seth, and I knew something was up with him. He wasn't acting like his normal self.

"I can start as soon as I fill out the paperwork. I just need your insurance information because mine don't cover the full expense."

He sat up in the chair and he dug in his back pocket to retrieve his wallet. "I'm all for you getting better, baby," he said. "So whatever you need to make that happen, let's do it." He handed Ms. Debra his insurance card.

Smiling, Ms. Debra said, "Okay, well, let me go and get the paperwork that you'll need to fill out. Once you read through it, she'll be good to go." As she walked out the room, Seth slouched down in his seat.

"Baby, you sure you're okay?" I asked, hoping that he would just talk to me.

"Gabby! Baby, I'm fine. I just need a nap before I go to work. You asked me to bring Jacob, and I did. So do me a favor, and let me get a quick nap before I have to go to work."

Jacob pulled on the strings from the balloons that Williamson had sent me. "Come here, baby, I want to show you something," I said to Jacob as I grabbed the remote.

He stepped onto the bed, being careful not to bump my legs. "What does it do?" he asked.

I smiled. "Anything."

"What do you mean?" he asked. "You press this button," I said, pointing to the kitchen button. "It orders any food you want," I added.

He pressed the button and said, "Can I have an ice cream, with almonds? Oh, and some McDonald's." He looked up at me.

I laughed and said, "They don't have McDonald's." Seth laughed while pretending to be asleep. Jacob was the heart of our relationship. Even when we were mad at each other, Jacob would bring us back together. After all we've been through, I only hoped that he could keep us together. I could feel us growing apart.

Hotboy

"Hey, Cali, bitch, you still got that nigga on payroll that be working in the hallway?" I asked.

Cali looked up from his letter. "Yeah, why? What's up?"

"I need to get off this wing. Shit is about to start moving for me. I don't want the laws watching all my plays. I can't take no losses right now."

"I feel you, so what, you tryna leave me already? Bitch, we just linked back up," he said as he sipped his coffee.

"My nigga, with all that pull you got, I was sure you would have since left."

"I thought about leaving, but bitch, don't tell nobody. I made parole. I'm about to go home in a few days. That's why I've been riding the cell a lot lately. You my nigga, but you know niggas don't be wanting to see a nigga do nothing, especially go home."

"Damn, that's wassup, my nigga," I said. "Don't forget about me when you touch down."

"Bitch, you my nigga. We've been riding since before this penitentiary shit. I don't even need your TDC number, I know yo' name by heart. Gianni Kingsley. Do I need to spell it out for you?

We embraced. I was always happy to see a real nigga go

home. "So were you gon' go when you get out?" I asked.

"I'm going back to that nutty li'l buddy. It ain't no place like it out there." Cali was originally from California. Moving to Dallas as a teen, he fell in love with the city and adopted Dallas as his second home. That was how we first met. The fast streets of north Dallas. "I'll see you again. I'm right behind you. I see parole in, like, sixty days. If God says the same, I'll be out there before the summer."

"My nigga, how are you still tryna hustle and you about to see parole. You know I'm all for a nigga getting to some money. But bitch, you moving like you don't wanna go home. The least you can do is put another nigga on and play the background."

That was a good suggestion. He was making a lot of sense. The one thing about dealing drugs in the penitentiary—you never put a nigga too much on your business. And I never put a nigga in my pockets to be able to count my money either.

"I feel what you're saying. I'll give it a little thought." I lied.

"So what, the li'l bitch broke the other day or what?" he asked.

"Who you talking about? Oh, that light skinned bitch? Hell naw, she stuck up than a bitch. I came at her with some of my best shit too. The bitch was so blind, she didn't even see the worm on the hook. I swear she can't think past go. She gon' get a lot of niggas fucked off watch. She think she know it all." Cali laughed at me. "What's so funny, li'l nigga?" I asked.

"Bruh, you always do that shit. You always talk down on a bitch when she don't like you."

"You full of shit, I don't do that."

"Name one bitch that you shot at, that didn't fuck with you, that you ended up cool with."

I sat back and tried to think of a time. When I couldn't think of one, I burst out laughing too. "Damn, you right. I don't care though. To me it's like this, if them hos ain't with me, then they against me. If a bitch don't bite the bait I be spitting, then the bitch a lost cause."

Cali kicked his feet up as he couldn't control his laughter. "You retarded, my nigga. Do you hear yo'self sometimes? That shit ain't gon' fly in the free world. The only reason that shit working now is 'cause these hos from the country, they don't know no better. They will accept anything in hopes of getting wifed up."

He wasn't lying though. I had won plenty hos just by shooting them a dream. They knew I was lying. They just figured that they would give me everything I wanted, with hopes of winning me over. They had to be stupid. I wasn't a game, I couldn't be won.

The doors rolled as inmates filed out of their cells to go to the dayroom. "Come on, bitch," I said to Cali. "I need to holla at yo' partner. I need him to make this happen before shift change." He folded his letter up before placing it under his mattress, then he put on his clothes.

"Coming out or what?" a short female C.O. asked.

"Hold on one second, my celly coming out too," I said, stopping her from closing the door on Cali.

Cali grabbed his shirt, walking out the cell with it in his hand. As he walked down the stairs, I looked at his back tattoo. Luckily, he was with me. But if he wasn't, someone would've called him out to fight.

Cali had a man with a gun tat'd on his back. The man held a dog's head in his hand with the words, "Every Dog Has Its Day" around it. To every blood that saw his back, it could be offensive to them.

"Bitch, put your shirt on before a nigga beef for yo' bitch ass," I said as we stood downstairs.

"My nigga, you know fighting ain't nothing but recreation to me. I do that type of shit."

I laughed because he didn't have shit from the shoulders. "Whatever you say, my nigga. Let's just find a way to get out the door without a nigga calling you out." I laughed.

"If a nigga call me out, you better step up for me," he said. We walked to the door in hopes of getting off the wing without any conflict.

"L-wing out!" I yelled, hoping we had a good law on the keys.

Officer Adams walked up to the gate with the keys in his

hands. "What you want, li'l guy?" he asked, laughing. Adams was a cool ass white boy. He was tall and lanky, but he was cool as hell. All he wanted to do was play. He was one of the coolest C.O.'s on the farm.

"What's up, big bitch?" I said, playing with him. "Nothing much, you li'l turd, when did you get back?" he asked.

"I got back a few days ago. Yo' whole Klan family tried to hang me, but you know I got slave feet in my blood." I laughed.

"You stupid fool, so wassup?" Adams asked.

"I need to hit the streets, who working down there by the chow hall?"

He looked down the hallway. "You got a sergeant on the chow hall door; other than that, everything is everything."

"Well, let me out then bitch," I said, laughing.

He laughed. "Fuck you!" he said as he unlocked the gate to let me out. Cali tried to follow behind me, but Adams stopped him. "Where you think you're going, li'l shit?" he asked Cali, playing with him.

"Come on, bruh."

Adams was just playing, but he wanted Cali to think he was serious. "Come on, bruh," Adams said, mimicking him. Cali got quiet as he started to get upset.

I laughed to lighten the mood "Come on, Adams, he with me."

Adams moved out the way as he unlocked the gate to let Cali out. "Looking like a teenager. You need to make sure you're old enough to be in here, see you looking like Benjamin Button." Adam cracked at him.

I laughed in Cali's face all the way down the hallway. "That shit wasn't that funny, homie," he said as we walked past the sergeant. "Aye, Big Will, have you seen Scratch today?" Cali asked.

Big will looked around, making sure there wasn't any rank in the area before he came over to us. "My nigga, why you looking around like that?" Cali asked him.

"Y'all can play dumb all y'all want. Y'all hotboys, I ain't trying to get put in that category." That was just like Big Will. Big and scary.

"Ayyyyeeeeeee!" Cali yelled loud as hell, as people looked at us crazy.

The sergeant looked over his shoulder to get a good look at who was causing a disturbance in his hallway. "Now you a hotboy, too." Cali laughed.

Just as Big Will was about to tell him off, Scratch walked out of the Lieutenant's office with a trash bag. "Scratch," Cali said, calling him over.

Scratch was a tall light-skinned guy who was really cool with almost every C.O. and ranking officer. He had been on Beto so long, that they practically got trained by him. He had done so much dirt for them that they practically owed him favors. "What's up?" Scratch said as he leaned against the wall.

"You still working the bed books?" Cali asked.

"Yeah, shit just slow right now. They got a bunch of new people in the count room, why do you ask?"

Cali looked over at me. "My guy is trying to get moved."

"Who? Hotboy? Why he just didn't come to me himself?"

"I never told him it was you that did the moves," Cali said. "I know how to keep my mouth shut."

"Where's he tryna go?" Scratch asked.

"Ask him, he's right there," Cali said.

Scratch moved between the two of us. "Where you tryna go, homie?"

My reply was prompt and specific. "I'm tryna get to H-wing. I don't care which row, but I prefer the back half. It don't matter if it's a top, or bottom bunk."

"You know shit's been fucked up, I'ma need a li'l time to make shit happen. You know I charge fifty dollars per person."

I pulled out the $100 that I had got from T-man the other day. "Here is a hundred dollars, make it happen tonight, and I'll bless you with a fifty sack of ice tomorrow." His eyes lit up.

It was amazing how so many people played with their nose. Fucking with ice didn't make you less cool on Beto; it just made you less like me. He snatched the Saran-wrapped money up, and tossed it in his mouth. "Go and pack your shit, I'll get it done today," he said, walking off.

I smiled at Cali. I had a motto. *Never be denied.* If someone had something, and I wanted it, I would always pay what the next man couldn't afford to pay. And I would always pay what the seller couldn't afford to let pass up. Money talks!

Chapter 14

Seth

My balls were sweating so damn much I was sure that the pack was going to fall. I stepped up in line as I clutched my grocery bag with my lunch in it. My appetite was so fucked up I knew I wouldn't be able to eat what I brought.

"Your turn," an old Caucasian lady said, smiling at me. She stretched her gloves over her hand as I placed my things in the bin to move through the metal detector machine. The metal detector wasn't my biggest fear. My biggest fear was the roaming hands of a cougar. I walked through the metal detector in a hurry as I tried to walk past the pat search.

"Uhhh—ahhh, my turn," the old lady said. I sat my bag down and walked over to her to get searched. Turning my back to her, I held my arms straight out. "You new here, darling?" she asked. She patted my legs as she moved her hands down.

I opened my legs a little to give her some room. As soon as I did, I could feel beads of sweat running down my legs. I was nervous as hell. "Come on, sweetie, spread them for me good, she said, breathing on my ass. "Don't be shy."

I spread my legs as far as I could without the risk of the pack falling. She moved her hands up and down my right leg as she squeezed my calf. "So are you?" she asked again.

"Am I what?"

"New, are you new here?" she asked, moving to my other leg.

"Not really, I've been here for almost three months." She gripped my other calf as her hands moved up between my legs. I was sure she had touched the pack, so I jumped to pretend that she had actually touched my penis.

"Oh I'm sorry. Little old me sometimes forget you youngins are hung like a horse. You are packing something nice down there, sweetie." She winked at me.

I let my arms fall, and I grabbed my food off the floor. "You take care," I said, rushing off.

Looking over my shoulder, she was still looking at me, smiling. I let out a sigh of relief as I walked up to the sergeant while he handed out our job assignments. I wondered, *was I that good at wrapping the pack, or did she actually know what I was really packing?*

Instead of placing me at least close to Gianni, I was placed on H-wing to work. That was on the other side of the unit from him. I was so irritated that I announced myself as I walked on the wing. "Shift change! Angry white man!" I yelled. The dayroom erupted with laughter as if they had never heard a C.O. announce themself like that.

Unlocking the officers' closet, I tossed my food on the shelf and sat on the ice cooler. I sat and thought about how I was going to get this shit to Gianni. Hopefully, he would come down here to get it. It wasn't like he was new to this. He had to have a plan, because I didn't. Looking down in my lap I could see the bulge sticking to my leg like a penis. In a woman's eyes, she would think that I was blessed. In a man's eyes, he would think that I was on some gay shit.

"Ice coolers! The keyboss yelled. I stood up as I dragged the half-full ice cooler to the gate.

"House call, boss man! I just got back from work, I'm tired as hell, I'm trying to go in the cell," an inmate said as he stood in the dayroom by himself. I was happy once I heard that H-wing was on a 23-hour dayroom restriction. That was until they told me they only had an hour left before the restriction came up. Here, this inmate was worrying about a house call while I was worrying about how in the hell I was going to get this damn bomb off of me.

I was walking around with a felony sticking to my leg. "Once I do my security check, I'll drop out, it's almost time for chow anyways," I said as I locked the closet back. Tucking the keys in my pocket, I announced myself again. "One row crawling, security check! The big bad wolf!" I screamed as I adjusted the pack.

Hotboy

"Who is that?" I said to myself. I stopped unpacking my property as I tried to make out the person's voice. Scratch had moved faster than I thought. After I paid him, an hour later, the buggy—which we called the black hearse—pulled up to my cell. I didn't expect him to get me where he got me though. Not only did he get me back on H-wing, but he got me a bottom bunk on three row, in the very last cell. That was like being in the sky box with Robert Kraft, sitting next to Tom Brady's wife.

"Two row, the big bad wolf is coming!" the voice screamed again. "Three row, I'm about to blow your house down," the voice said, getting closer. When I saw who it was, I felt like I could shoot a basketball pure net from half court, and pick a four-leaf clover with my eyes closed.

I was just stressing my head off about how I was going to get the bomb from Kiles, and he walked right up to my door. Walking up to my cell, he looked at me, and was about to walk away until he recognized it was me. "What the fuck, how'd you?—" he said.

I used the situation to my advantage. "Don't worry about that. Did you bring the shit?" I asked.

He nodded. "It's right here," he said as he tried to unzip his pants.

"Ayyee, you tripping. Chill out, my nigga. Not right here, look, all you have to do is pretend to do a cell search. When you come in my cell, put it in my locker, and put the lock back on the locker. Here go the key, put it back in the shoe when you finish." I placed the key in a pair of my shoes, making sure he saw where I placed it.

He nodded and said, "I put my info in there too."

"That's a bet, let me get everything situated, and I got you. Go and do a house call so you can get that shit off of you. I know you gotta be nervous as hell walking around with that shit on you." I laughed.

He grinned as he walked off, then he turned back again. "Just so you know, there is some weed in there too, it's not yours. Make sure you read the letter inside, and get the weed to who it belongs to." After telling me about the letter and the weed, he walked off.

He walked away so fast that I almost thought he said he had brought some weed for someone else.

As the doors rolled for the house call, I walked to C-lo's cell to see if he was still in there.

"Hotboy, is that you?" Eastwood said as he noticed me.

Looking over the rail, I said, "What's good?"

"Bitch, when did you get back? I thought you were still fighting that case," he said as I walked down the stairs. We embraced and shook up. It had been a few months since the last time we saw each other. He had gained at least fifty pounds since then.

"Damn, nigga, what you been eating?" I said.

"Shid, everything, cheese cakes, tacos, you name it," he said, laughing.

"Where is everybody at? I didn't see C-lo in his cell. When I pulled up, everybody was racked up, what happened?"

"We just came off of a 23-hour lockdown. One of them niggas got caught smoking on the run. Instead of locking him up, they put us on a 23, hoping we would beat the fool up. You know how they do it, try to make us do the dirty work. C-lo on medium custody now. That nigga was the first person in history to piss dirty for hooch."

To say I was astonished was an understatement. "Damn, where everybody else at that was here a few months ago? This bitch then flipped."

"Everybody gone," Eastwood said.

"Have you heard from Lakewood?" I asked.

Eastwood laughed. "Yeah, I heard from that nigga. He said he was staying with his baby mama. They ended up getting into it, so he moved in with his mother."

"Okay, um, when you see C-lo, let him know I got some business that I need to line up." I said. "Bet, aye, who my celly is? He wasn't in the cell when I pulled up."

"You in which cell?"

"Three, thirty-four."

"Oh, you and Li'l Chris cellies."

I tried to think about who he was talking about. "Li'l Chris, who is that?"

"My nigga, you know who Li'l Chris is. Badass Li'l Chris that used to be on P-wing."

When he said P-wing, I remembered the guy in question from being the youngster that was always fighting. "Li'l Chris, the one from Houston," I said.

"Yeah, he from Southbank, I think."

Li'l Chris was bad as hell. Quick-tempered, with a lot of heart. He reminded me of myself when I first got in the system. I was quick-tempered, and always ready to fight. I was quick to buck the laws, even fight them when given the opportunity.

That was until I touched my first pack straight out of a bitch pussy. It was something about the combination of two factors: Getting money in a place where it's forbidden, and fucking a C.O. that's supposed to be making sure I'm obeying the law. That type of shit always made a young nigga sit down. It was either hustle and stay away from the bullshit, or crash out and be broke.

If Li'l Chris had any hustle about himself, we would end up being good cellys. "That's live then," I said to Eastwood. "Especially for what I'm trying to do. When they get done with this house call, I need to show you something."

"You might as well stay on the run with me. I'm the porter second shift now. I doubt if the lawman will trip."

"Naw he ain't gon' trip, I got him!" I said.

Seth

"Picket boss, can you roll three, thirty-three, and three, thirty-four, so that I can do my cell searches?" I had to make sure I cleared both cells so that I didn't have to worry about anyone seeing me.

"Sure, just a sec," the picket boss said.

I walked up the stairs as I noticed Gianni sitting on the trash can. He looked at me as I walked to three row. I couldn't believe I was helping him just to get some revenge.

"Three row, cell search!" Gianni yelled. I stood at the cell doors as I waited on the picket boss to roll the doors.

"I need for you to step out and go downstairs until I finish my cell searches," I said to an inmate in three, thirty-three. He looked around as he gave up trying to conceal a stinger that was made for heating up water.

He knew he wasn't supposed to have it, so he tried to hide it. "Leave it. I'm not going to take it, or write you up. Just step out so that I can get this done." He stepped out as the doors rolled. He slowly walked down the stairs in his shower shoes as he peeped over his shoulders. Once I saw that he was out of sight, I ran inside Gianni's cell.

I didn't have a time limit on how long I had to search a cell, but the way I was sweating, it felt like I was racing against the clock. I unzipped my pants and pulled the pack from under my nuts. I thought about washing if off before placing it in his locker, but instantly killed the thought.

I wasn't trying too hard to convince him I was on his side. What I wanted to do was get out of his cell as fast as I could. Reaching inside his shoe, I retrieved a single key to the lock that was on his locker. As I opened the lock, a few soups fell to the floor. Kicking them to the side, I tossed the package behind a bag of chips and locked the locker back. I had to wipe the key off before placing it back in his shoe, which was covered with sweat.

As bad as I just wanted to destroy everything in his cell, I couldn't. I still had ways to go before I could destroy his entire life. Looking around, I tried to find something that I could take with me to make it look like I had really done a cell search. Grabbing an empty chain bag, along with a sheet, I walked out the cell, locking it behind me.

"Three row, back half!" Gianni yelled as I walked down the stairs. I tossed his sheet on the floor along with the chain bag, knowing he would pick it back up.

"You can go back to your cell whenever you're ready," I said to the inmate from three, thirty-three. He walked off and headed to his cell.

I looked at Gianni. "I closed your door."

He walked over with the broom in his hand. "Bet, I'ma go in when they run chow. Did you lock the locker back?"

"My part is done, just do yours," I said as I walked to the closet.

He walked behind me and said, "Look, I'm not new to this, remember you came to me for help. As soon as I touch the pack, rest assured it's gone."

I looked at him. He was cocky, a deadly kind too. I could usually read someone when I first met them, but him, he had so many hidden agendas you couldn't really tell. I only had to play this role for a few more days, and then I could sit back and laugh until my stomach hurts.

"Talking about it ain't going to solve anything. My pockets are still flat, and my tricking bill is sky high."

He looked at me. "You think I'm bullshitting, watch how I turn this bitch upside down," Gianni said with a serious look.

I laughed. He had no idea. What he planned on doing to the unit, I was planning to do the same to his life. I guess we did have more things in common than I thought.

Hotboy

"Damn, bitch, why haven't you finished unpacking your shit yet?" Eastwood asked as he stepped over some soups, as we walked in my cell.

"Coz I had other shit to do at the time."

"Ayyeee! Who is that in my shit?" Li'l Chris said as he walked up to the cell door. He looked from me to Eastwood. "What's this? You my new celly or som'?" Li'l Chris stood at an even six feet. He was a little heavier than me, but his tall frame made him look smaller than what he actually was. The women always considered him a pretty boy because he had deep dimples that showed on both sides. The dimples were the bait, 'cause as soon as they bit, he reeled them in.

"Yeah, I came from L-wing," I said.

Li'l Chris looked at me as he studied my face. "Ai'nt you the nigga that supposedly popped that law and that lame ass nigga that was on G-wing?" he asked.

"Ain't you the nigga that shot up them niggas' spot on South Lawn?" I shot back.

He looked at me, wondering how I knew. "Overstood, I peep game, my bad," he said.

Eastwood laughed "Li'l Chris, you bad as hell."

"You tryna come in?" I asked Li'l Chris as I heard the guard closing the doors.

"Naw, I just came to grab my cup. You know they running chow." Eastwood handed him his cup.

"Yeah, I know, I'ma chill," I said. He walked off as the C.O. stood beside him.

As Li'l Chris was walking down the stairs, I could still hear him talking shit to somebody. "Look out, Reese. You eat that shit, don't you, boy!"

"Y'all staying in?" Kiles asked as he stood in front of my cell. Eastwood tucked his head, trying to hide his face.

"Yeah, we staying in," I said, laughing. Kiles closed the door as he looked at me, then he turned his gaze to the locker. He was as green as they came. I nodded just to get him to walk away. "Scary ass nigga," I teased as Kiles walked away.

Eastwood stood up and said, "My nigga, I don't know that fool like that. He might know where I stay. I don't need no cases, I like my commissary."

He was serious. "Don't worry, after today, we ain't gon' ever have to go to commissary."

"What, we gon' rob the commissary room or what?" he asked.

I tossed him the key from out my shoe. "Grab *that* from out my locker, and I'll show you."

He stepped on the side of the bunk as he unlocked the lock. "Damn, your locker smells like a gym," he said as he moved some commissary around. "What am I supposed to be looking for?" he asked.

I stood on my tiptoes as I tried to see inside the locker. "A bomb," I said.

He looked around some more. "That's why yo' locker smells like that. That bitch needs to wash her pussy." He tossed me the bomb.

Catching it with my shirt, I tossed it on the desk. "That ain't pussy you smell, that's dick butter." I laughed.

His face was priceless as the shock registered across his face, "My nigga, you bullshitting. Dog, that's foul, why you ain't tell me?"

I couldn't stop laughing. "My nigga, ain't nobody tell you to stick yo' nose in the damn locker. You might as well bust this bitch open, you already had the bitch in yo' hand." I continued to laugh. Grabbing a loose razor, he sliced it open down the middle slowly. "Be careful, it's a lot of different shit in there. I don't want them to get mixed up." I was looking over his shoulder.

The bomb was so big I couldn't figure out how in the hell Kiles made it through with it.

"Damn, who brought this?" Eastwood asked as he opened the pack, revealing a Ziploc bag full of ice, weed, and tobacco.

"That fool there," I said, amazed.

"Who? That nigga that's working the wing?"

I smiled. "Yeah, that fool a gangsta."

"My nigga, how you pull that shit off? He look like a straight cop."

Looking at all the dope, I said, "Them be the ones. The ones that look like they gon' smoke a nigga. They be low-key looking for a gangsta to get some money with." Eastwood took the three different Ziploc bags out of the wrapper. He placed the tape inside a piece of paper, throwing it over the run.

"You might want to wash yo' hands," I said, laughing.

"Keep on, bitch, that shit better not leave this cell either," he said as he tossed some water in my direction.

"I ain't gon' let it leave this room. But I am gon' tell my celly as soon as he comes in." I laughed.

"So check it, how you want to play this? How much do you

owe the fool for bringing this shit?" Eastwood asked, getting down to business.

I looked at the dope. As I picked the ice up, a kite fell to the floor. I picked it up and unfolded it. *The weed goes to a guy name Los. He is supposed to have some diamonds in his mouth. It came from his cousin Dub, can you make sure—*" I read out loud.

"What's that?" Eastwood asked.

I shook my head. "It was with the pack. The fool was trying to tell me about the shit earlier, but I couldn't understand what he was saying."

"So the nigga been dropping off?"

"I don't know, I'm not really sure. Whoever that nigga Los is, he definitely jacked.

I was getting upset. "I'm not about to look around for another nigga and say, aye, this came from my mule. The fuck I look like!"

"Los? Wait, let me see that. Oh, it's Los with the diamonds, that's the homie Los. The one with the whip. Ain't no jacking the homie, fam. That nigga from H-town, you know how them niggas be rocking together, plus he a Muslim. He also a homie, they will politic the shit outta you."

I didn't know who the hell Eastwood was referring to. The only Los I knew was a Hispanic, but he didn't have any diamonds, and he wasn't a homie. "Do I know him?" I asked.

Eastwood leaned his head back as he tried to remember. "I don't think so. The nigga just really came to the unit not too long ago. He came from Bill Clemons. He cool though. Laid back, he ain't like most young niggas that come from Bill Clemons. You know them young niggas don't be tryna hear shit. All they comprehend is fighting, and gang banging."

He was right too. Bill Clemons was a young nigga unit. There really wasn't too many old convicts over there that could pass some game along. So if they didn't have any game before they went in, they damn sure wouldn't get any while they were there. "So you say the nigga who shit this is, is the same nigga with the phone?" I asked Eastwood.

"Yeah, Los, he a live li'l nigga."

"Bet, set it up. Tell him I got something for him. Tell him we need to talk business ASAP. Tell him to pull up on me next house call."

Eastwood nodded as he looked at all the ice and tobacco. "Bitch, you ain't gon' ever stop, is you?" He laughed.

"Why stop? So I can go home broke, just to start hustling again so they can catch me again, and throw me back in here? I might as well hustle now, stack it up, so when I go home, I can chill. I'm already in prison, what more can they do to me? Nothing! We gotta get it while the getting's good!"

Chapter 15

Newton

"Oh God, I didn't think it'll be this hard!" I cursed as two male nurses held me up.

In the course of two days, I had took four steps total. To make matters worse, they had me strapped by my shoulders with a pair of resistance bands. They were made to have resistance so that it would be harder to move. The doctor said that using the resistance bands builds muscles. I'm sure that my legs will be stronger than before, seeing how hard I'm working.

"Are you tired yet, sweetie?" Ms. Debra said. "We can take a break if you want to. Or we can start again tomorrow if you like." Ms. Debra was so sweet. Even though it was her job to care for me, she went out her way to do things for me when she didn't have to. She bought Jacob toys to play with while he was here visiting. She would constantly encourage me to keep pushing myself, even when I felt like giving up.

My chest heaved as I tried to catch my breath. I was exhausted, but determined. "No, I'm fine, let's go one more time."

Ms. Debra smiled. She could see that I was exhausted. I was sweating like I was in a sauna. I was determined to walk again, there was no giving up. "Y'all heard her, let's do it one more time," she said as the two male nurses looked at me, concerned. I guess they could see how tired I was, too.

Holding the rails, I raised myself with my shoulders, letting my feet dangle. As they reattached the resistance bands, I tried my best to catch my breath.

"All set," a nurse said. Taking a deep breath, I let my feet touch the ground, just to my tiptoes. As I felt my toes touch the ground, I closed my eyes. I said a silent prayer while I let my right leg touch the ground fully. As my left leg touched the ground, my entire body began to shake. "Come on, God, be my strength," I whispered. Easing my foot forward a little, I shut my eyes tight.

"Come on, Gabby! Relax your mind, think of a happy place,"

Ms. Debra said.

I closed my eyes as she said that. It was iike something took over my body. I imagined Gianni, I don't know why, but the picture was clear as day.

He was standing far off with his back to me as he cradled something in his hands. "Kingsley—Gianni," I said.

He looked back at me with tears in his eyes, and they started to pour down his face. I took a step closer, closing some distance between us. I could see his face clearer now, but I couldn't see what he had in his hands.

"Why, Gabby, why did you leave me?" he asked.

I stepped closer. "I had to, we couldn't be together," I said. He looked down in his arms as he rocked back and forth. Stepping closer, I could see the baby's feet, but the face was still hidden.

He wiped his tears away! "You took everything that I loved. Our baby, our memories! For what? For this!" he said as blood spewed down the baby's leg.

I took two steps closer as I looked over his shoulders, then I saw Jacob bleeding from his neck. "Noooo! What did you do?" I yelled.

"I did to you what you did to me—I broke your heart, and ripped it out," he said, tossing Jacob's body on the floor. I collapsed on the floor and I crawled over to the body. Rolling the body over, I jumped as Jacob's face was replaced with mine.

"Ms. Newton, are you okay?" one of the nurses asked as they helped me on to the wheelchair. I looked around the room. There was no Gianni, or Jacob. It was only me, the two male nurses, and Ms. Debra.

"You okay, sweetie?" Ms. Debra asked. I nodded. "You gave me quite a scare. Are you sure you're okay?" she asked again.

"Yes, I'm fine, I swear." I lied.

Her face didn't look convinced, but she didn't dig deeper. "Before you passed out, you did awesome. You took six big steps. You didn't even have to hold the rail. I don't know who Gianni is, but he sure motivated you." Ms. Debra smiled.

A tear escaped my eye. What I pictured wasn't close to a happy place. It was Gianni destroying everything that made me happy.

Hotboy

"You Hotboy?" asked a tall inmate with diamond encrusted teeth.

"Come in, the door open," I said as I sat on my bunk, leaving him the choice of sitting on the toilet or the stool.

"Eastwood said you had something for me," he said, getting right down to business.

"Yeah, but first I need to ask you something."

"Wassup?"

"You got a cousin out there that be messing with some live work?"

He looked at me, wondering where I got my information from.

"What?" he said, caught off guard.

"Your cousin, I got a package from him. At least he claims some nigga by the name Los is his cousin. Now before I give it to you, I want to make sure I'm giving it to the right person."

He relaxed a little. "Yeah, I got a cousin that be messing around, but I don't know how you ended up with something from him for me."

"Look, homie, that's beside the point. I'm just trying to fulfill my end of the deal. Now if I got the wrong person, I'll smoke this shit myself." I pulled out the bag of weed. "I'll tell the nigga I couldn't find who he was talking about." Once I said that, his eyes lit up. His diamonds sparkled as he smiled at the sight of the dozier,

"That shit had to come from Dub, he the only one with them big ass buds," he said.

That was all I needed to hear as I tossed the sack into his lap.

"I appreciate you, homie. Damn, that nigga know everybody. How y'all know each other?"

"We don't, he knows my mule," I said.

Los looked at me, then back to the weed. "Oh yeah, you live

like that?"

"Naw, homie, *we* live like that," I said, including him.

He looked at me and laughed. "You speak French or something?"

"I heard you a homie, I also heard that you know how to move," I said.

He nodded. "You know you can't always believe everything you hear, I only show niggas what they need to see. They don't really know me like they think they do."

"Trust, I know the real. I see all them diamonds in yo' mouth. How long you been locked up?"

"Almost seven years," he said.

"So you had them diamonds when you were a teenager. The normal young nigga would've spent his money on some Jordans or some bullshit. You, you were thinking bigger than the normal young nigga. That's why I want to do business with you."

He stared at me. "Business? What kind?"

"Yo' cousin got the dope, I got the mule. You get yo' cousin to fuck with us on a regular, I'll pay for the drop, we gap everything down the middle." I hoped he would accept my proposition.

"You know, Hotboy, I heard about you when I first pulled up. They told me you was a real nigga. That you're about that life, that you will pop that steel if you have to. I want to let you know something. With all due respect, I don't listen to all them war stories niggas be telling. All that ra-ra shit don't faze me. I can look at you and tell you're about yo' money. I could also see that if I was green, you'll try to get over on me, I see you got some game. All is fair in love and war, I couldn't be mad. Because surely, it'll be vice versa. I'm not like most young niggas. I don't jump when a big homie say jump. I don't stick my fork on another nigga plate because mine is empty, and his is full. I get mine on my own, by any means."

I sat back and listened to what he had to say. So far, he was just what I was looking for to help me get this money. "Like you said, you can't listen to what everybody tells you. Yeah, I'm about getting to some money. Ain't that every nigga agenda? At least I hope so. Yeah, I'm about that action, if need be. I don't speak on what I did in the past. That shit is long gone. What I want to talk about is money."

He smirked. "But what makes you think that I need you to get some money. What makes you think that I need you to get some dope in? Who says I couldn't get my cousin to get your mule—to bring my shit! As you can see, he can make it happen."

He was right, he could easily push me out the way. I would be a damn fool to let him know that though. "Yeah, maybe you can, maybe you can't. I doubt you'll do it though."

He raised his eyebrows. "Why you say that?"

"Because you're a real nigga, and real niggas do real shit. You ain't no fuck nigga."

He smiled, showing all his diamonds. "Enough said, so what you need me to do?"

I relaxed a little. I guess he wasn't like most young niggas. Any other nigga would've pushed me out the way. If he wanted to, he could've took my mule too. "I need for you to hit yo' cousin up. We need some tune, bad. Ain't no K2 on the whole farm. Whatever he can wrap up, we need it, I want this bitch to be a one-stop shop."

"Overstood, I gotcha. I'ma get on it right now." He stood up.

"Oh, Los, one more thing," I said, stopping him in his tracks. "I need to touch the world; I heard you was the man to talk to."

He looked at me and shook his head. "I ain't even gon' ask how you know. Give me a minute, and I'll shoot it to you." As he walked out, I rubbed my hands together. I had less than sixty days to see parole. Until then, I was gon' chase that sack!

***

"Aye, is this Lakewood," I whispered into the phone.

"Yeah, who's this?" Lakewood asked.

Damn, my li'l homie didn't even remember my voice. "It's me, bitch, Hotboy!"

"Wassup, nigga! You out or what?"

I looked over my shoulder to make sure Li'l Chris was still watching out. I damn sure didn't want to get caught up with a phone right before I saw parole. For some reason, Los sent Li'l Chris in the cell with me. I guess the trust wasn't there yet.

I whispered into the phone, "Naw, I'm still locked up. I just got back to Beto."

I looked over my shoulder again as I leaned into the phone. "I took care of that bitch that fucked my nigga Gangsta over, and I popped that other fool too."

"Yeah, I heard. I also heard about Uncle Marvin too, he a real nigga for that."

"Hell yeah, he came through in the clutch," I said, thinking about what he did for me.

"Don't he always!" Lakewood said.

"Damn, bitch, I miss y'all niggas. This bitch then flipped. Ain't nobody here no more. It's only me and Eastwood now. Everybody else got shipped, or went home."

The phone went silent. "Which one are you trying to do?" Lakewood asked.

"What you mean?"

"You tryna get shipped, or come home?" he asked.

"What you mean, bitch? I'm tryna come home!"

He sighed and said, "At what cost?"

"My nigga, I'm not on that type of shit no more. I'm just tryna stack, that's it. I ain't got no choice, I ain't tryna come home broke."

"I feel you on that. It's hard out here, for real. Shid, I'm staying with my T-Jones until I can find a job." T-Jones was his mother.

"I already heard, what, you need some money?" I offered.

"My nigga, I can't take yo' money. I should be sending you money."

"I tell you what, I'll pay you to do something for me. I need a favor anyway."

"Like what?" he said.

"I need you to make a CashApp, so that I can send all my money there. You the only one that I can trust right now."

"That ain't hard, I just gotta get a bank card. I can do that first thing in the morning. I'll check with my tajones, she might have one."

"Bet, oh before I forget, I need you to do something else too."

"Name it."

"Write this address down. You ready?"

"Hold up, let me get a pen," he said, and the phone went silent. "Yeah, I'm back. What's the address?"

"3431 Chimey Lodge, Rusk, Texas. The nigga name is Seth Kiles. He's a C.O., I need you to see wassup with the fool." I looked over my shoulder.

"Who is the fool?" Lakewood asked. Li'l Chris peeped over his shoulder at me.

"Just some fool that thinks he can't be touched." I lied. I couldn't say what I really wanted to say. Even though Li'l Chris was cool, I didn't know him like that just yet.

"How'd you get his address?" Lakewood asked, laughing. I had paid Scratch to sneak into the captain's office when no one was around. In the captain's log is every C.O.'s number and address, for emergency purposes. "I had to sell my soul to get it, and that's all you need to know," I said, looking back at Li'l Chris. Li'l Chris laughed as he looked to make sure no one was coming.

"So what you want me to do? Watch him or something?" Lakewood asked.

"Naw, just scope his spot out, see who he be hanging out with. For some reason, I think McFee sent the nigga my way to set me up, I'm not sure yet. Make sure he on the up and up."

"Anything else, big bro?"

"Matter of fact, yeah!"

"Name it, and it's done." Lakewood says. "Find that bitch—Newton!"

Seth

"Go get in the bath while I get dinner ready."

Jacob tossed his jacket on the couch as he ran to his room. "Why couldn't we just eat McDonald's, dad?" he yelled from his room.

"Because we ate McDonald's for the last three days. It's about time you ate some real food."

"You're the dad," he said sarcastically. He was just like me when I was younger. Too smart for his own good. Just as I was about to start dinner, the doorbell rang at the same time as my phone did.

"Daddy, the doooorrrr!" Jacob yelled.

"I know, smart guy, I'm on it!" Grabbing my phone, my CashApp notification popped up, saying that I had just received three hundred dollars from $KingShit$. Gianni moved faster than I thought. "Dammit, I'm coming!" I yelled as the doorbell rang constantly. "What the fuck!" I said after opening the door.

The sight brought back so many memories, as well as regrets.

"Seth," she said, smiling.

"Kelly, what are you doing here? How do you know where I stay?"

"You're not even going to ask me how I'm doing, or even invite me in?" she said.

I peeped over my shoulder to make sure Jacob wasn't around. "What are you doing here?"

"I went by Dub's spot. I saw your old car in his driveway. I broke into it and found a piece of mail with this address on it. I wanted to see you, see Jacob." She sounded sincere.

"Kelly, you shouldn't be here. Jacob shouldn't see you."

"I'm clean, Seth, I swear. I've been clean for almost two months now."

I looked her over. She didn't look high, and her clothes looked clean. She didn't have the same look from when we first met, but neither did I. She was still sexy as hell, standing at five feet four. She kept herself up to par as her jeans hugged her hips like a newborn does a nipple. Her dirty blonde hair flowed down to her ass. I could see why Dub said that she still looked good.

"If you're clean, then why were you at Dubs?" I asked.

"I was looking for you. I asked him if he knew where you were. He said the last time he saw you, you came by and traded your car in."

For some reason, I believed her. I don't know why, but I did. Maybe because I needed someone to believe in me when I said I was clean.

"Daddy, who's at the door?" Jacob asked, walking up to the door. He peeped around my legs and smiled. "Hi, I'm Jacob." That was the first time he actually spoke to someone without being shy. It was like deep down, he knew she was his mother.

I looked at Kelly as she clasped her hands around her mouth. "Hi, I'm Kelly. It's nice to meet you." She began to cry.

Jacob looked up at me. "Why is she crying, daddy? Did I do something wrong?"

I shielded him behind me. "Kelly, it's time for you to go," I said.

"Seth, please! Just let me spend a little time with him. Give me thirty minutes, that's all I ask."

"Why? So you can abandon him again, no! It's time for you to go."

She wiped her face. "Seth, I never got the chance to tell you this, but I am sorry. That dope, it took me fast. You should know how it does people."

"Kelly, leave—please. I don't want to have to call the police." She had warrants for her arrest, so I knew that's all it took.

"Don't, okay, I'll leave." She tried to take another look at Jacob. "He looks just like us," she said before walking away. I watched her as she walked away, to make sure she didn't double back. I closed the door and rested my back against it. After all these years, she still had a hold on me.

"Jacob, get your ass in the damn tub," I said as he stood in front of me.

"Ohhhh, you cursed. That's one dollar for my jar," he said, running to grab his jar. I shook my head at him. Sometimes I thought he did stuff just to make me curse so that I would have to put money in his curse jar.

My phone chimed as I was walking by it. It was a text from a random number. The text read: *This is King. Go by Dubs and* *grab that issue. Check your CashApp too. You should have close to $400 by now. Be careful too."*

"How in the hell do he know my number! And how the fuck do he know Dub?" I shouted at the top of my voice.

Jacob ran into the room with his jar and a big smile. "Ohhhh, daddy, you're on fire tonight. That's two more dollars."

Hotboy

"Bitch, you stupid!" Los said to Li'l Chris as he had us all laughing.

Li'l Chris stood on the dayroom bench as he addressed the entire dayroom. "Dayroom, dayroom! Look, I got a proposition for y'all. I got a fat-ass line of ice for whoever let me slap them ten times in the face. Naw, look, five times. And I won't even draw all the way back. Look, I'ma do it like this." He imitated a slow slap.

The dayroom busted up laughing. "I tell y'all what," Li'l Chris went on, still standing on the bench, "just give me one, Eastwood get a slap, Hotboy get a slap, and Los get a slap."

"Hey! Please sit down! The benches are made for sitting, not standing," a C.O. who was working on the wing said.

Li'l Chris lay into the C.O. right away. "Fuck you! That's why yo' booty hole suck dick! Ya mama booty hole suck dick, ya daddy booty hole suck dick, ya whole family booty hole suck dick, bitch!"

We all fell to the floor, laughing. He was bad as hell, and funny as hell too. "Bitch, you retarded as hell, for real," Los said, laughing.

Li'l Chris looked out the window as a group of C.O.'s were changing shifts. Then he said, "Look at Li'l Chucky. Big head ass, watermelon head ass, with them li'l ass boocheeniees!" This time he made tears come out of my eyes as we all laughed at him.

"My nigga, what the fuck is a boocheeniee?" I asked.

"Booty and cheeks. That's my own little recipe. I call 'em boocheeniees!"

We couldn't control our laughter.

"There go that li'l bitch. What's her name?" Eastwood asked, pointing out the window. I looked out the window as she was passing by. I hadn't seen her since that day on L-wing when she was talking to Sanderfield.

I stood up to get a closer look. "What's her name?"

"*Stupid dumb bitch*, that's her name!" Li'l Chris said.

I laughed. "Naw, for real, what's her name?"

"That's that bitch Ms. Grain," Los said. "She be policing though. Little bitch always yelling and screaming and shit."

As she walked by, we locked eyes. "I bet that little bitch pussy good as hell," I said as I sat back down.

"Good—and angry," Li'l Chris added.

Los threw a water bottle at him. "Bitch, shut up!" he said, laughing.

An inmate walked up to the window and started tapping in with his knuckles. He looked over at Eastwood, trying to flag him down.

"Eastwood, phone call!" I yelled. Eastwood walked over to the window, placing his ear to the glass so that he could hear through the thick glass window.

"Yeah, how much? Okay, I gotcha," Eastwood said. He looked at me without saying a word. I knew it was a money call. I didn't have to move to make money. I had blessed each homie with a sack to do whatever they wanted to do with it. Some of them thought small and sold theirs for commissary. Eastwood, on the other hand, flipped his, and hadn't stopped since. My celly even scored with me, he made most of his money back off of it, but he used some for the entertainment.

As for Los, he silently made a killing. He had stockpiled his dope on another inmate that nobody knew about, not even me. All he did was collect, and dish out.

Los said, as he sat beside me, "My people say that's a go. He said yo' boy picked that up earlier, he say it's a whole thang, and some tabs too."

I nodded and replied. "Bet! We should get it in a little bit then. They already changing shifts. Everything good with you?"

He understood what I meant. "Yeah, my *ese* handling business as usual. He waiting on me to bring that tune by. When that shit lands, a nigga pockets gon' swell."

"Fa sho, it'll be here tonight. We'll wait until third shift if you wanna bust it down tonight. It don't matter, however you wanna do it."

"One hunnit, just keep me posted when it gets here. Let me go grab this phone though, I gotta call baby back." With that, Los excused himself.

Li'l Chris said to me: "Damn, my nigga Hotboy then spoke the li'l bitch up on the wing. Let me find out you want that ho booty hole to suck yo dick."

I looked back to see what he was talking about, as Ms. Grain walked on the wing. I walked over to Eastwood. "Do she know who you are?" I asked him.

"Naw, why?"

"Because, I'm about to pretend to be the porter. The li'l bitch might be game."

"Shoot yo' shot. I'm chilling. I gotta watch this window anyway. Niggas been pulling up like a pit stop."

"Bet, let me see if she let me out," I said, walking off. As I walked to the dayroom bars, I could feel a hundred eyes on me. Niggas was nosey when it came to a female. You couldn't pay a nigga to talk to one, but they damn sure didn't want to see you talk to one either.

"Boss lady," I said, making her turn around. She placed her things into the closet before walking over.

"Yes?" she said.

"You going to let me out?" I asked.

"And why would I do that?"

"Because, I'm your porter," I said.

"Sure you are," she said, not believing me.

Pulling my ID out my pocket, I stretched my hand out to her. "Check the roster if you don't believe me." Normally, an inmate wouldn't produce his ID when he knew he was lying, so I took it upon myself to give it to her.

She took it. "I believe you," she said, unlocking the door. I looked over at Eastwood as he laughed. He had read my mind. I was back with the shit.

"So tell me something, shorty, what—" I managed to say before she cut me off.

"Don't call me that," she said.

"Okay, well, tell me this. Why do people say that you're mean?" I had finally got her to myself. The whole night she had dodged me as she walked the runs, pretending to do security checks, so that she wouldn't be stuck talking to me. After she did her house call, I saw her sneak a peek at the roster to see if I was really a porter. Seeing that she didn't say anything, I knew she was game.

"People can say, and think, whatever they want about me. I'm here to get paid, and go home."

"Then what?"

"What do you mean, then what?" she asked.

"What do you do when you go home?" I asked as she stared at me.

"Wasn't you just on L-wing?" she asked.

I smiled. "So you remember me."

"You were that boy that was out there with Sanderfield. Yeah, that was you."

"It wasn't what you're thinking."

"Okay, if it wasn't what I was thinking, then tell me what I was thinking," she said.

I grabbed the broom and rushed off as I pretended to be sweeping. I knew it seemed to her as though I looked retarded as hell. But at the moment, I was looking out for my own good.

"Lieutenant McFee on the block, y'all get right!" I yelled over the run. I peeped over my shoulder to see if he was still there as he walked towards his office. "Everything is everything, he gone!" I yelled, putting everyone at ease. Mc- Fee was like a Robocop who everyone feared.

"Boy, I was, like, what the hell—I thought you were retarded until I saw McFee walk by," Ms. Grain said as I walked back up.

"I can't let him see us like this. I had to walk off to protect the both of us. That nigga is top flight security of the world Craig." I was imitating Mike Epps, and she laughed at how I sounded just like him.

"How'd you see him coming?" she asked.

"You see that C.O. that's standing right there. He was sitting down at first. When he saw McFee, he jumped up. That's what made me look."

She looked impressed. "That's good, you watch your surroundings. I like that." She blushed.

I checked my watch to see if today was Sunday because this shit was too easy. "Tell me about you. Look, I didn't even call you shorty that time."

She smiled. "No, you didn't. I can't really say much. I'm not supposed to tell y'all my personal life."

"You can trust me."

"Yeah, like I can trust you to really tell the truth. You said that you were my porter. You're not even on the roster."

"I didn't lie, I never said I was on the roster. I also didn't say I was the porter. What I said was that I was *your* porter. Therefore, I didn't lie because I am here to service you."

She shook her head as she bit her bottom lip. "They told us about inmates like you."

"Couldn't have, there is no other inmate like me. I'm the last of a dying breed."

She smiled as she looked past me. As I turned to see what she was looking at, there was an inmate posted up on the bars, eavesdropping. "Aye, you need something?" I asked him.

"No, just bored is all," he said.

"Do me a favor, and take yo' bored as somewhere else." He just stared at me like I didn't say anything.

"Look out, Li'l Chris!" I yelled. Li'l Chris stood up to see who was calling him. As he looked my way, I flagged him down.

"What's up?" he asked. I leaned in close to him so that no one could hear what I was about to say. As I whispered in his ear, he nodded. "I gotcha," he said. He wrapped his arm around the nosey inmate. As he walked off, whispering in his ear, I walked away from the bars. He leaned in his ear closer as he continued to whisper. He stopped whispering, then he screamed in the inmate's ear: "Go sit yo' bitch as down!"

The inmate wiggled his finger in his ear as he rushed to find a seat. Li'l Chris threw me the thumbs up and walked away.

"What did you tell that boy?" Ms. Grain asked.

"I didn't tell him nothing."

She shook her head. "What am I going to do with you?"

I looked dead in her eyes. "You could let me explore your mind the way no other man has ever done. You could let me step inside your heart where the spot needs to be filled. Truthfully, I don't want anything from you financially, or physically. But spiritually, and emotionally, I want your smile to help brighten my dark days. Because until I saw your smile for the first time, I didn't have anything to smile about."

She looked at me and smiled, as she was at a loss for words. She didn't know how to take what I had just said. When Los had said that she was a cop, that was all I needed to hear. I turned good girls into bad girls for a living.

"You know that I can write you up. That's an attempt to establish a relationship."

"I know you could, but you will never get a chance to find another real nigga like me again. Why risk the chance of me not making parole when you know you deserve a good man like me at home with you. Every night I hold you tight as we sleep, with my arms around you." She blushed and put her head down. I knew I had her then!

Seth

"Anything else, Mr. Kiles?" an inmate asked as he placed some oatmeal cookies in a brown paper sack. I figured I'll grab something from the O.D.R, so that I could have access to put the drop in to send to Gianni. I had already known my task.

As I walked past H-wing, I looked into the dayroom to see if I could see him. I didn't want to make it look so obvious, so I kept walking. As I walked to H-wing's door, I noticed him posted up with a female C.O. as he held the broom in his hand.

"Hey, porter, do you have any gloves on you that you can spare?" I asked to throw the C.O. off.

"What's up?" he said, walking to the gate. "I got that for you. It's a lot too." He nodded as he looked over his shoulder. The C.O. that he was talking to walked off. "I shot another five hundred dollars to you. That way, you can re-up on your tricks." He laughed.

"I got it. But what about the one that's on me now? How are you going to get it? I'm working on A-wing."

He looked around as he tried to figure out a plan. "I got some-body that will pull up. You just be ready."

"It's going to be in this johnny sack," I said. He nodded before walking off. He killed me, always trying to be so discreet. Here I was panicking with a big ass bomb under my nuts, and he was over here chilling. Probably flirting with another man's wife.

"Hey, Kiles, are you my relief?" a female C.O. asked.

I shook my head at her and said, "No, I'm sorry. I'm headed to A-wing."

"I'ma pray for you," she teased. A-wing was known as a grown-up T.Y.C. There was nothing but youngsters on that wing. All they wanted to do was fight, and smoke. As I walked on the wing, there was at least ten inmates walking the run. When they saw me, they all scattered.

"Shift change, hard head," the porter yelled.

Someone yelled over the run: "Tell him to take his bitch ass somewhere else. We ain't had a female C.O. work the wing in over a week." They were complaining about not having a woman working the wing. They were running around like animals, and they wondered why they didn't have a female working the wing. Surely, a woman couldn't control them by herself.

"Wassup, bossman, you good?" a short dark-skinned inmate asked. My face was covered with sweat. I was exhausted because I hadn't been able to sleep. Ever since I saw Kelly, my mind had been all over the place.

"Are you the porter?" I asked. He looked around.

"I can be."

"Good, then get these assholes off my run before I start shaking houses down," I said as I placed my things inside the closet. He walked off as he took his state shirt off. He then bellowed orders to the rest of the inmates:

"Aye, man, y'all need to either get in your cells, or come to the dayroom. The law man says if he can't get y'all off the run, then he gon' start shaking niggas houses down. If y'all know, y'all can't stand up under that thunder when a nigga calls you out, then take yo ass in the cell, or the dayroom." He looked at me. "Open the dayroom so they can go in," he said as a few inmates walked down the stairs.

"What about the rest of them? I know I saw more than these three."

"Trust me," he said, "you ain't gon' have to worry about seeing them anymore. If they show their face, you'll hear about it."

Locking the door back, I glanced down the run to see if anyone else was coming. "Fuck!" I said as I leaned against the closet wall.

The inmate walked over. "You good? You need some water or something?"

I looked at my food. I had left my water in the car. Being nervous about that big ass bomb, I must've forgot. "Sure, what's your name, by the way?" I asked.

"Call me Dame," he said, walking off. I stepped out the closet to see how far down the run he was going to get the water. As he walked up the stairs, I stepped inside the closet, closing the door behind me, to give myself some cover. I fumbled with my zipper as I rushed to get the pack out before he came back with the water.

Just as I got it out, the door swung open. "I thought as much," he said as he noticed the bomb in my hand. I was caught red-handed; there was no playing it off. Tossing the bottle of water on the shelf, he looked over his shoulders to make sure no one else could see. "You good, I don't see shit," he said, closing the door back.

I stood in the tight space, wondering what I had got myself into. Tossing the pack inside the johnny sack with the cookies, I threw it on the top shelf, all the way in the back. As I walked out the closet, I felt like everyone was watching me.

When I noticed Dame, he was coming out of the mop closet with a wet floor sign. "Wassup?" he said.

"I know you saw what I had. I would look out for you, but it's not mine."

He laughed. "I know it ain't yours."

"Maybe I could bring you something, maybe a pack of cigarettes. That's as long as you can keep this between us."

"My nigga, you good. I'ma gangsta. I ain't gon' say shit." In a casual tone of voice, he asked me: "By the way, who shit is it?"

I stayed quiet. I didn't know if I should tell him or not. Then it all came to me. Instead of having to wait for my plan to fall through, I could just skip to plan B. "He goes by Hotboy," I said, giving him up.

"Hotboy, you talking about the nigga that just got back on the unit. The nigga that supposed to have popped the law?" I nodded.

"You fucking with that snitch ass nigga. That nigga told on Marvin. Got my nigga another L for that shit." He was upset.

I smirked. The little bastard was playing right into my hands. Determined to add fuel to the flames, I said: "I didn't know that. I was told that someone took the rap for him."

"Come on, for real. A nigga ain't about to take a rap for a double homicide in the penitentiary. That nigga rolled on Marvin. Now he back to do it to another nigga. I wouldn't be surprised if he ain't setting you up. That nigga a snake."

My gaze moved towards the closet, then back to him. "You think he snitched so that he wouldn't mess up his chances of making parole."

"Fuck that nigga. I got fifty years, parole can eat my dick. I should take that nigga shit! He flared his nostrils, his eyes flashing with anger.

"Why take it, when I could just give it to you, instead!" I said, catching him off guard.

"Huh?"

"Look, you say that he's a snitch. He might be trying to set me up for all I know."

"So what?" Dame asked.

"Look, if you want, I can give you what I brought for him. Plus, I'll bring you another one just like it. All you have to do is take care of him. Get him out the way. That way, my name will be clear, then we could take care of business together." I observed his body language intently as he took it all in. I opened the closet to grab the bag. "You do understand what I'm talking about when I say get him out the way?"

"Come on, my nigga, I ain't dumb," he said, snatching the sack.

I laughed in my head. *Sure you're not dumb at all!*

Hotboy

"What did he say?" I asked Scratch as he came back from A-wing. I sent him down there to grab the pack from Kiles. He finally came back ten minutes later, empty-handed. "He said he had to flush it. He said that McFee walked on the wing. He said that he thought McFee knew what was up."

I grilled Scratch. It took everything in me not to punch him through the bars. Even though he didn't have anything to do with it, I still wanted to hit somebody.

"Here he comes now, he must've just got his relief," Scratch said, walking off.

"Aye, come here!" I raised my voice, not caring who heard. Kiles walked over slowly, looking both ways before stepping to the gate. "What happened?" I asked him.

"I had to flush it, bro, I had to. McFee came over. I thought he was going to make me strip out. You know how he is." He gave the explanation with a scared look on his face. If he wasn't in the main hallway, I would've knocked him the fuck out. He obviously took me for a fool.

"My nigga, how did you flush it? If you fumbled the pack, just say that, stop lying! I hate when a motherfucker just dry lie!" I yelled in his face.

He raised his hand to his heart. "I swear!"

I knew he was lying, I could see it all over his face.

"I tell you what. You owe, I'm one up on you now. Hook up with Dub again. This time I'm not paying you shit!" He just stared at me. "Get the fuck outta my face," I said, forcing him to walk off. I could've sworn I saw him smile when he walked away.

"Wassup, bitch?" Los asked as he walked up behind me. I shook my head. "Bitch ass lawman talking about he flushed the pack."

"You think he lying?"

I sighed. "I don't know. The way he's describing it, I could tell he's lying about that. I told him though, the next pack, he ain't getting shit."

Los put his arm around me. "My nigga, always remember, don't panic. We making money, free bands, in the penitentiary. Look at that over there. You see that?" He pointed to a Hispanic C.O. that was working the wing. "That's for us, a little celebration for tonight," Los said, his breath smelling like straight weed.

I looked at the C.O. as she sat on the cooler. From the side, she looked decent. Long silky hair, chubby cheeks. She looked like she was sitting on something fat back there.

I was so fucked about Kiles fumbling the pack, I wasn't really in the mood.

Los whispered on my ear. "See that right there? Li'l mama is down on her luck. She says she'll do anything for the right price. She's even down for a *choo choo*. Li'l Chris and Eastwood is setting up right now, you down with it?"

I shook my head as I gazed at the female. She looked zoned out. "I'ma chill. I'll hold Jigga though. Y'all go ahead."

Los looked at me, bewildered. "Fa real? You scared or what? Man, that bitch is game, she's full of Ecstasy."

"You know how I play it. I'm already working on one, and I

don't fuck with two females that work on the same card."

"Suit yourself." Los shrugged, and then he directed me over to her.

With arm still around my shoulders, in a close homie way, he made the introductions. Her name was Saucadena. After telling her my name, Los bounced. When Saucadena stood up to follow him, I stopped her.

"Hold up, ma! You can't just follow right behind him. Niggas be watching. Give it a minute, then you can go," I cautioned her.

"Okay." She nodded.

"Wassup, you alright?" I asked her. She smiled. When she did, her lips rose above her teeth as her braces stood up like some razor wire.

She quickly covered her mouth with her hand to hide her smile. "I'm okay," she said with her hand still over her face.

I noticed a gold ring on her left index finger. *Bitches ain't shit,* I thought.

Obviously, she noticed me staring down at the ring. Because she quickly said, "It's not what you think. I'm not married, the names on the ring are my children's names."

"Oh yeah? I damn sure ain't fucking with you. You a regular breeder." I laughed.

"Boy, shut up, you so stupid," she said. She rubbed her nipples, which looked like they were eating through her shirt. I could tell the Ecstasy was doing its job. "Can I go now?" she asked.

I couldn't help but laugh. I wondered how many she had taken. Probably one for every dick she was about to take. "Enjoy," I said as she walked off. She was in a hurry too. Her body was actually tight. She looked like she had an ass, the way she was switching, but it looked hard. As she walked, her ass never moved.

"Porter showers!" the keyboss yelled.

I looked at my watch. They had been going at it for at least an hour. The inmates in the dayroom had started complaining about a house call. I walked up the stairs as I went to get them. If they wasn't done by now, they were out of there. They were so high they wasn't gon' be able to bust a nut anyway.

As I was walking up to the cell, Eastwood was coming out with his forehead covered with sweat. "Damn, bitch, you scared the shit outta me," he said.

I looked in the cell as Los was sitting on the toilet. He was getting some head, and I could tell he was high. He had her hair down as he was playing with it. Li'l Chris was behind the ho, fucking her from the back. "Watch out, li'l bitch, watch out, li'l bitch," he said as he rammed her from the back. They were having a full-fledged orgy.

"Y'all be wilding." I laughed. Los started smiling as he noticed me.

"You not gon' sample that?" Eastwood asked.

"Naw, they calling porter shower. You know I only mess with one bitch per card. Her and Grain work on the same card. They probably know each other."

Li'l Chris must've finished, for he walked out of the cell. "Mane, that ho pussy got a mind of its own," he said, wiping his dick off. I see why she got so many babies," he added.

"You going back in or what?" I asked.

"Maybe before she leave for the night, why?" Li'l Chris said.

"I gotta go take a shower, I been out here working all night," I said.

Li'i Chris looked back into the cell at Los. Los had the ho's tittie in his mouth as she moaned. She was riding him as he gripped her ass. She was so gone that she didn't even know everyone had left. "Fuck, I'ma let my nigga rep out then—I'll hold it down, ya'll go 'head," Li'l Chris said.

I walked off and jogged down the stairs. "Bitch, wait for me!" Eastwood said at the top of his voice.

I yelled back at him as I walked off the wing. "Mane, I gotta go, they called it like five minutes ago. You know they bet I tripping." I held my shower shoes in my hand as I walked inside the shower.

"Wassup?" an inmate asked as we passed by each other.

I shook his hand. I didn't know him personally, but we had played basketball together before. "I'm straight," I said, as three inmates walked in the shower behind me. None of them had a towel with them as they clutched their shower shoes in their hands.

Placing my fresh clothes on the concrete slab, I stripped naked and placed my shoes under my clothes. "The water hot?" I asked an inmate that was coming out of the water.

"Hell yeah, feels good though," he said. Taking the shower all the way in the back, I placed my shampoo on the top. As I hit the button to cut the water on, three inmates walked into the shower area, and they found a spot not too far from me. Grabbing my shampoo, I poured some in my hair and placed it back.

I was lathering the shampoo in as Eastwood walked in. I could tell that he was heated because I had left him. He looked around the shower for me. I was so far in the corner that he didn't see me. I closed my eyes before taking my head under the water to rinse my hair.

"Hotboy, watch out!" Eastwood yelled as I felt something go through my side.

The sudden impact caused me to fall to the floor. The soap fell into my eyes as I tried to open them. Before I could see who my attacker was, a fist smashed into my face. I saw stars, and then the room fell silent.

To Be Continued
CONCRETE KILLA: PART 2
Coming Soon

Submission Guideline

Submit the first three chapters of your completed manuscript to ldpsubmissions@gmail.com, subject line: Your book's title. The manuscript must be in a .doc file and sent as an attachment. Document should be in Times New Roman, double spaced and in size 12 font. Also, provide your synopsis and full contact information. If sending multiple submissions, they must each be in a separate email.

Have a story but no way to send it electronically? You can still submit to LDP/Ca$h Presents. Send in the first three chapters, written or typed, of your completed manuscript to:

LDP: Submissions Dept
Po Box 944
Stockbridge, Ga 30281

DO NOT send original manuscript. Must be a duplicate.

Provide your synopsis and a cover letter containing your full contact information.

Thanks for considering LDP and Ca$h Presents.

Coming Soon from Lock Down Publications/Ca$h Presents

BOW DOWN TO MY GANGSTA
By **Ca$h**
TORN BETWEEN TWO
By **Coffee**
THE STREETS STAINED MY SOUL **II**
By **Marcellus Allen**
BLOOD OF A BOSS **VI**
SHADOWS OF THE GAME II
By **Askari**
LOYAL TO THE GAME **IV**
By **T.J. & Jelissa**
IF LOVING YOU IS WRONG… **III**
By **Jelissa**
TRUE SAVAGE **VIII**
MIDNIGHT CARTEL III
DOPE BOY MAGIC IV
CITY OF KINGZ II
By **Chris Green**
BLAST FOR ME **III**
A SAVAGE DOPEBOY III
CUTTHROAT MAFIA III
DUFFLE BAG CARTEL VI
By **Ghost**
A HUSTLER'S DECEIT III
KILL ZONE **II**
BAE BELONGS TO ME III
A DOPE BOY'S QUEEN III
By **Aryanna**

Kingpen

KINGPIN DREAMS III

By Paper Boi Rari

CREAM II

By Yolanda Moore

SON OF A DOPE FIEND III

By Renta

FOREVER GANGSTA II

GLOCKS ON SATIN SHEETS III

By Adrian Dulan

LOYALTY AIN'T PROMISED III

By Keith Williams

THE PRICE YOU PAY FOR LOVE II

By Destiny Skai

CONFESSIONS OF A GANGSTA III

By Nicholas Lock

I'M NOTHING WITHOUT HIS LOVE II

SINS OF A THUG II

By Monet Dragun

LIFE OF A SAVAGE IV

MURDA SEASON IV

GANGLAND CARTEL III

CHI'RAQ GANGSTAS II

By **Romell Tukes**

QUIET MONEY IV

THUG LIFE II

EXTENDED CLIP II

By **Trai'Quan**

THE STREETS MADE ME III

By **Larry D. Wright**

THE ULTIMATE SACRIFICE VI

Kingpen

IF YOU CROSS ME ONCE II

ANGEL III

By **Anthony Fields**

FRIEND OR FOE III

By **Mimi**

SAVAGE STORMS II

By **Meesha**

BLOOD ON THE MONEY III

By J-Blunt

THE STREETS WILL NEVER CLOSE II

By K'ajji

NIGHTMARES OF A HUSTLA III

By King Dream

THE WIFEY I USED TO BE II

By Nicole Goosby

IN THE ARM OF HIS BOSS

By Jamila

MONEY, MURDER & MEMORIES II

Malik D. Rice

CONCRETE KILLAZ II

By Kingpen

Available Now

RESTRAINING ORDER **I & II**

By **CA$H & Coffee**

LOVE KNOWS NO BOUNDARIES **I II & III**

By **Coffee**

RAISED AS A GOON I, II, III & IV

BRED BY THE SLUMS I, II, III
BLAST FOR ME I & II
ROTTEN TO THE CORE I II III
A BRONX TALE I, II, III
DUFFLE BAG CARTEL I II III IV V
HEARTLESS GOON I II III IV
A SAVAGE DOPEBOY I II
HEARTLESS GOON I II III
DRUG LORDS I II III
CUTTHROAT MAFIA I II
By **Ghost**
LAY IT DOWN **I & II**
LAST OF A DYING BREED
BLOOD STAINS OF A SHOTTA I & II III
By **Jamaica**
LOYAL TO THE GAME I II III
LIFE OF SIN I, II III
By **TJ & Jelissa**
BLOODY COMMAS I & II
SKI MASK CARTEL I II & III
KING OF NEW YORK I II,III IV V
RISE TO POWER I II III
COKE KINGS I II III IV
BORN HEARTLESS I II III IV
KING OF THE TRAP
By **T.J. Edwards**
IF LOVING HIM IS WRONG…I & II
LOVE ME EVEN WHEN IT HURTS I II III
By **Jelissa**
WHEN THE STREETS CLAP BACK I & II III

Kingpen

THE HEART OF A SAVAGE I II

By **Jibril Williams**

A DISTINGUISHED THUG STOLE MY HEART I II & III

LOVE SHOULDN'T HURT I II III IV

RENEGADE BOYS I II III IV

PAID IN KARMA I II III

SAVAGE STORMS

By **Meesha**

A GANGSTER'S CODE I &, II III

A GANGSTER'S SYN I II III

THE SAVAGE LIFE I II III

CHAINED TO THE STREETS I II III

BLOOD ON THE MONEY I II

By J-Blunt

PUSH IT TO THE LIMIT

By **Bre' Hayes**

BLOOD OF A BOSS **I, II, III, IV, V**

SHADOWS OF THE GAME

By **Askari**

THE STREETS BLEED MURDER **I, II & III**

THE HEART OF A GANGSTA I II& III

By **Jerry Jackson**

CUM FOR ME I II III IV V VI

An **LDP Erotica Collaboration**

BRIDE OF A HUSTLA **I II & II**

THE FETTI GIRLS **I, II& III**

CORRUPTED BY A GANGSTA I, II III, IV

BLINDED BY HIS LOVE

THE PRICE YOU PAY FOR LOVE

DOPE GIRL MAGIC I II III

Concrete Killa

By **Destiny Skai**
WHEN A GOOD GIRL GOES BAD
By **Adrienne**
THE COST OF LOYALTY I II III
By Kweli
A GANGSTER'S REVENGE **I II III & IV**
THE BOSS MAN'S DAUGHTERS I II III IV V
A SAVAGE LOVE **I & II**
BAE BELONGS TO ME I II
A HUSTLER'S DECEIT I, II, III
WHAT BAD BITCHES DO I, II, III
SOUL OF A MONSTER I II III
KILL ZONE
A DOPE BOY'S QUEEN I II
By **Aryanna**
A KINGPIN'S AMBITON
A KINGPIN'S AMBITION **II**
I MURDER FOR THE DOUGH
By **Ambitious**
TRUE SAVAGE I II III IV V VI VII
DOPE BOY MAGIC I, II, III
MIDNIGHT CARTEL I II
CITY OF KINGZ
By **Chris Green**
A DOPEBOY'S PRAYER
By **Eddie "Wolf" Lee**
THE KING CARTEL **I, II & III**
By **Frank Gresham**
THESE NIGGAS AIN'T LOYAL **I, II & III**
By **Nikki Tee**

Kingpen

GANGSTA SHYT **I II &III**

By **CATO**

THE ULTIMATE BETRAYAL

By **Phoenix**

BOSS'N UP **I , II & III**

By **Royal Nicole**

I LOVE YOU TO DEATH

By Destiny J

I RIDE FOR MY HITTA

I STILL RIDE FOR MY HITTA

By **Misty Holt**

LOVE & CHASIN' PAPER

By **Qay Crockett**

TO DIE IN VAIN

SINS OF A HUSTLA

By **ASAD**

BROOKLYN HUSTLAZ

By **Boogsy Morina**

BROOKLYN ON LOCK I & II

By **Sonovia**

GANGSTA CITY

By **Teddy Duke**

A DRUG KING AND HIS DIAMOND I & II III

A DOPEMAN'S RICHES

HER MAN, MINE'S TOO I, II

CASH MONEY HO'S

THE WIFEY I USED TO BE

By Nicole Goosby

TRAPHOUSE KING **I II & III**

KINGPIN KILLAZ I II III

Concrete Killa

STREET KINGS I II

PAID IN BLOOD **I II**

CARTEL KILLAZ I II III

DOPE GODS I II

By **Hood Rich**

LIPSTICK KILLAH **I, II, III**

CRIME OF PASSION I II & III

FRIEND OR FOE I II

By **Mimi**

STEADY MOBBN' **I, II, III**

THE STREETS STAINED MY SOUL

By **Marcellus Allen**

WHO SHOT YA **I, II, III**

SON OF A DOPE FIEND I II

Renta

GORILLAZ IN THE BAY **I II III IV**

TEARS OF A GANGSTA I II

3X KRAZY

DE'KARI

TRIGGADALE I II III

Elijah R. Freeman

GOD BLESS THE TRAPPERS I, II, III

THESE SCANDALOUS STREETS I, II, III

FEAR MY GANGSTA I, II, III IV, V

THESE STREETS DON'T LOVE NOBODY I, II

BURY ME A G I, II, III, IV, V

A GANGSTA'S EMPIRE I, II, III, IV

THE DOPEMAN'S BODYGAURD I II

THE REALEST KILLAZ I II III

Tranay Adams

Kingpen

THE STREETS ARE CALLING

Duquie Wilson

MARRIED TO A BOSS... I II III

By Destiny Skai & Chris Green

KINGZ OF THE GAME I II III IV V

Playa Ray

SLAUGHTER GANG I II III

RUTHLESS HEART I II III

By Willie Slaughter

FUK SHYT

By Blakk Diamond

DON'T F#CK WITH MY HEART I II

By Linnea

ADDICTED TO THE DRAMA I II III

IN THE ARM OF HIS BOSS II

By Jamila

YAYO I II III

A SHOOTER'S AMBITION I II

By S. Allen

TRAP GOD I II III

By Troublesome

FOREVER GANGSTA

GLOCKS ON SATIN SHEETS I II

By Adrian Dulan

TOE TAGZ I II III

By Ah'Million

KINGPIN DREAMS I II

By Paper Boi Rari

CONFESSIONS OF A GANGSTA I II

By Nicholas Lock

I'M NOTHING WITHOUT HIS LOVE

SINS OF A THUG

By Monet Dragun

CAUGHT UP IN THE LIFE I II III

By Robert Baptiste

NEW TO MONEY, MURDER & MEMORIES

THE GAME I II III

By **Malik D. Rice**

LIFE OF A SAVAGE I II III

A GANGSTA'S QUR'AN I II III

MURDA SEASON I II III

GANGLAND CARTEL I II

CHI'RAQ GANGSTAS

By **Romell Tukes**

LOYALTY AIN'T PROMISED I II

By Keith Williams

QUIET MONEY I II III

THUG LIFE

EXTENDED CLIP

By **Trai'Quan**

THE STREETS MADE ME I II

By **Larry D. Wright**

THE ULTIMATE SACRIFICE I, II, III, IV, V

KHADIFI

IF YOU CROSS ME ONCE

ANGEL I II

By **Anthony Fields**

THE LIFE OF A HOOD STAR

By Ca$h & Rashia Wilson

THE STREETS WILL NEVER CLOSE

BOOKS BY LDP'S CEO, CA$H

TRUST IN NO MAN

TRUST IN NO MAN 2

TRUST IN NO MAN 3

BONDED BY BLOOD

SHORTY GOT A THUG

THUGS CRY

THUGS CRY 2

THUGS CRY 3

TRUST NO BITCH

TRUST NO BITCH 2

TRUST NO BITCH 3

TIL MY CASKET DROPS

RESTRAINING ORDER

RESTRAINING ORDER 2

IN LOVE WITH A CONVICT

LIFE OF A HOOD STAR

CPSIA information can be obtained
at www.ICGtesting.com
Printed in the USA
LVHW082302061021
699714LV00009B/329

9 781955 270014